SIGN OF THE RAVEN

*A Case from the Files of
Cheyenne Bruce, Private
Investigator, Book Four*

Lella Rae

MasterPieces Unlimited

To artists everywhere. The world would be a drab and unhappy place without you.

CONTENTS

PROLOGUE

There had been three murders and most likely more by the time I realized that death was again stalking Washington. It seemed to lurk around every corner. It seemed to watch quietly and bide its time, waiting for an opportunity to strike again.

In that summer of 1984, fear was already flooding the cities, towns, highways and forests of Washington State. We residents of the Pacific Northwest, by then, were well familiar with serial killers. In the 70s, Ted Bundy had terrorized Seattle by charming and then killing young women. In the 80s, Gary Ridgway murdered and hid his female victims along the banks of the Green River only to return to their remains again and again. He, of course, became known as The Green River Killer.

These men were able to fulfill their horrible goals because they appeared to be average, ordinary, normal people and were able to hide in plain sight. They had families, girlfriends and jobs. They stood next to us in the grocery line and sat behind us in the movie theater. They were our neighbors. They were there, in plain sight, unnoticed because they didn't look like the deranged monsters they were. They acted like us. They looked like us. They were just like us.

What drove these killers to do what they did? Complicated forces and emotions, yes. Certainly, repressed memory, pain, jealousy, lust and greed played a part as well. Ted Bundy's and Gary Ridgway's childhoods, emotions and motives have been analyzed again and again by those who know far more than I. They were discussed in restaurants and bars, at baseball games and dinner parties and, especially, in the press.

Unknown to everyone, though, there was another killer lurking in the state during those years. One who remained unnamed by the press, unrecognized by the authorities. An unknown, free to pursue and eliminate whomever the mystery killer wished. So skillful were the murders, they were not believed to be murders at all.

The press never did name the perpetrator nor did the authorities ever recognize the fact that a third killer roamed the area. I knew though, that in the colorful world of the local art scene, someone was watching, making plans and waiting for the moment to strike. I knew about the killer I came to call the Raven.

ONE

I was a private investigator in the summer of 1984. My name is Cheyenne Bruce. I was thirty-nine years old, single and psychic.

I didn't advertise the paranormal part of myself, especially in my business. It gave potential clients the wrong idea. I can't predict the future, nor do I know which numbers are going to win the lottery. I do get "feelings" from people and places and know when someone is lying to me or telling the truth. My "talent" made my work somewhat easier and I took advantage of it. To me it's natural, a part of who I am. Not everyone sees it that way, however. The name of my business, The Sign of the Cross, came into being when a police officer who fancied himself a comedian, put his fingers into a cross when he found out about my ability.

That summer, as usual, was a slow time in my business. I had just completed a case. I had spent the weekend locating a runaway teen who had absconded to Oregon. I don't know who was more relieved when I returned him to his parents; them, him or me. It had been a hot and uncomfortable two days for the both of us.

I had gotten home late the night before, thankful for the comfortable cottage where I lived. I had two more small jobs to finish, a couple of reports to write and then I could spend a little time with my two newly discovered hobbies.

In May I had completed a case working undercover in a writer's colony where I had discovered a joy in writing. In addition, a few months prior to that, I had been made an apprentice in a local West Seattle stained glass shop and found that I had an affinity for that as well.

The sun flooded my office that morning when I padded in, still brushing my teeth. My office was in my home, a charming house, surrounded by trees, on the grounds of a mansion in West Seattle. Rumor was that it used to be the caretaker's cottage and, in fact, that was what it was still called. My landlady, a retired film actress named Magda St. Martin, rented it to me when I had solved two cases for her. She lived in the big house when she was in town but her new career as film director kept her out of the state most of the time.

It was the sunshine that made me decide that my last two cases could wait one more day. I showered, dressed and, skipping breakfast altogether, climbed into my car and headed down to Avenue Art Glass.

The brilliant light coming through the sample window made rainbows on the floor when I pushed through the front door. Ab Eberstein, the proprietor, looked up from his soldering iron and grinned.

"Hey," he said. "Find the kid?"

"He's all safe and sound," I told him, and went up the two steps to the workroom. I put on my apron that was only slightly cleaner than Ab's and circled the table until I reached the lamp that I had been working on. The air smelled like metal, flux and wooden bins with a little cork from the bulletin board mixed in. That scent would stay with me for the remainder of my life and evoke pleasant memories every time I caught it.

"Are you all ready for the show?" I asked him.

He was headed to the Washington coast in a little more than a week to attend a five day art show. There he would mix with other artists, sell his wares and, I hoped, enjoy the beach. I would stay home and run the shop for him while he was away. He was also entered into the contest sponsored by the Pacific Coast Arts Collective, or the PCAC for those in the know. They held a contest every summer with the winner to be announced at the show in July. The week before, Ab had learned that he was a finalist.

"Got that peacock window all polished up and ready to go?" I asked.

He laughed. "Don't get your hopes up too high, babe." (He called all women "babe".) "There are artists there who are way better than I am."

I doubted it. Ab had been working in glass for most of his fifty-five years. He had once told me that when he was a child, his mother scolded him constantly for carrying pieces of broken colored glass in his jacket pockets. Even at five, he had wanted to "do something with glass."

"I know you're coming home with the first place prize," I told him. "I have every confidence in you. I'll be waiting right here ready to pop the champagne cork. It's a prestigious prize, I have discovered. There was an article about the show in the Sunday paper."

"I don't know about prestigious," he said. I thought he looked a little chagrined, like he *did* think it was important and that he wanted it more than he was letting on. "The prize money would be nice, though." When he smiled his eyes crinkled around the edges.

"I'll be here raking in the bucks for you and you'll be winning untold amounts of loot. You'll be rolling in it," I said, laughing.

He put down his soldering iron, looking serious. "I need to talk to you about that," he said.

"That sounds ominous." I put down the piece of glass I was foiling. "What have I done? Am I fired?" I frowned. "Can you fire an apprentice?"

He laughed again. "You're not fired. In fact, I need you to go to the show with me."

All I could do was raise my eyebrows. We had been discussing the plan for months. I was to stay behind and keep the shop open while he attended the show.

"As you know, I'm on the PCAC board of directors," he said. I nodded. "They're worried because there seems to have been an increase in thefts from the last several shows. Small but valuable pieces have been stolen."

"They have security, don't they?"

He nodded. "Sure. And they've tightened that up a little. Even so, the thefts seem to have picked up. The board is worried because the artists in the Everett Art Council shows have been noticing things going missing too." He rubbed the top of his head, making his frizzy gray hair stick up. "Between thefts and artists dying, it's a wonder we can get anybody to sign up for the shows."

"Wait," I said. "Back up. Artists dying?"

"After the EAC winter show, one of their artists died of carbon monoxide poisoning from a malfunctioning space heater."

"Yikes," I said. "I've heard you have to be careful with those things."

"She had complained about having a rather expensive piece stolen just prior to that," Ab continued. "Or at least, she thought it was stolen. It was missing anyway. That's how I found out about it. The Everett Art Council contacted our board and warned us about the increase in thefts and happened to mention the loss of the artist." He looked at me with a sheepish grin. "I don't mean to imply anything. The death doesn't have anything to do with the shows or the thefts."

"Let's hope not!" I said. My mind turned to the coming show. I had been looking forward to being in charge of the shop while Ab was gone, but *going* to the show was even better.

"Anyway," Ab continued. "I mentioned to the Pacific Coast Collective that you are a private eye. They would like you to attend and see if you can figure out who the villain is."

I nodded but didn't say anything, so he went on. "I would be glad to have your help anyway. I thought we could bring along a few pieces of your work, too."

That was icing on the cake. I think I gaped at him.

"You'll go, won't you?" he asked when I still hadn't said anything.

"Of course! I would love it. But who's going to run the shop?"

"We can leave it shut for a few days. I'll put a 'gone fishing' sign on the door or something. I've left it closed before. No problem."

He picked up his soldering iron again and, in a moment, some of that hot metal and flux smell wafted from the piece he was working on.

I picked up the piece of glass I had been foiling

and finished it. Could life be any better? I asked myself. I was thrilled at being invited to help at the show and score an investigation job at the same time. I gave a happy little sigh and Ab looked up at me and smiled.

Funny how we make plans and things turn out so differently from what we thought.

TWO

Tuesday, July 10, 1984

The next morning, while I was still in my PJs and working out the strategy for the two cases that were hanging over my head, I got a phone call.

"I'm sorry to call you so early, Miss Bruce. My name is Kirk Nielsson. I'm the event director of the Pacific Coast Arts Collective. I spoke to Ab Eberstein this morning and he said that I should give you a call."

"I'm glad you did, and it's not too early at all," I told him. We chatted for a while about the job I would be doing for them and he invited me to join a board meeting scheduled for the next afternoon. I promised to be there and bring the paperwork for him to complete to make it official that the PCAC was hiring me to take the case.

"And there's one more thing," he said, hesitating. "Ab said he had told you about that Everett artist who died. A potter?"

"Yes," I said. "Do you have more information about that?"

"Nooo—" he said, dragging the word out until it meant "yes." "I was talking to Ab and mentioned that we had a booth space that we hadn't anticipated. One of our artists had applied to the show, had been accepted but was remiss about securing her booth. I tried to contact her only to find out that she had died. I don't know why Ab thought you would be interested in that, but he wanted me to mention it to you." He sounded apologetic, as though he was bothering me about some trivial matter. "Her husband tells me that she died last month."

"That's terrible!" I said. "I'm so sorry!"

"Well, I don't think it has anything to do with anything, but Ab said you might be interested in hearing about it anyway."

"Yes, I am," I said. The man probably thought I was a ghoul. That made two deaths. My mind ratcheted into high gear and I made a quick decision. "You said she had a husband? Do you think it would be possible for me to speak to him?"

"Well, I guess so..." He sounded so doubtful I wondered if I had overstepped. It wouldn't be the first time. "There's no reason to think her death has any connection with, well, anything that's going on in the collective."

"I'm sure not," I said. "But I think that if I'm

investigating a crime which also is happening to another local art organization, I should cover all the bases." I tried to sound businesslike and not like I was discussing someone's death. I don't think I did a good job.

He left the phone for a moment and returned to give me the number of the artist who had lived in Ballard. He told me her name was Barbara Robertson and her husband's name was Tyler.

I called the number and the man at the other end agreed to meet me at his house in Ballard. Even over the phone he sounded utterly defeated, and I wondered if I would be making things harder for him.

❊ ❊ ❊

Tyler Robertson confirmed that his wife had died in an auto accident. He told me about it at his kitchen table. He had set out a plate of vanilla wafers and had made some weak instant coffee. It was a sad little attempt at hospitality from a man who could think about nothing but the empty years ahead of him.

"Was she driving alone, sir?" I asked.

"No," he said, his voice cracking just a little. "She wasn't driving at all. She was walking. She went out for a walk every morning." He stirred his coffee even though he had added nothing to it. I don't think he knew he was doing it.

"She was walking up 15th and they think she was going to cross the street. Someone…someone going way too fast hit her. She died at the scene, they said." He continued stirring. I took a sip of my coffee and put it down.

"What about the person who hit her?" I asked.

He shook his head. "They haven't found out who it was. He sped away from the scene. They say they're still looking for him but I don't think they'll ever find him if they haven't by now."

"So, they know it was a man?"

He nodded. "There were two witnesses. Some guy who was filling newspaper kiosks caught a glimpse of him. Said it was an old man, but couldn't see him very well. He said he thought the car was dark blue. The other witness was a woman who had just arrived at her hair salon. She didn't see the guy at all but said the car was black." He sighed and put down his spoon at last. "She's the one who called the police. I called the police every day for a couple of weeks but there was never anything new. 'The case is still open,' they always say." He picked up a cookie from the plate and broke it in half then put the pieces back on the plate.

"Did she walk the same route every day?"

He nodded. "She walked 15th because, in the

winter, it was pretty well lit and she got to know some of the people along there."

I was about to decide that Kirk Nielsson had been right after all. What had happened to Barbara was an accident that had nothing to do with the other death. Then he spoke again.

"The police won't take me seriously," he said. "They think I'm some crazy guy who keeps pestering them."

"I'm sure they don't think that, sir," I said. I knew many of the Seattle Police officers and couldn't think of a more dedicated and caring bunch.

"I don't know," he said, sounding tired enough to die himself. "She was always very careful. She looked out for cars. She wore a reflective vest, even in the daylight. I made her promise and she did. Maybe I'm just trying to find some sort of reason why a perfectly healthy woman could be...destroyed like that. So fast...So...stupidly." His voice shook again. "Will you be investigating her...this?

"Yes," I told him, even though it would only be peripherally. Nevertheless, he seemed relieved at my answer.

"Is her studio intact?" I asked after a few moments. When he said that it was, I asked him if I could see it and he agreed.

❋ ❋ ❋

"I just don't know what to do with all of this stuff," Tyler said miserably when we were standing at the door of the upstairs studio where Barbara had done her paintings. He was flummoxed that she had died, and that he had been left to pick up the pieces.

The room was at the very top of the house, an early-century craftsman with a peaked roof. It was an artist's dream of a studio, with large north and south facing windows. A paint spattered apron hung from an easel. There were paintings leaning against every wall. It looked like the artist had stepped out for a moment. There was the faint aroma of wood, paper and some sort of rose scented candle in the air.

I could feel a trace of Barbara, too. I knew that she had been content in her studio, but I got the impression that something had worried her. Something significant and frightening had loomed in her mind. Before I could capture the feeling and search it for anything further, it was gone.

I stepped into the room and was surrounded by Seattle street scenes; some of the downtown area, some of the waterfront. Many were of neighborhoods that I didn't recognize; buildings and homes, gardens and parks while others were places that I had been myself.

"Do you mind if I take some pictures?" I asked him.

He shook his head but said nothing. I wasn't sure if he meant "no, I don't mind" or if he meant "no, don't take any pictures." I chose my answer and pulled the camera from my bag.

Barbara's watercolors were beautifully done. I believe she had captured the essence of Seattle with her sometimes misty looking paintings. I snapped photo after photo of rainy downtown streets, glowing sunshine on the waters of Lake Union, the distant, almost lavender Olympic mountains.

I stopped and stood gazing at a group of paintings that seemed to be separate from the others, lined up against the far wall. They appeared to be the underside of Seattle; abandoned buildings, alleys, homeless men and women and the part of downtown where the bawdy shows flash more than neon through the rainy twilight.

"Those were her 'Skedaddle Seattle' series." Tyler's voice brought me back to the studio that would soon have a forlorn, neglected feel. "She felt like people were leaving the downtown core and that it was a shame because it has so much to offer."

I wondered how pictures of the worst of the city were going to help bring people back, but maybe that had not been her intent, after all. Perhaps she had been merely making commentary.

I wasn't sure what I was going to accomplish with the photos I was taking, but I felt that there may be something in the woman's studio that would lead me to a larger truth. I couldn't afford to ignore my instincts and they were beginning to flash red. Also, I was inclined to believe the instincts of a husband when he said that he couldn't fathom why his wife had died. Even though that is a natural reaction, for some reason, I felt he was justified.

"I have no idea what I'm going to do with the paintings, let alone the supplies," he said, shaking his head. "I'm half inclined to leave them here for now." He glanced at me. "In a way, it makes me feel that she will come back to it. To her things, her work."

I told him I thought that was a good idea; that, in my experience, it was best not to rush into any decisions after a loved one passes. If, in the future, he *did* decide to get rid of it all, the Pacific Coast Arts Collective might be helpful in finding homes for the supplies and maybe the paintings as well.

On the way home, I made a stop at the Fotomat with the rolls of film I had shot.

The more I thought about it, the more I thought two deaths were significant. My psychic sense had shot into overdrive.

THREE

Tuesday, July 10, 1984

When I got home, I headed for the phone book in my office and called the Everett Art Council. I identified myself to Gale Jens, the president, as a private investigator working for the Pacific Coast Arts Collective. I told her I wanted to know more about the thefts.

Gale told me that several of the artists had been complaining about their work being stolen at shows. She tried to brush it aside, saying that small things go missing from shops and shows all the time. I thought it must be more than an ordinary amount for her to have mentioned it to the PCAC in the first place. And I was intrigued about the death, though I didn't want to mention it to Gale at that point in case my imagination had finally run amok. I asked her instead if I could meet with her.

"I have an hour this afternoon about one," she said, almost reluctantly, I thought.

"One, it is," I confirmed. "I'll be there. I'd like a

list of the artists who've had things go missing, if possible."

She agreed and I ended the call.

I looked at my watch. I had to allow for at least an hour to get to Everett and find the address.

I had a serious conversation with myself while I made a quick sandwich. Was I jumping to irrelevant conclusions? I didn't know enough about either the thefts or the deaths to think they were connected, but I knew that if they were and I did nothing, I would have trouble living with myself. I needed to find out as much as I could.

"That's exactly what I intend to do," I said aloud while I grabbed my keys on the way to the car.

❉ ❉ ❉

It was two minutes to one when I found the building where the Everett Art Council was housed.

Gale and I introduced ourselves and she led me to her office. She was a thin, nervous looking woman, tightly wound with energy to spare. Even her curly dark hair seemed to have a kind of frenetic liveliness. It bounced against her neck as she talked.

She gestured for me to sit. "I hope you didn't come all the way up here for no good reason," she said when she had settled in her desk chair. "We've always had a few thefts, although they seem to be escalating."

"That's what the PCAC is finding too," I told her. "They're interested in hiring me to come to the summer show so I can keep an eye out. I thought I'd come up here so I could pick up that list and try to get as much information as I can."

"Hiring a detective may not be a bad idea," she said. "The articles that have gone missing are small things, mostly, but they *are* original works and worth something." She stopped for a moment and looked out the window. "It could be, after all, that the artists are just reporting it more than they used to." She rose and went to a file cabinet behind her desk and riffled through some files until she found the right one. "I started keeping a log of the reported thefts about a year ago," she told me, slipping it into the copier. "That's when I noticed they were escalating. I'm sure there are more than these. Many times, the artist doesn't realize anything is missing or believes the item was sold unless he or she keeps careful inventory. Frankly, very few of them do that."

I nodded and scanned the list she handed me. It looked like quite a lot of theft to me, but what did I know?

"I understand one of your artists has died," I said.

She looked taken aback. "Well, that doesn't have

anything to do with the thefts, does it?"

"I don't know. What can you tell me about it?"

"All I know is what I've heard from her husband. Her name was Ramona Rainey. She was a wonderful potter!" She stood and fetched a small vase from the shelf above the file cabinet. When she handed it to me, I felt the velvety smooth texture of the almost luminescent turquoise glaze. I turned it over and looked at the artist's signature on the bottom. She had used glaze to paint an R in flowing script. Her signature was almost as lovely as the vase.

I handed it back to Gale. "Ab said that she died from carbon monoxide poisoning."

"I believe so," Gale said.

Just then a tall man about my age stopped by the office door. "Oh, sorry, I didn't know you were busy," he said.

"Rod, come in a moment, will you?" She looked relieved to be interrupted. "This is Cheyenne Bruce. She's a detective. You knew Ramona Rainey better than I and you know Pete. Would you be able to tell us what you know about Ramona's death."

"Sad, sad thing," he said, as he came in and leaned on Gale's desk. "It was a terrible accident. It was in the winter, you know, right after the Magical Wonderland Studio Tour. She was using one of those propane space heaters. Apparently, she used to spend the night in her studio now and again if she had a firing to do over night. Anyway, something went wrong with the heater and she never woke up in the morning." He looked at me as if just now realizing I was there. "I thought the police already..."

"I'm working for the Pacific Coast Arts Collective," I sort of lied. They hadn't hired me yet. "I'm investigating the increase of thefts the collective has noticed."

"So, you think there's a connection? I'm sure there isn't," he said, shaking his head. "I don't think there's any... It was an accident." He looked at Gale and they both nodded.

"There probably isn't," I said, "but I'm investigating a series of crimes and I want to cover everything. Would it be possible to get her husband's phone number?"

They looked at each other, both reluctant to open what they obviously considered a huge can of worms.

"I'm not sure Pete..." Rod began.

At the same time, Gale said, "I don't think..."

"No problem, I said, with a smile. I stood. "What was the woman's name again, Ramona Raleigh?" I knew that Gale had said Rainey but I wanted to know how to spell it.

"Rainey," Rod said, looking relieved.

"R-a n..." I prompted.

He bit. "R-a-i-n-e-y."

I shook hands with both of them and thanked them for their time. Then I left, leaving them, I was sure, satisfied that they had somehow protected Pete Rainey from my intrusion.

I found a phone booth a couple of blocks away. Pete Rainey had listed his name, address and phone number in the phone book. Ramona's was there too.

Ramona's husband agreed to meet with me. He asked me the same questions that Gale and Rod had asked and I answered the same, that I was merely covering all the bases.

Pete lived in a newish modest house near the marina. When he answered the door, I was surprised to see that he was younger than I had thought. He had blond hair that was a bit in need of a cut and his shirt was rumpled, as though he had slept in it.

He seemed eager to talk. I wondered how much of a support system he had to help him with his grief. Most people have some family, some friends or neighbors who are willing to help out. I wanted to tell him that a bit of grief counseling might be helpful to him but it was none of my business. Instead, I listened and nodded in the appropriate places and added condolences where necessary.

When he began to wind down, I declined the coffee that he belatedly offered and asked, "Did the police take any photos of the scene?"

He shook his head. "It wasn't a crime," he said. "Just a terrible accident. They *did* suggest suicide, but Mona would never have done that." He turned his head away from me and I let him have a moment to compose himself.

"How did it happen?" I asked. "I mean, where was she and why was she using a space heater?"

"She was in her studio," he said. "It's a converted garage and has no heating. In the winter, when she had the kiln going, it used so much electricity that if she used an electric heater, a fuse would blow and ruin the whole firing. We had this old propane heater and sometimes, if she had to spend the night in the studio, she used it."

"Did she ever have problems with it before?"

"No! It worked fine." He put both hands to his forehead. "She was always careful with it. Even so, I didn't like her using it."

"Did anyone else besides you and Ramona have access to it?"

He shook his head. Then something occurred to him. "You don't think it *was* a crime, do you? Oh, my God, if it was, I couldn't... They said the heater malfunctioned! You don't...oh my God!" he said again. "You don't think she was *killed*, do you?"

"No, no I don't, Mr. Rainey. I never meant to suggest that she was." I put my hand on his shoulder and was not shocked at the amount of searing pain that washed from him to me. He was suffering and I was sorry I had come to his home to bring it all back to the surface.

"I couldn't stand that," he said, seeming to calm a little. "I couldn't accept it if it was anything but a pure accident. Suicide, no. Murder, absolutely not."

I wondered why an accident was preferable. It seemed to me that a motiveless mishap would be worse somehow. For some reason, he felt he could only accept her death as an accident.

"I saw one of Ramona's pieces at Gale Jens' office," I told him. "It was stunning. I was very impressed." I paused for only a moment. "Gale also mentioned that Ramona had had a piece stolen and I was curious. Gale said it was a rather valuable item and since I'll be investigating the thefts, I wanted to find out what I could."

"It was a small vase, but Mona had experimented on it with some difficult technique. I'm not sure what it was all about but I do know that she also used a purple glaze that's no longer available. Since it was unique, she wanted a little more for it."

"Her work is lovely. Would I be able to see her studio?"

He nodded. "I've been dismantling it," he said. "You're welcome to see it. What's left of it. It's slow work. I can only stand to do it for short periods at a time. My heart just isn't in it."

"One more thing, Mr. Rainey, if you don't mind," I said, thinking. "I understand that Ramona was selling out of her studio. Gale mentioned that she had a studio tour just prior to her death."

He nodded. "She did studio tours three or four times a year," he said.

"I'm not familiar with studio tours," I told him, though I was sure I could figure out what they entailed.

"They're pretty common. And popular too. Mona always did well. Artists in the area get together and open their studios to visitors. They organize a tour, print a little map and people get a close up view of how the artist works. They can purchase items too. Lots of the artists do it. Mona used to let the visitors mess around with the clay or paint an unfired piece. They loved it."

He led me out the back door to a single story building in the back yard. Someone had made the yard a peaceful sanctuary, paved with square stones and surrounded by potted trees and climbing vines. I commented on it and Pete only shook his head. I had to assume that it had been Ramona's work too.

He unlocked the door for me then stepped back, opting to wait outside.

When I walked in, I was surprised that I couldn't find much of Ramona's essence in her studio. Normally, I get the sense of people when I enter the spaces where they spend their time. But though I felt that Ramona had deeply loved her home and her work, I believed that she had lavished her passion on her garden. If I had spent any time sitting among the plants and flowers that Ramona had loved, I thought I would find more of her.

I took some photos of the remaining pieces of pottery. There weren't many, maybe a total of twenty or thirty items, all glazed in a rainbow of colors and in a variety of textures and shapes.

I noticed one item that was out of place. It wasn't a pot or a bowl or a plate. It was a little house, well-crafted and detailed and made out of clay. It was charming but I could tell it wasn't Ramona Rainey's work. I picked it up and looked at the bottom. The script R was not there. Instead, there was a carved BJ.

Outside, I thanked Pete and once again offered my condolences.

"I found a piece that is not Ramona's work," I told him. "It was signed BJ. Do you know who that is?"

He nodded. "She had a friend who lived on the Oregon coast. Brynn Jagger. They both learned from the same teacher. Ramona went into pottery while Brynn branched into sculpture. They did a swap one year and exchanged some of their work." He shook his head. "The world has lost two wonderful artists now."

"I'm sorry," I said. My ears all but pricked up, like a dog's. "What happened to Brynn?" I asked.

"She died." He seemed almost startled at his own words. "She died, too," he whispered again. "She lived outside of Seaside, Oregon. She was in a car crash coming home from the grocery store one night. I thought Mona was going to make herself sick, she was so upset when she found out. Their booths had been next to each other at the Cannon Beach Art Festival just a few weeks before."

"I am sincerely sorry," I said, again. "I hope I didn't trouble you too much, although I'm afraid I did." I laid my hand on his shoulder again.

"They tell me it's good to talk about it," he said. "They also tell me that I'll feel better one day. I don't know. I don't think I'll ever get over it."

"I know it's hard to believe if you've never been through it before," I told him. "But you *will* find peace." He didn't seem to notice my failure to tell him that he would "get over it".

He looked at me and managed a shaky smile. "I hope so."

❋ ❋ ❋

After I got home, made a few calls and told a couple of white lies, I was able to contact Brynn Jagger's husband. He didn't want to talk about it.

I explained to him that I was an investigator looking into the art thefts. "I'm sorry, sir, but can you tell me if Brynn had anything stolen from her booth at the Cannon Beach Art Festival that year?"

"Yes, she did, but that happens all the time. Look, her death didn't have anything to do with her sculptures, or the show or anything else. It had to do with a drunk driver and she's dead and that's all I'm going to say."

I couldn't blame him. I gave him my number and asked him to call me if he thought of anything at all. I very much doubted that he even wrote it down.

I called the Oregon Highway Patrol and they told me that it had indeed been an accident, a hit and run. Most likely a drunk driver. Either way, the person who had forced Brynn Jagger off the road and killed her had never been found.

That was three deaths out of how many countless thousands? All accidents, all presumably unrelated to art or art shows. Nevertheless, there was a certain little psychic buzz in the back of my brain that was getting louder all the time.

* * *

I had at least part of the afternoon left so I stopped by Avenue Art Glass.

Ab was selling glass to a customer and there was another waiting to buy supplies. I stepped behind the cash register and did what I could to help.

At last, he was free and I trailed after him as he went to his office to put the day's receipts into his desk.

"I think there may be more going on than anyone realizes," I said when he had a fresh cup of coffee in front of him and I had a mug of tea.

"Naah," he said, then stopped when he saw my face. "Like what?"

"I think there's at least a slight possibility that we might be looking at another serial opportunist at work."

"Opportunist?"

"A killer."

He laughed. "You don't think that you're looking for mystery in some random happenings?"

I didn't laugh.

In a moment he said, "I'm sorry, babe. It just seems incredible."

"It seems incredible to me that three artists are dead. When I have feelings about something, they generally are true. Not always, I admit. I hope that this time I'm wrong, but, Ab, I don't think I am."

Neither of us said anything for a moment, both lost in thought.

"I understand why you think I'm jumping off the deep end here," I said. "There are three deaths with nothing in common except that the dead were artists. Women artists. Artists are dying all the time all over the country for one reason or another. I realize these deaths have legitimate causes. Accidents happen all the time. I have nothing more to go on than my own intuition."

He watched me another moment over the top of his coffee mug. His eyes told me that he was beginning to take me seriously. He was well aware of my psychic ability.

"Then, babe," he said. "I'm grateful that you are coming along to the show with me. I'm glad and the board will be glad."

"Speaking of the board, I'll be going to the meeting tomorrow afternoon. Kirk Nielsson asked me to attend."

He nodded, still ruminating. "A serial killer," he said. "Don't we have enough going on with the Green River Killer? Now another one? For once, I hope you are wrong, Cheyenne. I hope you *are* wrong."

He had dropped the "babe" and called me by my name. He was serious. So was I and I hoped I was wrong too.

FOUR

Wednesday, July 11, 1984

The next morning was another glorious one in Seattle. When Seattle has good weather, it's spectacular. The sun glints off of the water and lights up our world. Seattleites aren't bothered by the rain—very few natives even own umbrellas—but we revel in the sunshine. That day was starting out to be one of the better ones.

I headed over to Avenue Art Glass. On the way, I felt those last two jobs jangling around in my head. I had finally gotten the go-ahead for one and could begin that before the weekend. The other, having worn on for two weeks with no resolution, was beginning to weigh more heavily in my mind than it deserved to.

Ab's mind and shop were full of the show. Even though it was a week until we would leave, he had begun crating a few of the larger pieces he would be taking along. Two crates already stood in the back of the shop ready to load into the van when we left.

"So, where will we be staying? Are there any hotels in Oceanside?" I asked when I had helped him maneuver the last crate into the back room and we had settled down to work on projects. I had been building a lamp for several weeks and Ab was repairing a small window.

"One hotel. The town is mostly locals' homes and small cabins and a few big old houses with lots of rooms that the owners rent out. I've taken a couple of rooms in one of them," he said. "It should be interesting. There will be three or four other artists staying there."

"It must be some house to fit five or six strangers. I hope we don't have to double up." I was half kidding. I don't care much where I sleep.

"It's a seven bedroom, turn of the century house. There are three bathrooms and a kitchen where we can do our own cooking, or not, and we're not far from the venue. It even has a name. 'Beachhouse'. I think *you'll* like it."

I soldered a seam. "Wow," I said. "Imaginative name. Why do you think I will like it in particular?" I looked at him. He was grinning.

"It's supposed to be haunted. The owner made a point of telling me that when I talked to him. I think he thought it was an attraction. I understand it's pretty rustic. The price was a lot better than staying in the hotel."

"Speaking of which, let me know how much my

35

share is and I'll write you a check."

He nodded but didn't say anything. I knew that he would never mention the money again. He probably knew, too, that I would never let it go.

After a few minutes of soldering, I said, "Haunted. That should be interesting."

"I wouldn't get too excited," he said. "I think the guy just thought it would be more desirable if it had a couple of ghosts hanging around."

"So, what kind of clothes should I bring? Remember, I've never done this before."

He stopped working for a moment. "Thanks for reminding me. I have to take some stuff to the cleaners. Some people wear their 'shop' clothes. That is, I know a wood worker who always wears jeans and a plaid shirt and an apron. He likes to look the part. I'd say most people dress up a little. The customers expect to buy high end art from high end looking artists." He grinned. "I wear slacks and a shirt, but I refuse to wear a tie."

I laughed. I didn't think I had ever seen him wearing anything but jeans and a t-shirt—short sleeved in the summer, long sleeved in the winter. In extreme cold weather, I have known him to put on a sweatshirt. "So, I guess I'd better spruce up my wardrobe a bit too," I said. The best thing I owned was a wrinkle proof black dress that I had gotten at a discount when some travel store had gone out of business. By then it had seen better days. "I have a decent pair of pants and a jacket but I'll go shopping and do my best to look like a respectable representative of the art."

When the time came to leave for the board meeting, Ab offered to drive. I turned him down and headed for my own car. I had a couple of errands to run afterward.

* * *

Ab introduced me to Dak Washington who told me that the board members were amenable to the idea of having an outsider in their midst. "For the most part," he added after an almost imperceptible pause. He then introduced me to the board secretary, Yvonne Garafeld, a sweet looking woman of about forty five. She asked me at least four times how to spell my name. When I told her it was spelled the same way as the city, she looked baffled.

The treasurer, Hank Franklin, was just the opposite. He seemed much more focused. For the board's sake, I hoped so. I met a young man named Lagan something or other, who seemed disinclined to either talk to me or look at anyone at all. An artist named Julia didn't seem the least bit interested either. The last member turned out to be Kirk Neilsson, the event coordinator who had called me the day before.

We sat around a rectangular table in one of the conference rooms at the main branch of the library downtown.

First, Yvonne, the secretary, went through a giggle-studded and rather endless reading of the minutes of the last meeting. When she finished, Hank stood up, straightened his tie, cleared his throat and began the group's financial report. Long ago, I learned to yawn while keeping my mouth shut and I got to practice my skill several times that afternoon.

While Hank droned on about incomprehensible topics, I tried to be circumspect while I observed the other members. I noticed that Lagan kept his head down most of the time. I wondered if he felt as sleepy as I did. He had dark hair and skin and I thought, given his name, he must be East Indian. Julia, a lady with salt and pepper hair that she wore in an attractive short style, looked as though she smelled something unpleasant. Dak sat with his arms folded, glowering until the preliminaries seemed to be winding down.

Just as Hank was bringing his report to a conclusion, he was interrupted.

"We have a crowded agenda, so I think we should proceed," Dak, who turned out to be the president, said. Everyone seemed to come back to consciousness at that point and sat up a bit straighter. I heard Hank Franklin mutter something but couldn't catch what it was. There did seem to be some tension between the two men.

"As you know," Dak began. "Cheyenne Bruce is a private detective who has joined us to help us get to the bottom of our theft problem." Everyone's attention turned from Dak to me and I offered a small nod, hoping I looked competent.

"Cheyenne," Dak said. "I'll let you take it from here."

Oh, fine, I thought. Extemporaneous public speaking is not one of my strengths. Nevertheless, I stood and looked at each member in turn. "I know that the Everett Art Council is having a theft problem too," I said, "So, you're not alone." I smiled. No one moved a muscle so I plowed ahead. "Ab tells me that you will hire security for night time. Is it inside security or a company that patrols the outside?"

"Outside, isn't it, Hank?" Dak asked. Hank, taken by surprise, looked up and nodded. He seemed to be brooding about something.

"I think you should have someone patrolling the inside as well. Are the thefts occurring during the night or during the day?"

"We think they're during the day," Dak said. "Although we can't be sure. The artists haven't been able to pin down when things have gone missing."

"One of my bags went missing during the day," Julia said. "It was there one minute and gone the next."

"I think it would be wise to hire a uniformed guard," I said.

Dak and Kirk looked at each other. "Isn't that what we're hiring you for?" Dak asked me.

"Yes, of course, and I will do my best to keep an eye on things during the day, but I will not be in uniform and I think a more visible presence would go much further as a deterrent." I stopped for a moment while they gave my proposal some thought, then I said, "Unfortunately, I think there may be a bigger problem than a few thefts."

They all looked at me. Dak threw an impatient glance at his watch, but I continued. "Three artists have died within the last six months. One in Everett, one in Seattle, in the Ballard district, and one on the Oregon coast. They are all artists that have participated in local shows and have had items stolen."

Dak surprised me by bursting into laughter. "Ridiculous!" he said. "Are you telling us there's a crazed maniac going to art shows and killing artists? That's preposterous!"

I put up my hands to calm the murmurs. "None of them, that we know of, has been killed deliberately.

They died from accidents. I'm not saying that there is a 'crazed maniac'. I'm saying that three artists have died. They have all had items stolen while attending art shows. The deaths may not have anything whatsoever to do with each other or the art shows. What I'm proposing is that a warning be given to the artists to be careful and that they be advised to be sure to report any thefts, certainly, but also any unusual behavior by customers."

Yvonne looked terrified. Julia was smirking. She obviously agreed with Dak. Lagan offered no opinion at all and Kirk didn't seem to be listening. Ab stayed silent. He seemed to be waiting to see how the discussion would work out. Hank was the only one, other than Yvonne, who seemed alarmed in any way.

"I don't think we want to frighten the artists," Dak said. "They would cancel the show in droves. We wouldn't have a show left."

Ab stood up. "I think that what Cheyenne is proposing is reasonable. I have known her for some time and I trust her intuition. I think you should too."

"You're saying that we should tell the artists that there is a possible crazy maniac killer on the loose and to be alert for anything unusual?" Dak shook his head. "Not a good idea."

"I don't think it's necessary to use the word 'killer'," I said. "Nor do I think 'crazy maniac' is appropriate. I could be wrong. I think you should make it known that three artists have died and to be careful. They should take this seriously."

Hank spoke up at last. "I agree with Dak," he said. He seemed reluctant to speak.

"I don't think it would be a good idea to mention it to the artists," Dak said. "We'll talk about hiring a second guard to patrol the venue." He closed the notebook he had open in front of him and I gathered that his would be the last word.

In the end, they took a vote and decided to hire a uniformed guard and to say nothing to the artists.

"Now, we must get back to the agenda," Dak said, dismissing the three dead artists as not important. I gave them the standard paperwork and a contract for them to sign and asked that it be returned prior to the first day of the show the following week. Then I left.

I didn't like their decision at all. It worried me, but it was not my decision to make. It did make my attendance at the show all that much more important.

Before I left downtown, I debated about a trip to the Seattle Police Department to get the report on Barbara Robertson. It was about one-thirty and I had a couple of errands to run. There would be plenty of time, I knew, to grab that report before I left for the coast.

Instead, I headed north to pay a visit to my friend Molly. Whenever I need a voice of reason or someone to restore me to serenity, I turn to her. Molly has been a stabilizing influence for me since my mother died. She is the most comfortable person on the planet and has made her home a nest of contentment.

At her front door, she smothered me in a hug, like she always did, then offered me a poppyseed muffin.

While we ate, I told her about the board meeting and the tepid response I had gotten. Surprisingly, Molly tended to agree with the PCAC board.

"Everyone would panic," she said. "Look how they make a big deal out of everything in the papers and on TV. They make up nicknames for killers. People panic over nothing. Besides, you may not even be right. It might be nothing but a few coincidences." She frowned and looked doubtful. "I'm not sure I remember a time when your intuition was wrong, though."

"Well," I said, polishing off the last of the muffin. "This time, I hope I am wrong and everyone else is right. Either way, I have to buy some decent clothes for the show. Want to go shopping?"

Molly did. There was nothing she liked more than shopping, unless it was eating. For all that she tried to get me to eat and succeeded more often than not, I was continually surprised that we both were not overweight. In fact, Molly had a remarkably good figure for a woman on the other side of fifty.

We headed out to Northgate and milled around in The Bon Marche and Nordstrom until I had found a couple of jackets worthy of an artist. One was a wonderful lavender silk and the other looked like an artist had made it. Beautiful stylized Asian characters in red were set against black with dabs of a gorgeous French blue. I loved it. The salesclerk assured me that it was hand painted. Molly tried to get me to buy a scarlet beret to go with it, but I put my foot down about that.

"Want to get dinner out here?" Molly asked when we were heading out of Nordy's.

"Can't," I said. "Sorry. Easy's coming for dinner tonight."

"I'm not sorry!" she said. "Say 'hello' for me. These Wednesday dinners have gotten to be a regular thing, haven't they?" I could see that her eyes were sparkling with mischief. "Has Easy made any more moves toward an engagement yet?" She wanted me to be married in the worst way. God only knew why. I had tried it once and it hadn't worked. I wasn't about to do it again.

"I don't know. I don't know what 'moves toward engagement' look like," I told her. "Besides, I'm not inclined to get married." Not long before, I had told Molly that I knew Easy had been thinking about proposing. I had nipped that right in the bud and he and I had come to a détente. He wouldn't ask me and

I wouldn't have to say no.

On the way home, my mind returned again and again to the board meeting. I wondered if, having not taken me seriously, they were going to ignore my recommendation. Not the one about warning the artists, they had already shit-canned that one. But would they take my advice and hire an inside security guard? They had voted to but would they follow through? I hoped so, although I didn't know how much good it would do. At least it was better than nothing.

When I reached West Seattle, I chugged up Admiral Way and made a stop at the Fotomat in the Safeway parking lot. I picked up the two packets of pictures from the film I had dropped off the day before then headed into the store to get groceries for Easy's dinner.

Molly was right. Wednesday dinner with Easy *had* become a regular thing. It was comfortable being with him as long as he wasn't having thoughts about marriage. Sometimes being psychic was a pain in the ass.

I was looking forward to seeing Easy. He was another of my stabilizers. I had known him for many years, first as the Chaplain of the Seattle Police Department when he was still Ezekial to me, and then as a beloved and faithful friend who had turned into Easy. I knew that Molly was right, that he still wanted to marry me. He, in turn, knew that I wasn't interested in marriage. It wasn't him. I couldn't think of finer husband material than Easy. He was smart, handsome, friendly, honest, devoted, funny – in fact everything that I considered important. It bothered him a teensy bit that he was two years younger than I. I hadn't the slightest idea why. He wasn't without flaws by any means. Easy had a bit of a sexist streak and thought that I would be better off in a less dangerous job. He might have been right, but that wouldn't be happening any time soon. And he could be a little overprotective which, on occasion, drove me insane.

For a moment, I tried to imagine being married again, only this time to someone whom I could trust, but I shied away from the idea almost immediately. Sometimes I wished that Easy would just give in and have a comfortable, casual sexual relationship with me, but he was too ridden with religious guilt for that. I knew it and did my best to stay out of intimate situations with him. I sighed, knowing that there were no perfect relationships and that I should be happy with what I had.

❋ ❋ ❋

I had just put a chicken salad together and slid some garlic bread into the oven when Easy arrived. I opened the door to his wonderful smile. He gave me a hug like he always did and I had to resist the impulse to kiss him. He was extremely kissable, but doing it had gotten us into sticky situations before.

While the bread heated, we set the table and talked about Walter Mondale's likely nomination by the Democratic party for President.

"I would like to see him win the whole damned thing," I said. "Especially if he picks Geraldine Ferraro as his running mate." I set the salad in the middle of the table and went to get the bread out.

"Are you sure it isn't just because she's a woman?" he asked. I knew he was teasing, but it nettled me a little bit. What's more, I think he knew it.

"We're long past due for a female in a high government office, don't you think?" I asked. "Other countries have women in power. I think the US is the last country that doesn't. That strikes me as somewhat backward, doesn't it you?"

"What strikes me as backward is that we've had an actor for President for the last four years. I don't understand the obsession with celebrity. Who's next, Donald Trump?"

We laughed and while he served the salad and bread, I took a bottle of Chardonnay out of the refrigerator, held it up and lifted my eyebrows.

"Nope," he said. "I'm on call." I put the wine back and we sat down to dinner.

The food was good and so was the company.

It was a pleasure to laugh and watch him enjoy everything right through to the slender slice of cheesecake I served him. He took a bite and his eyes rolled in pleasure.

When we had finished, we lingered at the table unwilling to let the evening end.

"Next week, come to my place and we'll make that pizza you like," he said.

"I won't be able to have dinner with you next Wednesday," I told him while I stacked the plates but made no move to get up and put them in the sink. "Ab has asked me to attend the art show with him."

"I thought you were going to mind the shop," he said, frowning. "Why the change?"

I told him some of what the Pacific Coast Arts Collective board had said about the thefts that appeared to be escalating.

"So, what do they think you can do about it?" he asked.

I shrugged. "I suppose I'm a deterrent. They've agreed to hire a uniformed guard too." I was about to tell him about the three artists who had died but there was something about his demeanor that stopped me.

He pressed his fork onto his cheesecake plate where there were no more crumbs to collect. "Wouldn't that be enough—a guy in uniform? Why do they need you too?"

"A security guard doesn't investigate. They want me to investigate the thefts." I started to rise but Easy's next words made me sit back down. It wasn't so much the words but the tone in which he said them.

"So, you're going to be spending a week with Ab Eberstein?" He didn't look happy.

"I'm going to be on a job," I told him.

He made a dismissive gesture.

"It's not going to be a romantic interlude. It's work," I said, hoping I was still sounding patient. "I wouldn't have mentioned it at all except I won't be able to have dinner with you next Wednesday since we will be leaving that day." I watched him carefully. "Easy, you aren't jealous."

"I think you spend quite a lot of time with Ab," he said. "You're down there at the shop almost every day and now you're going to spend a whole week with him." He wasn't looking at me.

I was amazed. He *was* jealous. "That would be funny if it wasn't so pathetic," I said and laughed a little. I shouldn't have, I admit. I started to put my hand on his arm but he pulled it away. It didn't matter. I could feel his jealousy from where I sat.

"You *do* spend a lot of time with him, Chey. You *know* you do." He spoke with slow and deliberate words as though I was having difficulty understanding the language. He began to tick things off on his fingers. "You cancelled our Wednesday dinner that night he held the open house at the shop," he said. "And you went to him when your car wouldn't start last week. Now, you're planning to spend a week with him. I'm saying that I don't like to be second on your list. There's nothing 'pathetic' about that at all. I don't like it that you spend most of your time with that guy."

"*Most* of my time? Hardly. Besides, I work for the man. What on Earth has gotten into you?" I asked. "I'm at the shop because he is teaching me how to do stained glass. You know that. This is a slow time in my business. You know that too. I'm going because the board asked me to look into the thefts they and some of the other arts organizations have had lately." I shook my head in real bafflement and I thought he looked a little ashamed. "Seriously, Easy."

"I suppose I'm being possessive again," he said. It wasn't an admission of guilt, nor was it anything approaching an apology. It was more a challenge than anything else.

"No shit," I said. I no longer felt like laughing.

"Look, Cheyenne," he said. "I think I've done a good job of keeping silent about this. But when you call him instead of me when you have car trouble, I have to wonder."

I was astonished that he had used my full name. I don't think I had heard him use it since he had first met me. I wondered if it signaled real anger.

"I don't think you're being quite fair," I said trying hard to sound patient. "So, what you're saying is, that you don't trust me."

"I trust *you*."

"I don't think you do," I said. "Last year, you gave me a bunch of grief about my job and now you're doing the same thing about a man I work for."

"I never gave you a 'bunch of grief'!" he said. "I merely said that I thought your job was dangerous. After all, you came home from San Francisco with your face all bruised and cut. You were almost killed! Then I find out that you were almost killed *again* because some guy tried to push you into a volcano crater."

I guessed I wouldn't be telling him about my serial killer theory.

"I agreed to keep quiet about that, yes," he continued. "But it's a little harder for me to keep quiet when you go off for a week with a guy that I know you care about."

"Of course, I care about him. He saved my life. Also, he saved my sanity after that Hawaii thing, Easy," I said, putting my hand out to him. He declined to take it. "You saved my sanity too. I'm surprised at you. What? Do you think I'm going to sleep with him?"

Immediately he said the wrong thing. "I don't

know what to think," he said.

"Easy, for God's sake! What is wrong with you?"

"Lots, apparently," he said.

"Easy," I said. I couldn't believe what was happening. What had happened to easy going Easy? This was a different man altogether.

"I think I should go," he said. "I'm apt to say something I would be sorry for."

"You've already said something you should be sorry for." I was suddenly furious, yet I tried to keep my voice down.

I was dumbfounded when he got up from his chair and left.

I sat at the table long after he had shut the door behind him. His essence seemed to linger; his bigness, the smooth sound of his voice, that shock of dark hair that was constantly falling into his denim blue eyes. There was an emptiness in the house. Or, perhaps, the emptiness was in me.

I was still angry later that evening after I had cleaned up the kitchen. I kept having inner dialogs with Easy and thinking of the perfect things I should have said.

I decided the best thing for me would be to plow ahead with the cases I had pending and the art show case which I hoped would prove my theory wrong. I was confident that, within a day or two, Easy would call me with a shamed apology and we could continue our friendship as usual.

I began by setting up a casebook. I didn't know if I would need one or not. If I was wrong about the deaths, it could be a waste of time, and that would be fine by me. But if I was right, I would be glad I had it. My casebook is a notebook divided into sections. I got into the habit of making a casebook long ago. I took a novel writing class once and found that the bones of a book are similar to the innards of an investigation. In it, I list the people involved, and clues I get, suspects and other assorted information. In the back I set up a time sheet and an expenses list. It makes writing the report a breeze once the case is done.

I needed to think about what clothes I would be taking with me and make sure that my bag of detective tricks was well stocked. I used an old doctor's bag that Easy had given me years before. Looking at it gave me a little twinge of regret which I tried to brush away. I checked to make sure the camera, flashlight, rubber gloves, swabs, plastic bags, binoculars and small empty bottles were there. I had added a couple of hats and scarves for quick disguises and anything else I could use should I need it. I never knew what I might run into and it was best to be prepared. I had a gun but I rarely, if ever, carried it. I had found myself in a dire situation in the volcano case that Easy had referred to. In the course of it, even though I had not carried my weapon, I had been forced to kill someone. I never wanted that to happen again.

It was still a week until I would be leaving and there were those two cases that I needed to finish before-hand.

Had I known what was ahead, I may have made different decisions.

FIVE

Thursday, July 12 through Monday, July 16, 1984

The next morning, I got an early start. I was pretty sure I could complete the two cases I had pending in one day. It turned out I was wrong.

One was a case of fraud. Jackson Dry was on paid leave while he dealt with a back problem suffered on his job with Henderson Brothers Construction. His co-workers at HBC had been complaining to management that he was not hurt as badly as he claimed. One of them had reported that he saw Jackson carrying a fifty pound sack of dog food out of the pet store and putting it into his truck. HBC's insurance company had hired me to try to get pictures of him doing something similar. I had his photograph and had staked out his house but so far, had seen nothing. I had, however, noticed the sounds of sawing and hammering coming from the backyard.

Jackson lived in the Greenwood area of Seattle. His house did not have an alley and there was a six foot fence around the property. Needless to say, I could not see what was going on back there much less take photographs. I couldn't haul a ladder into the next door neighbors' yards nor stand on their garbage cans to peer over the fence so I had to figure out something else.

As I sat in my car across the street from the Dry home, I noticed a new apartment building that was just being finished up in the next block behind Jackson's property. I drove by the front of the building and pulled over. There was a sign on the fence surrounding the place with a name and phone number on it. Interested parties were invited to call Marlene Bainbridge for more information. I jotted down the name and the number then headed back out to locate a phone booth.

I met Ms Bainbridge at nine o'clock in front of the Lake Vista Apartments. As far as I could see, the building had no vista of any lake.

We introduced ourselves and she launched into her spiel about the apartment's amenities. Apparently, there was a gym downstairs and, for an additional fee, pets were welcome.

"Will it be just you?" she asked, "or is there a family? There is a single unit on the third floor and a two bedroom on the second."

"There's just me," I told her.

She pushed the button for three and in a moment, we stepped onto the third floor.

She led me into a brand new apartment, so spotless that there was still cardboard covering the carpeting in the hall. The one she showed me was the single bedroom unit that, alas, looked out over the territory opposite Jackson Dry's back yard. We were, in fact, on the Puget Sound side.

"What do you think of that view? Isn't it gorgeous?" she asked. "I think this is the nicer unit of the two left."

By standing at the far left side of the living room window, I could see a tiny glint flash off the waters of the Sound through the trees. What little of the water I could see was a clear blue and I could catch a glimpse of the mountains that still held some of the winter's snow. Not exactly "gorgeous". Nothing is prettier than Seattle on a summer day though, even if you have no view to gaze at.

She was surprised when I asked to see the two bedroom unit on the second floor. "This one is much nicer," she told me. "Even with the view the rent is very reasonable. These view units have gone fast. Also, I don't believe the units on that side of the building have been finished yet." I thought I saw the first glimmer of suspicion flicker in her eyes. I didn't say anything. At last, she sighed and we rode the elevator again.

The suspicion flamed brighter when I bypassed the bedrooms and headed for the front window. There was a splendid view in this unit too. Two large pines framed a fine view of Jackson Dry's backyard complete with a half-built deck. No one was in the yard, but I was willing to bet that Jackson was the one building it.

"Now, of course, you wouldn't be able to move in for a little while," Marlene was saying. "They're still finishing this one. The appliances won't be installed for a few more weeks." She gave a guilty little laugh. "In fact, no one has been here for a while. They can't do anything further until the washer and dryer and kitchen stuff comes. But the installation is the last thing to be done and it will be ready."

"Perfect," I said. "That doesn't matter to me. I would like to rent this space for just a week."

Marlene Bainbridge opened her mouth and shut it again.

"I don't want to live here." I pulled my PI license out of my wallet. "I'm a private investigator and I'm doing some surveillance. I won't be putting any wear and tear on it at all. In fact, I would only be here an hour or two each day until I get what I need. Maybe not even that much."

The intrigue dawned on her face and quickly replaced the skepticism in her eyes. I saw it and took advantage. "This would be an off the books deal between the two of us," I said. "I'll give you $25 for the week. Cash. If you like, I can give you another $25 for a damage deposit."

I could see the little war that was going on in poor

Marlene's mind, but I also saw the gleam in her eyes. I would be willing to bet that she had read plenty of Nancy Drew when she was a kid.

* * *

That afternoon, I brought my camera, a notebook, some water and a lawn chair and set up my base of operations in the front window of Apartment 202 of the Lake Vista. I sat there for two hours but was rewarded only by seeing Mrs. Dry come out of the back door with a sack of garbage and deposit it into the trash bin. It looked like Jackson wasn't even home. I decided to call it a day. I had another task to finish.

My other case involved keeping an eye on someone too. A guy named Mannheim Samuelson had been dodging my friend Link, a process server I knew, for a week. Link had at last given up and had handed the case off to me so he could grab a few days with his girlfriend in Hawaii. I didn't mind. He had done all the hard stuff anyway. I was sure I could take care of it in one evening. First, though, I needed to make a quick stop at the thrift store.

The Goodwill had exactly what I needed; A pair of shiny black pants that were so tight they almost qualified as leggings, a ridiculous little purse and a stretchy tube top that had sequins dangling all over it. I also found a pair of what could loosely be classified as high heeled sandals obviously made by the FuckMe Shoe Company.

Like I said, Link had already done the hard part. He had discovered that Manny—he liked to be known as "Sam"—hung out at the Golden Dragon Bar and Restaurant in Chinatown. Except for the fact that I hate the Golden Dragon with a hot purple passion, my job promised to be easy.

I dressed with care. I had some old make-up that had belonged to my mother in another decade, and I put on as much as I could. The sequins on the tube top made it extremely uncomfortable for me to put my arms down to my sides and the shoes were almost impossible to walk in, but I looked great. Or, if not great, I looked like the kind of tart that could get Manny's attention.

The Golden Dragon was a sleazy dump that I tried to stay away from. The carpet in the lounge looked like it had been there for a century and had never seen a cleaning. Bar fights and drug deals were frequent occurrences.

The second I walked in the door, I spotted Manny/ Sam at the bar. I had never seen the man in person, but he was the only one at the bar and he looked like the picture Link had shown me. He had been gnawing on some kind of sandwich. As I got closer, I saw he had a pickle and a slice of tomato on his plate along with half of a burger. I stopped at the end of the bar and ordered a glass of water with lime, then made my way to the stool next to Manny.

When the bartender brought my water, Manny turned to me. I took a sip and winced a little as if it were straight vodka or gin. Then I gave him a long look, raised one eyebrow and turned back to my "drink."

He said "I've never seen you here before." Or some shit like that.

I said nothing.

"I like that star," he said, referring to a scar that I had gotten in an altercation with a guy who wore a star-shaped ring. It had occurred during the infamous San Francisco encounter Easy had mentioned. Again, the thought of him made me sad.

"Thanks," I said and felt like a fool when I tried to flutter my eyelashes.

I gave him another long look and took another sip of my water.

He turned on his stool to face me. "So, what's your name?"

"Bruce," I told him. "Cheyenne Bruce." I thought I sounded like James Bond and thought it was funny but he didn't get it.

"Which one is your first name?" he asked. I knew the guy was never going to win any quiz shows.

"Cheyenne," I said. "But you can call me Ms Bruce. You are Mr…?"

"Sam," he said, looking a little baffled.

"Just Sam? No last name? Doesn't matter, I always liked the name Samuel."

"My last name is Samuelson," he said, "but everyone calls me Sam."

"So, what's your first name? Or don't you want to be on a first name basis?" I tried the eyelash thing again and, I thought, failed miserably.

He laughed. "It's Mannheim. Now do you see why I like to be called Sam? It's better than Manny, and much better than Heimy."

"Wait. It's Mannheim...Sam..." I tried very hard to look confused.

"Mannheim Samuelson," he said, and put out his hand for me to shake.

I laughed and leaned into him while I reached into my handbag. With my left hand, I took the pickle from his plate and bit off the end. With my right, I put the subpoena into his outstretched hand. "It's nice to meet you Mannheim Samuelson," I said. "You've been served."

He looked down at the envelope in his hand. "What the hell?" he said and stood up. He looked like he had just awakened from a long coma and he was furious about it. "What the hell?" he screamed again. Then, muttering, he started to drag his wallet out to pay for his food. He looked at me and shoved the wallet back into his pocket.

"Fuck you, lady," he said. "You can pay." He turned around and headed for the door. The other bar patrons, always looking for entertainment, watched as he picked up a chair that was in his way and threw it aside. It crashed into one of the minuscule tables and toppled it.

"What's his problem?" the bartender asked when I handed him a ten.

"He's just mad because he got caught in some illicit activity. I have his address if you want to send him a bill for any damage he may have done. I'm sure he'd be delighted to pay for it."

He laughed. "Yeah, I'm sure he would," he said. "Don't worry about it. The furniture in here has been through worse." I didn't doubt that for a moment.

I went home. I still had to write a declaration attesting to the fact that I had served Mr. Mannheim Samuelson with his summons. I could do it that night and drop in at my client's office the next day to get it notarized and delivered at the same time. Then, when I had finished with Mr. Jackson Dry, I would be in the clear for the art show case.

On the second day sitting in the Misnamed Apartment, I was rewarded. Just after I arrived at ten am, Jackson himself came outside and proceeded to work on the deck. I took picture after picture of him, kneeling, sawing, carrying boards. At one point, Mrs. Dry came outside and talked to him. He stopped sawing and went into a small shed in the back yard and came out with what looked like a fifty pound bag of potting soil which he obligingly opened for his wife.

At about ten-thirty I was ready to pack it in. I called Ms. Bainbridge from home and told her answering machine that I had gotten what I wanted and wouldn't be needing the apartment for the full week. I had left my key on the kitchen counter as she had instructed and thanked her again for her accommodation. Even though I had used the apartment for only two days, the week's rent and the damage deposit I had given her were well worth it.

* * *

The weekend passed with no word at all from Easy. I knew that I could call him and probably would at some point, but I thought he owed me a call at least and an apology at most. I spent my time cleaning my house, washing clothes, returning phone calls and packing. And, yes, I went to Avenue Art Glass too. The stupid guilty feeling I got from seeing Ab made me even angrier at Easy. I had never given one moment's thought to Ab as a romantic partner and now I couldn't seem to get the idea of it out of my mind. "Thanks, Easy," I said to myself.

I had gotten into the habit of walking or jogging every morning. It was always a good way to clear my mind. That Monday, I was determined to clear it of both Easy and Ab. I ran until all I could think about was getting into a cool shower and dry clothes.

In the afternoon I did a couple of quick jobs that required nothing more than a phone call and a trip downtown to the County-City building to look up records. While I was there, I stopped in at the Seattle Police Department and found my friend Perce O'Dell working at his desk.

He looked up and his long face wreathed in a smile that was balm to my sore heart. "Hey!" he said. "Where have you been keeping yourself?"

He stood up and then bent his great height to give me a hug. I've known Perce longer than I can remember and we've been good, close friends. His warmth and kindness were legendary and exactly what I needed right then.

"Here and there," I said. "I came down to find out what I could about the Barbara Robertson hit and run case. Any chance of getting the report on that?" I gave a quick glance toward Easy's office but the door was shut and the light was off. I didn't ask Perce where he was.

"No problem," Perce said and opened a nearby file cabinet. "To tell you the truth, I don't think this is going anywhere. Even though there were two witnesses, neither one of them saw a thing." He headed for the copier and fed sheets into it.

"The husband told me it was a man driving. One of the witnesses noticed that at least," I said.

Perce nodded. "An older guy. Bald. The witness…" he shuffled through the papers for a second. "Henry Fiske said that. The woman didn't see anything except Mrs. Robertson being hit." He handed me the copies. "We're trying to work with pretty much nothing here. There's not much we can do." He sighed. I knew he hated being unable to solve a case.

We chatted for a while and I hoped both that Easy would and wouldn't come in. He didn't. And, though it was refreshing to talk to Perce, there was work to be done, so at last, I went home.

There was nothing at all unusual about those few days, except that they felt empty because I knew that Easy and I were out of sympathy with each other.

SIX

Wednesday, July 18, 1984

I got up early on the morning we would leave so I would have time for a little exercise before the long car ride to the coast. It was the perfect morning for it, still cool but with an undercurrent of coming heat. I headed down California Way toward the water and alternately walked and jogged until my face was warm and moist with sweat. Then I tackled the long walk up the hill and headed home.

As I turned the corner toward my house, I saw Iola Graft from across the street, still in her pajamas and a pink robe. I jogged toward her as she looked around as though she were studying each of the houses on the block.

"Mrs. Graft," I said when I had caught up with her. "Are you lost? Is something wrong?"

I hadn't seen her for a couple of weeks. For months, her son had been talking about putting her into what he called a "care home" and I thought he might have made good on it, although I didn't think she would go without a goodbye for me. It appeared he hadn't. Iola looked at me and seemed to come to attention.

"Just the person I wanted to see," she said. She was a sweet, grandmotherly looking lady. Her permed white hair was thin and her pink scalp showed through. She had merry blue eyes that formed into crescents when she smiled. She usually wore those white cat's eye glasses that had been popular twenty years before, but that day she wasn't wearing them.

I was surprised that she had wanted to see me. I knew her, but had only talked to her three or four times. She couldn't seem to get it into her head that my name is Cheyenne and not Diane.

"Are you lost?" I asked again.

"A little bit," she said, nodding.

Mrs. Graft didn't know it but she had been instrumental in helping me to solve one of my cases. But that's a whole other story. I took her arm and turned her around so she was facing the right direction and we started walking at her slow and deliberate pace toward her son's home.

"What is it you wanted to see me about?" I asked.

She stopped walking. She looked both ways up and down the block then leaned in to me. "There's something going on around here."

"Oh?" I asked. I had learned at our first meeting to not dismiss Iola's ramblings out of hand. She had once told me that she had seen some ghostly activity at Magda St. Martin's house which, in the end, had turned out to be true. Just not in the way Iola had told it.

"I think there's a monster running loose," she whispered.

"What kind of a monster?" I tried giving her elbow a little tug to propel her forward again but she wasn't having it.

"Well, *I* don't know," she said, putting an emphasis on the "I". "That's why I wanted to talk to you. You're a detective, aren't you?"

"I am." I was surprised that she remembered that.

"I've seen some strange goings on," she said. "I think you should investi—" She stopped when she saw her neighbor, Frank Granger, step onto his front porch to fetch his newspaper. He gave us a brief look then retreated back to his house.

"Oh, dear!" she said. I was surprised at how distressed she was. I could feel the fear blossom as I held onto her arm. "He saw us! Oh, no! We'll both have to be very careful now!"

"Is it something about Mr. Granger?" He seemed a pleasant man in his sixties who lived with a quiet wife and a cocker spaniel. I had seen him often enough to nod to but had never spoken to him.

"I don't know *which* one it is," she said, impatient, as though I were a somewhat backward child. "We have to be careful of them all."

We had reached her porch by then and I could see that the door was ajar. I hoped her son had not discovered her missing yet. If he had, he might step up his plan to move her to the "care home" and I didn't want her to leave the neighborhood. I knew she didn't want to go either.

"We could have tea this afternoon, and I can tell you all about it," she said.

"I'm sorry, Mrs. Graft, but I'm leaving this morning and will be gone for several days. I would love to have tea with you when I get back. Okay?"

She thought for a moment. "I hope that won't be too late," she said. "I think I'll write down everything I know. That way, if I'm gone when you come home, you'll at least be able to find out what happened."

"That sounds like a good idea," I told her, trying to steer her in the door.

"They're going to put me away, you know?" she said.

Her son appeared in the hallway and came toward us.

"Was she out wandering again?" he asked. "Mom, I told you that you can't go out alone."

She muttered something I didn't catch and headed toward the depths of the house.

"She wasn't wandering," I told him. "She and I were just having a little chat." I turned to go across the street to my own house.

"Thanks for bringing her home," he called and I threw him a wave.

I didn't know it then, but that was the last time I would see Mrs. Graft alive.

*　*　*

I was still thinking about Iola when I grabbed my suitcase, bag and garment carrier with my new jackets and headed down to Avenue Art Glass. I was early, but hoped to help Ab with whatever needed doing to finish loading the van for the trip. He had already crated the big pieces so I helped him wrap and pack the last of the smaller items.

"Hey!" I said when he handed me a small box to wrap. "I made this. You can't think it's good enough to sell!"

"Of course it's good enough to sell," he said. "I've already sold two of those five you made. I'm going to take the ones that are left to the show. I'm taking those oval suncatchers you made too. Don't underestimate yourself, babe."

I thought for the first time since I had started the previous January, that I was, at last, contributing to the shop. I was pleased beyond all rationality.

We worked through the rest of the morning

packing, wrapping, checking and rechecking.

We loaded the smaller pieces into the van along with the crate containing the big window that was Ab's contest entry as well as the tables, chairs, booth components and décor that would transform a ten by ten square of concrete into an inviting, attractive booth. Long ago he had worked out a lighting system that he could hang from the booth framework that would shine through the glass and make it glow with color. He had been working shows for years and had a plastic utility chest—a "drawer thing" as he called it—loaded with sales receipts, order blanks, cords, hooks and anything else that could be needed for the five day sojourn.

When we had stowed our luggage in the very back, it looked as though there was room for not one more thing. It was after two o'clock and I was already running out of gas.

At last we started out and I felt like a kid on the way to camp. I didn't know what to expect but knew it would probably be fun.

"We should get there around five," Ab said when we had crossed the bridge and hit I-5 going south. "Barring any major traffic or the unexpected." He turned to look at me. "Excited?"

"Yes, I am," I told him. I didn't tell him I was a little nervous too. I kept thinking that we had forgotten something vital. "Did you remember the extension cords?"

He laughed. "Yes, I got the extension cords. That's the reason why I keep the checklist. I've been doing this for a long time and I still question myself. One time, way back, I forgot to bring the 's' hooks." He laughed again. S hooks were indeed vital for hanging the stained glass pieces. Without them, there would be no booth. "I was lucky, the show was in Everett and not out in the sticks so I could stop at a hardware store and buy some."

The day was sunny and the air sparkling. Again, I had that kid-like feeling as if I was starting out on a vacation or an adventure. I settled back and began to relax and enjoy the ride.

"How do *you* feel, Ab?" I asked him. "Are *you* excited?"

He thought for a moment. "Yes, I guess I am. I used to be nervous as a cat right before a show. Worried about how much I was going to be able to sell. That was before I had the shop and selling at shows was my livelihood. This show is indoors, so it's much easier. And it's in a touristy area. Usually, the sales are pretty good in places like that."

"An indoor show is easier?" I asked. "How come?"

Toward Tacoma the traffic grew heavier and I could see darkening clouds off to the west. In a few minutes we were inching along the road.

"Outdoor shows are much harder," he said. "You've got the weather to deal with. It might be so hot you think you can't breathe or so cold that your fingers are too numb to make change. You need a canopy and weights for the canopy. I was at a show in Ilwaco one summer and a gale whipped up so bad that they had to shut down the show after two of the canopies blew into the water. I heard about a show in Marysville one year—thank God I wasn't there! The people who were, had all kinds of stories about the street drains backing up in a torrential rain and their booths being flooded." He shook his head. "Most of the artists are too poor to have insurance so they just had to eat the loss."

He talked on about various shows he had attended or heard about while I relaxed back in the comfortable bucket seats.

Finally, we left I-5 and the traffic behind and headed for Highway 101. That would take us to the quiet little town of Oceanside. The clouds had, at last, caught up to us. We stowed our sunglasses and Ab put both hands on the wheel when the rain hit about four-thirty.

The rain bashed the van and sheets of water sluiced sideways on the window next to me. I felt the tension growing in the car and thought a little chitchat might help to ease it.

"How much do you think we should tell our housemates about why I'm there?" I asked him. "Should I just be an assistant who came along to help you or should we warn them?"

Ab seemed to give it some thought. "What do you

think?"

"If they know I'm keeping an eye on them all, it might make for a pretty uncomfortable few days. They might act differently than they normally would."

"Makes sense," he said, with his gaze still riveted on the road ahead.

"Not that any of them are under any kind of suspicion. I know that people get a little twitchy if they think they're being watched."

Ab's only reply was a small nod as another gust of wind hit us.

"I guess we won't be getting there at five," I said. Ab didn't answer.

The rain came harder and battered the van, the windshield wipers swished at a frantic pace to keep up. Occasional gusts hit us broadside making the van rock. The heavy clouds seemed to come almost to the ground and it grew as dark as it would be on a late afternoon in winter. All around us, huge evergreens sighed, moaned and twisted as if trying to get away from the storm.

"'The woods are lovely, dark and deep,'" I said.

"That's for damned sure," Ab answered, his jaw tight.

The highway had become a two lane road with twists and turns that forced us to slow, sometimes to less than twenty miles an hour. On one side was a sheer rock face where the road had been cut through. The other side was a drop off with a view of the tops of trees that grew far below.

It wasn't long before a car came up behind us. At first, the driver stayed a car length or two behind but soon began to creep closer.

"Oh, get off my ass," Ab muttered at the rear view mirror.

The car stayed in back of us, so close it looked like it was touching the van's back bumper. At least it appeared that way from the mirror on my side.

Ab tried slowing down even more but the car stayed put.

Grumbling something that I didn't hear—I think it was in Yiddish—Ab pulled over to the side of the road, stuck his arm out the window and waved the car on. As it passed, going way too fast for the conditions, I could only get a glimpse of the driver, just a vague outline. The car was dark but so dirty it was impossible to discern what color it was. The rain and gloom didn't help.

"Could you see the driver at all?" I asked Ab. He shook his head but said nothing.

"Crazy to drive like that in this weather," I said.

For a while we didn't speak at all. Ab was concentrating on keeping the van on the road, negotiating the twists and turns and trying to peer through the struggling windshield wipers.

It was just after we passed a sign that said "Oceanside 45 miles" that I looked at my side mirror. The headlights, the left one a little dimmer than the right, looked familiar.

"Is that the same car behind us?"

"Pretty sure," Ab said through clenched teeth.

"What in the hell...?" I muttered.

The car remained about two car lengths behind us for a mile or more then began to creep closer.

"I'm not pulling over," Ab said. "Not doing it, buddy." I knew he wasn't talking to me.

The car inched nearer until it was so close, I could no longer see its headlights. A second later, I felt a small jolt and the van fishtailed a little.

"Jesus Christ!" Ab said. "Hang on!" His knuckles were white as he gripped the wheel.

He began to tap the brakes very gently and gradually slowed. The car behind us nudged the van twice more, the second time was not a gentle nudge. The van fishtailed violently and Ab had to struggle to keep it on the slick highway. I held on to the dash and watched where the edge of the road dropped off into the steep ravine. The guard rail, at that moment, couldn't have looked flimsier.

Suddenly, the car pulled into the oncoming lane and sped past us. I tried hard to get a glimpse of the driver, but all I could see was a hazy outline through the pounding rain.

We didn't speak at all as we wound our way along the gloomy, narrow highway. Trees crowded each side of the road making the murky way before us even darker. It was a couple more miles before we saw the car again, waiting at the end of a logging road. As soon as we went past, it turned and followed us.

This time, Ab kept his speed as slow as possible. We had been going twenty-five on the slippery turns but he let the van slow to a crawl. The dark, dirty car behind us crept to within inches and once more began to tap the back of the van. It gave us a bump violent enough to cause us to skid closer to the edge even though we were barely moving.

With short taps on the brake, Ab eased the van to a stop. The car stopped behind us.

"I'm going to find out what's going on," he said, and began to open the door.

"No! Ab, wait!" I said, envisioning the driver crushing Ab between the two cars or smashing him into the side of the van as he sped past.

But, before Ab could open the door, the car pulled out and rushed away. It was gone in a blur of rain.

❋ ❋ ❋

I t was about five-fifteen when we pulled over into the parking lot of the tiniest diner I had ever seen. The sign above the door, spray painted on a piece of plywood, said "Ma's".

"How about some R and R, kiddo?" Ab said. "I can't guarantee food, but maybe we can get some coffee."

While I don't drink coffee, I would have welcomed it by then. We climbed out of the van and as soon as I stood, I realized how tense my muscles had been. I felt like I hadn't been on my feet in years. I stretched and threw back my head so my face was to the sky. The rain was beginning to taper off.

I followed Ab as he circled to the back of his van and we inspected the bumper.

"I don't see a thing," I said. The bumper was already so textured with scuffs, scrapes and dings, I didn't see how anyone could tell if there was new damage or not.

"No, I don't either. I'm going to call the police anyway, if there's a phone in there." He nodded toward the tiny building. "Let's go in before we get drenched to the skin."

It turned out there *was* a phone booth inside. It stood in the corner, elegant in its wood and glass walls. I thought it had been there since telephones were invented. Ab headed straight for it and I saw him riffle through the worn telephone book before I scanned the rest of the room.

Inside, "Ma's" looked much homier than it did on the outside. Red and white checkered tablecloths covered three small round tables and a bar with red barstools held three men, all wearing the same thing; jeans, plaid cotton shirts and boots. I felt like I had stepped back into 1958. A woman who could have been Ma herself greeted me and seemed delighted when I indicated that I was with the man making the phone call. The three men at the bar stared.

"Take any table you like," she said and handed me two menus. They looked hand typed and had charming misspellings and typos.

I chose a table and sat, watching Ab. He was scowling and, though I couldn't hear him through the walls of the booth, he did not look happy. In a moment he joined me, still wearing his frown.

"Special today is pot roast and noodles," Ma said just as Ab pulled out his chair.

He looked at me and I shrugged. Ma hovered while we looked at the menus.

Every selection featured meat in some form. Beef, it seemed was the food of choice in the neighborhood. I tried to avoid including meat in my diet, but I was hungry and enjoying the endorphin rush of being off the road. I had to admit, it looked appealing.

"I'll have the pot roast," Ab said and raised his eyebrows at me.

I shrugged again and said, "Sure, why not?"

Ma collected the menus and disappeared into the depths of the diner.

"Well?" I said.

"The sheriff's office can't do anything." Ab's glower was back. "They said that, if there was no damage to my car and I had no description of the car that followed us, their hands were tied." He shook his head then muttered, "Bastards."

"I, for one, feel grateful to be here," I said. "What do you think all that was about?"

"I have no idea. It was clear that guy wanted us off the road. Why? I don't know. You piss anybody off lately?"

"Well, I piss people off all the time," I said, "but not to the extent they would want to kill me and whoever I happened to be with as well."

"Probably just some crazy kid," he said, but I could tell that he didn't believe that.

"I'm not so sure," I said. "It was too dark and raining too hard to even tell what color the car was, let alone who was inside. I tried to get a look at the license plate but it was too dirty to see." I said it again for emphasis. "*Too* dirty."

"You mean you think someone had deliberately disguised it?"

I nodded. "A little dirt is normal. Too much

is suspicious. I would think the rain would have washed off simple dirt. Could you even tell what kind of car that was?"

He shook his head. "I don't know cars. It was a dark sedan, that's all I know. Dark red maybe?"

"I got the impression it was dark blue," I said. "At any rate, whoever you talked to was right. There's nothing the sheriff can do. We have no license, no make, no model, no color, no description of the driver. Nothing."

Right then, the door was flung open and two men strode in, both dressed exactly like the triplets at the bar.

I saw Ab flinch, then he scrutinized the men who had paid no attention to our presence. I watched as he continued to eye them with suspicion. I knew then that the incident with the car had unnerved him as much as it had me. I had never seen him act uncomfortable at all. Not with a demanding customer, not when his shop was vandalized. Never.

"Maybe it was someone who wants to make sure you're out of the contest?" I said, half kidding.

Ab tore his gaze from the men who had seated themselves at the table behind me. "Prize money isn't *that* good," he said.

Our dinners arrived then and he looked appreciatively at the chunk of meat and the mound of noodles.

The food was wonderful. The pot roast was as tender as butter and flavored with onions, garlic and some herb that I couldn't identify. I began to wonder why on Earth I was so averse to meat, especially if it was so good. The noodles were a golden brown, having absorbed the savory juices from the roast.

"So, how many people know my purpose for coming to the show?" I asked when we had eaten in blissful silence for a few minutes.

"Only the board members," he said, looking at me with surprise. "Why do you ask?"

"If it isn't you someone wants harmed, then it's me."

"You don't think it was kids?"

I shook my head. "No. And I don't think you do either. There was only one person in the car. I could see that much, at least. Kids prefer to travel in packs. They do things like that when they have an audience. Besides, it seems we were deliberately targeted. He waited for us twice. In my mind, there is someone who doesn't want one or both of us at the show."

"Say that's true," he said. "How would they know where we were and what we were driving? How would they know it was us in that van?"

"It's easy to discover personal information such as license plate numbers, addresses and such. Trust me. I'm an investigator. I do it all the time."

Ab shook his head. "I don't think it's a board member. Some of them are arrogant, some are insecure, but they voted unanimously to hire you. I don't think any of them would want you to be hurt or, God forbid, killed!"

I had to agree with him, but someone had tried to cause us to have an accident. I would have to give the problem more thought, but as I remembered the three deaths that I had learned about, I decided to keep my mouth shut for now. If someone wanted to keep us from the show, or at least to keep me from investigating, I thought there was more to the case than just a rash of thefts. Much more.

SEVEN

Wednesday, July 18, 1984

The rest of the trip went smoothly. The rain had eased up by the time we left the diner and the sky had begun to lighten again. For a summer squall, though, that one had been a doozy!

We talked little, both sated, I thought, by food.

"I think it was just someone playing around," Ab said finally. We hadn't been talking about the incident on the road but I knew we both had been thinking about it.

I was sure that it had *not* been "someone playing around". I wondered then, if, over the years, I had become a bit paranoid. But no, I thought. There had been three deaths, two by auto accidents. Why not a third? During that rainstorm, it would have been easy to run us off the road and kill two birds with one stone so to speak. But, again, for what purpose? Ab was an artist, yes, but I wasn't. I gave myself a good mental shake and told myself to be patient. I didn't know enough yet to be any kind of judge about the situation.

It wasn't long before we began to see signs that we were nearing the town of Oceanside. The winding road through the forest had ended and we passed small farms and clusters of homes. Before long, I spotted a sign that read "Black Lake" and a moment later I saw the lake itself. Surrounded by huge pines and marsh grasses, the water looked impossibly dark, as though the lake was filled with ink rather than water. I was used to the blueness of Lake Washington and the sea green waters of Puget Sound. Black Lake looked forbidding and cold. Even though it was mid-July, I saw no swimmers nor even picnickers at the lake's edge. It was impossible to tell how deep it was; the daylight did not reveal anything but black.

"The house isn't far now," Ab said, glancing at a piece of paper he had pulled from his pocket. I reached over and took it so he could concentrate on his driving.

We turned down a residential street that was lined with older homes. Some of them were run down with sagging fences and in need of paint and repairs. Some looked well kept. Many were large and of an earlier era. Amid the stately, handsome houses were small beach cabins as well.

"We'll have six roommates, I believe," Ab said as we crept down the street searching for the address. "They'll be other artists or show staff. There's a couple with a teenaged daughter and three others I don't know anything about."

I said nothing, wondering how that would go. In my experience, eight strangers in a communal living situation don't always work well together. I, once again, told my pessimistic, paranoid mind to shut up.

The house sat off the main street, down a quiet little dead end. It was by itself on the shortened block. Across the street was a vacant lot which trailed downhill into a wooded ravine. Only a half block away and around the corner was a pharmacy and a little old-fashioned post office/grocery with a leaning phone booth out in front. The store looked as though it had been there as long as the house. The pharmacy appeared more up to date even though it was at least thirty years old. On the far side of town loomed the Pacific Ocean. From where we were, we couldn't see it, but the smell of salt and tide rode on the air.

We pulled up in front of the house which had been impressive in an earlier day. There were three floors, bay windows and gables everywhere. Both it and the fence were in need of paint and repair but the porch looked sound and the grounds had been mowed. There were three huge crows sitting on the stained pickets of the fence. They eyed us as we climbed out of the van.

When we opened the gate, the birds continued to

watch us carefully but didn't fly off.

"Those are some big crows," I said, looking back at them.

"They're big because they aren't crows, they're ravens," Ab told me while he rummaged in his jeans pocket for the key. "You don't see many of them in Seattle but they live everywhere." That was news to me. I had thought crows and ravens were the same thing.

The inside of the house was old and though it was a little shabby, it was clean. The front door opened on a small entry hall. To the right was an arched entry into the living room. The dining room was through another arch to the left. Farther along, I could see a wide stairway that was sided with elaborately carved pickets and newel posts.

Ab had said that Beachhouse was "known" to be haunted and I had been curious to see what I could feel from it. Houses almost always have either a positive or a negative feel. Many houses that are purported to be haunted simply have negativity emanating from them, not ghosts. The auras of some buildings are quite strong and even non-psychic people can feel them at times, leading them to believe there are spirits present.

That day, my abilities seemed out of sync, a frightening thought for me. At the very least, I am able to get a sense of who had lived in a home. Beachhouse seemed to be soulless. Was it haunted?

I couldn't tell. If it was, it was not in the traditional sense. At that point, though, I could almost believe the place was populated by spirits, given the chill that came over me as I stepped inside. But, to be honest, that feeling was probably from moving out of a hot, uncomfortable vehicle into a shaded house.

Some past owner had left the wood door lintels and window frames unpainted. Instead, they were stained and varnished and glowed with a warm richness. I thought they were original to the house. The floors were wood and worn and most likely original too. The carpeting was old, thin with wear in spots but clean. Once again, I was struck with the un-homey feel of Beachhouse. It needed people in it, that was all, I told myself.

"Anyone here?" Ab called, but no one answered. "I guess not. Let's get out to the van and get our things. Since we're the first, we can have our pick of the bedrooms."

The ravens watched us as we made a trip back to the van. The glass pieces and booth paraphernalia could remain there. It was only our suitcases, my work bag and our garment bags that needed to be brought in.

We put our luggage at the foot of the stairs then went to explore the rest of the house.

The kitchen had all the modern conveniences; the stove was electric and the refrigerator was roomy. There was a microwave too and an ancient looking dishwasher. Stained, old linoleum covered the floor and lined the countertops. There was a metal strip along the edges where the seams joined. A scarred table sat in the middle of the kitchen with four chairs around it. The cabinets were high and old fashioned. In one corner was a small door in the wall that I recognized as something my mother had called a cooler. I opened it to find, as I had expected, a screen at the back so that it was open to the outside. Inside was a forlorn, almost empty jar of peanut butter. Such coolers had been used, before electric refrigeration, to keep things cool in the summer. I guessed one could also have used it for a freezer in the winter.

Beyond the kitchen was what, in modern times, would be called a mudroom. Back when the house was new it was more likely a pantry or a utility room. It had shelves for canned goods, a washer, dryer and water heater. Across the hall was a small bedroom, next to that a bathroom, and another bedroom was on the other side of the bath.

Ab and I went upstairs with our bags. At the top of the stairs, a long hall ran the length of the house. On the right was a library and across the hall from that, another bathroom. There were five more bedrooms and one more bathroom along the length of the hall. I imagined that this had been a rooming house in an earlier day.

Ab chose one of the two bedrooms in the front, simply for the reason that it was a corner room and looked out over the front yard, the street and the ravine. I chose one closer to the stairs. I knew that the other corner room's east window would allow the sun to stream in each morning much earlier than I wanted to wake. The bedrooms were all close to the same size, each furnished with a bed, a desk and chair, a small chest of drawers, a nightstand and a wardrobe. There were no built-in closets. Each one was close to one of the bathrooms and, except for the eastern exposure of the corner room, we could see no disadvantage of one over any of the others.

I put my suitcase on the floor inside the room I chose, shut the door behind me and walked down the length of the hall. There were more stairs leading upward to the third floor and I was eager to see what was up there. I had seen from the street that the windows were covered and knew that the rooms were probably unused, but I was, and still am, devoutly, insatiably curious. I was doomed to disappointment, though, because Ab called to me that someone else had arrived.

We both went downstairs to see that a dark sedan and trailer had pulled up behind Ab's van. I know we both had the same thought; that the car was probably not the one which had plagued us on our drive down. It was clean and the license plate was clear. Besides, it pulled a trailer and the car we had met had not.

We walked out to the gate as though we were the owners, ready to welcome visitors.

A man and a woman emerged from the front seats of the car and a young woman from the back.

"Hi!" the man called to us. "We're looking for Yellowstone Park."

The woman glanced at him and said "Don't listen to him. He thinks he's terribly funny." She put out her hand. "I'm Cassandra LaChance. This is my husband, Carson and our daughter Persis."

Ab and I introduced ourselves. As I touched her hand, I felt a buzz of energy from Cassandra. I had the feeling that she was never still for very long and I got the sense that she was nervous. She was tall – they both were – and her hair was short and reddish blonde and always seemed to be in motion because she herself was.

Carson seemed the opposite of his wife. He was tall too, but didn't seem as energetic. I felt a strong undercurrent of insecurity in him. He wore his gray hair short and a trim gray beard. Where his wife was stick thin, Carson was stockier and was beginning to develop a paunch. He seemed to have a ready smile.

Their daughter, Persis, looked like neither of her parents. Nor did she respond to my offer of a handshake. She had jet black hair that she wore short on one side and long on the other. She had a lethal looking earring in the ear that was not covered by hair. She wore a studded dog collar around her neck and black jeans and, in spite of the summer day, a long sleeved t-shirt. Her lipstick was dark red, almost black. Despite her attempts to look older, I judged her to be somewhere between thirteen and fifteen. She threw a quick glance at me and frowned.

They told us they were from Tacoma, and they had encountered the same traffic and rainstorm that we had.

"There are two bedrooms down here," Ab said when we had reached the entry. "The rest of them are upstairs. Come on up and I'll show them to you." He sounded like a tour guide.

Persis had gone off on her own, opening doors and peering into rooms. I heard her in the hall, then she returned without her suitcase.

"Come on, Persis," Cassandra said as she appeared again. "Let's go upstairs and pick our rooms." She and Carson headed up the stairs with Persis reluctantly following.

Persis muttered something under her breath and I heard Cassandra say, "Oh, no you are not!"

Just after Ab and the LaChances had gone upstairs, another car arrived. This one, an aging Ford station wagon, parked across the street. A tall man wearing an African *dashiki*, climbed out. I saw him speak to the ravens on the fence but I couldn't hear what he said. The colors of his clothing shone brilliant against the darkness of his skin. I opened the door, startling him.

"Hello," he said. His voice was rich and chocolatey, much like his complexion. "I am Ayubu Issay. We will be housemates, I believe."

"Cheyenne Bruce," I told him. "Come in." I stepped back to allow him into the entry. "Do you have anything more to bring in? I would be happy to help you."

He thanked me but declined my offer. I told him that he could find the bedrooms upstairs and he nodded. I heard Cassandra, Carson and Persis coming down the stairs while Ayubu went outside to fetch something from his car.

"It's too old," I heard Cassandra say.

Carson murmured something that I didn't catch.

"I don't see why," Persis said. Her voice was low and throaty. I thought it would be a true asset when she matured. It would have had a lovely, musical quality if she had not sounded so sullen.

"This house is cold and drafty," Cassandra continued. "It's probably unsafe and unhealthy too. And, Persis, if we *must* stay here, then you will take the bedroom we choose for you."

"I'm going to look around," Persis said and headed down the hall in the opposite direction.

"I don't understand why you couldn't have made reservations at the hotel, Carson. This is not—" She stopped when she saw me in the living room.

I nodded to them then retreated to the kitchen to

see if I could find the makings of tea. I didn't want to be present in case the conversation flamed into an out and out brawl.

I had no sooner started the kettle when Persis stepped into the kitchen from the hall with her arms clutched around herself. The voices in the living room had begun to rise. At least Cassandra's did. I didn't hear much from Carson. I heard Ayubu return and his greeting to the LaChances. They seemed to have declared a brief détente to greet him then resumed combat.

"I know," I said. "I hate it when people argue too."

Persis looked surprised but said nothing. She began to search the cupboards. In a moment she sat down at the table. She had found a box of hard little chocolate chip cookies.

"Would you like a cup of tea?" I asked her.

She shrugged but, again, said nothing. I took that for a yes and got out another mug. As I reached for a cookie, our hands touched.

Sometimes I can get a sense of what people are thinking by that brief connection. Sometimes not. But Persis, at that moment, anyhow, was easy to read. I knew that, though she was suspicious of me, she seemed to lean toward a more positive attitude. I could tell, too, that she liked the scar I had on my cheekbone.

Ab joined us at that moment.

"I met Ayubu upstairs," he said. "I'm going to the grocery store down the street to get some eggs, milk and bread so there will be food here for breakfast. Anyone want to go?"

"I just put water on for tea," I said. I gave a glance toward the living room. "Persis, you want to go with Ab?"

She shook her head. "Get some cereal, though," she said and Ab smiled.

"Cereal is on the top of the list," he said. "What's your favorite?"

Persis shrugged.

"I'll do my best," he said then left us, silent in the kitchen while the battle continued to rage in the living room.

After a minute, I said, "I love this house."

Persis gave me a quick look. "I do too," she said then seemed surprised that she had spoken at all. Her voice sounded like she wasn't used to talking. "It's spooky."

"I heard a rumor that the house is haunted," I said, hoping to get another response from her.

"I hope it is," she said.

"It could be, you know," I told her. "Old houses like this often have lots of history."

"Don't let my mother hear you say that." She glanced toward the living room. "Or we'll have to go to a hotel. Or back home."

I poured a mug of tea for Persis and set it on the table in front of her. She cupped her hands around the mug and breathed in the steam that lifted off the surface.

"Are you going to help your parents at the show?" I asked.

She shook her head. "They're going to let me use a little part of their booth to sell my own drawings."

"I didn't realize you were an artist, too!" I said. "I'd love to see your work! It's nice of them to let you do that."

"Yeah," she said. "My parents usually never let me do anything." She took a tentative sip of her tea. When she lifted the mug, the sleeve of her shirt drew up a bit and I could see an anarchy sign tattooed onto her wrist.

"I see they let you get a tattoo. It's hard to find anyone who is willing to do tattooing on people your age."

She smiled for the first time. I would find out that her smiles were rare. "It's fake. I bought as many as I could get so I can put on a fresh one every few days. My parents thought it was real at first and went berserk." She laughed softly at some memory. "They really won't let me do anything. You'll see. I have to wear fake pierce earrings because *she* won't let me get my ears pierced." She said the word "she" like it was her mother's name. "They don't want me to wear make-up either."

"But I see you defy that rule," I said. "How old are you, Persis?"

"I'm sixteen."

Of course, she was lying. I knew it without even touching her. I looked at her. "Don't be in such a hurry. How old are you really?"

"Fourteen," she said after a long hesitation, as though she had been forced to admit to something horrid.

I nodded but refrained from saying anything.

Our hands brushed again and once more I got the image of my scar coming from her.

I put my fingers to my cheekbone, remembering the night I got it. It was no wonder that Easy worried about me so much.

She stopped with the mug halfway to her lips and said, "I like your scar."

"Thanks," I said. "The guy who hit me was wearing a star shaped ring."

"It's so cool!" she said. "Do you mean you got it in a fight?"

I laughed. "Not exactly. I was mugged." That was my official story, and it was almost the truth. I had been in the middle of a case at the time.

I thought she would have questions and was

prepared to answer, but I think her shyness got the better of her. Instead, we started talking about the possibility of the house being haunted. She was quite pretty when she became interested and animated. It was something I didn't think her parents often saw.

In a little while, Ab returned bearing three large grocery bags. Persis didn't say anything more while we unloaded Cheerios, eggs, milk, white bread and rye, butter, sugar, bacon and coffee, pancake mix, fruit and enough other edibles to feed us all.

❊ ❊ ❊

Persis had staked her claim to one of the two bedrooms across from the kitchen and stood firm before her mother's disapproval. It helped her cause that Ayubu had appropriated the room that Cassandra had picked out for her.

Later, when Persis had retreated to her room and Carson and Cassandra, now at peace, had gone upstairs, Ab and I sat in the kitchen for a while.

"We have to set up tomorrow morning," I said. "There are still two bedrooms available. Do you think there will be more coming?"

Ab nodded. "The agent told me that I had gotten the last room when I booked yours." He looked at me with mischief in his eyes. "Otherwise, you'd be sharing, sister."

"Me? Why not you? You could bunk with the LaChances," I said with my voice low.

We laughed.

"I wonder why the others haven't arrived," I said.

He bent his head back to get the last few drops of his coffee. He had set up the pot to be ready for morning but then hadn't been able to resist a cup for himself. Now he would have to clean out the pot and make it all over again.

"Some of them may have to work and can't afford to take an extra day off. They'll be along in the morning. Or else they'll go straight to the venue and we won't see them until they come back after setting up. They all have their own keys, so that isn't a problem. A few people in the show won't get here until Friday early and set up the same day the show opens." He shrugged. "The board doesn't like that, but people do what they do. Some of them just can't get in gear until the last second."

"It seems to me you'd be much more relaxed the first day of the show if you were already set up and didn't have to worry about it."

He nodded again and pushed himself away from the table. "Speaking of relaxed," he said. "I'm going up. See you in the morning."

"Night, Ab," I told him. I sat on, relishing my second cup of tea. I listened to the quiet of the house, still surprised and uneasy that I felt none of the rich history that the house must have had. I wished that it would speak to me. Soon, though, the house's stubborn silence and my exhaustion from the stressful day chased me upstairs too.

I passed Ayubu's room. He had chosen the one next to mine. Carson and Cassandra were across from Ab and I was farther down the hall across from the library and next to one of the baths. The only room upstairs that was still vacant was the corner one with the Eastern exposure. Cassandra had complained about Persis being downstairs "by herself" but it appeared that Cassandra complained about a great many things.

Once alone in my room, I got out my notebook. I made a page for each of the occupants of the house so far and added them to the pages for each of the board members. I still hadn't solidified any plan for my investigation and that made me feel less confident than I usually feel at the beginning of a job. I didn't like the sensation.

I knew I would have to question the artists at the show. That was a daunting task since I knew there were over one hundred of them. I could skip most of the first timers but the number of long time PCAC members and show veterans was significant. I wanted to get a more accurate picture of how many thefts there had been. I suspected there were many. I knew that some of the artists had not reported them, thinking that theft was, sadly, a normal part of business.

I sighed. Any other time, I was excited to begin a case, but I wasn't feeling it that night. I felt unmoored. It was nothing more than fatigue, I thought. I was tired, wired from the harrowing incident on the road earlier and uncertain about the coming show.

My mind drifted and, not for the first time, I ran over the events of the afternoon. I realized that the person who had been trying to run us off the road could have been anyone, but my thoughts returned to the board members. They were the only ones who knew the real reason I was there. Was being discovered to be a thief motive enough to kill us? That didn't seem reasonable. However, if I considered my half-formed idea that the thefts and deaths were somehow connected, it made more sense. If whoever it was had been serious about causing us to have an accident, they could have easily done it considering the road conditions. I had begun to think it may have been someone trying to scare us rather than harm us. But why? Were they trying to frighten us enough to turn back and go home? Again, why? Or was Ab right and it was a kid thinking it was fun to terrify people? That made no sense in my mind either.

The house was quiet and I felt chilled when I put aside the notebook as well as my thoughts and began to prepare for bed. I put underthings and other paraphernalia in the dresser then hung my clothes in the armoire. It made a forlorn squeak—"e-e-e-e-e-e"—each time I opened and closed it.

After I turned off the light, the darkness was profound. I was not in the big city where there were street lights on every corner. I lay on my back and tried to let the history of the house surround me.

Persis had said that it was a spooky house, and I agreed. It was old and creaky but it was, after all, just a house. Even a dwelling that has been full to the brim with unhappiness and tragedy can still become a pleasant place to live once the unfortunate inhabitants are gone. But the house itself, while retaining a bit of the emotions that have been experienced there, is still just a house. This one had been built a long time ago and many people must have stayed in it. It no doubt held the voices and emotions of those who had lived in it over the years. But to me, that night, they were silent. I could not hear the echoes of the families who had lived in Beachhouse.

Just before I went to sleep, I thought with regret of Easy. I mourned the loss of his friendship, even though it would no doubt prove to be temporary. I wondered if he was missing me that night as much as I was missing him. It was Wednesday and, if not for my job, we would have shared dinner that evening.

I thought about him for what seemed like a long time.

Nevertheless, that night I dreamed about Ab.

EIGHT

Thursday, July 19, 1984

The next morning, I was up early, almost before the sun. It wasn't because sleeping in a strange bed is difficult for me. I can sleep anywhere. Instead, the culprit had been my dreams which refused to fade into those forgotten ghosts that none of us remember.

I dressed and slipped out of the house. I needed a little walk and I wanted to get a look at the neighborhood. In the back of my mind, too, I was reluctant to admit to myself, was a foggy hesitancy to see Ab. Even as my mind became occupied with other things, the residue of the dream was stubborn and hard to shake off, like a spiderweb caught in my hair.

I walked toward the west. Though the house's name was Beachhouse, it wasn't on the beach. Between it and the ocean was a main street, a small neighborhood of maybe two blocks and a wide wooded area that opened onto sand dunes. Beyond those, stretched a wide swath of sand at the edge of the ocean. I stood on the top of a rise and watched the gulls and the sand-pipers for a moment, then turned and walked back to the house.

Now that I felt rested, I found I was excited about getting to the show venue and eager to help Ab make our booth ready.

I joined Ab in the kitchen. He looked like himself, a fiftyish man with frizzy hair and a scraggly beard. Not at all the stuff of my dream. I felt myself shake off my fancies and relax. He was staring at the coffee maker.

"Watching it isn't going to make it work any faster," I said.

He glanced around as if he had not heard me come downstairs. "I am the master of the coffee maker," he said. "It is not the master of me." He turned back to it.

"Even so, you can't order it to work any faster. If you want quicker coffee, you'll have to submit to instant." I put a kettle of water on for tea and turned to him. "Want some eggs? I'm going to make scrambled."

He nodded and went back to watching the coffee maker as it began to make subtle gurgling noises.

I had just poured the beaten eggs into the buttered pan when Cassandra pushed open the kitchen door. She was followed by Carson who seemed as grateful for the prospect of coffee as Ab.

Cassandra peered into the pan where I was stirring the eggs and made a wry face.

"Want some?" I asked her. "I can whip up a few more."

Carson looked eager but Cassandra shook her head. "No, thanks," she said. "We don't eat breakfast." By then the coffee was ready and she poured generous mugs for Carson and herself while I steeped the tea.

"I think I'll have a bit of toast," Carson said and put two slices of bread into the toaster, ignoring Cassandra's frown.

I was dividing the eggs onto two plates when Persis pushed through the door and Carson began to scream.

Ab spun to face him, alarm alive on his face. Carson turned toward us with a knife sticking out of his hand and an ugly gush of red surrounding it. Then he began to laugh.

"Oh, honestly, Carson!" Cassandra said, disgusted. Carson had stuck the knife between two of his fingers and smeared raspberry jam around the "wound". He, apparently, thought it was hilarious. Persis rolled her eyes and Ab looked angrier than I have ever seen him look.

"Hey, man," he said. "That is not cool."

"Just tryin' to lighten the mood," Carson said, unperturbed. He washed the jam off of his fingers, still chuckling to himself. Cassandra looked angry too, but I was beginning to think that was her normal expression.

Ab said nothing further, though the look on his face told me that he was not at all amused by Carson's antics. I was surprised at his angry outburst. I thought he may be a little more nervous than he was willing to admit. Perhaps, though, it was nothing more than a sort of post-trauma reaction to the events of the day before.

Meanwhile Cassandra was eyeing Persis. "Oh no, young lady," she said. "You are not going out dressed like that."

I could see nothing wrong with Persis' outfit. She was wearing black jeans, a black shirt and a black denim jacket, essentially what she had worn the day before. She ignored her mother and reached for a mug. Her hair was every which way, and looked like she had done nothing to it after she had climbed out of bed. I was pretty sure, though, that she had spent time to get it that way.

"Persis, we are going to be meeting with our customers today. I don't think that outfit is appropriate." She looked Persis up and down. "And that hair! Oh, my God."

Persis continued to ignore her but I could see a pinkness beginning to suffuse her face.

"We won't see customers today. It's just…" Carson began, but Cassandra shot him a look.

Ab looked calmer after he had gotten a few sips of coffee and a forkful or two of eggs into him. He had lost his scowl at any rate. "I'm glad it's not raining for our load-in," he said. His voice sounded forced and unnaturally loud for him. It was obvious that he was trying to fill in the awkward silence. "Soon as you're ready, Chey, we can get going." He may have calmed, but I heard a hard edge lingering in his voice.

"I'll be glad to get set up today so we won't have to do it all tomorrow. We'll be all ready," I said, doing what I could to help him out in his efforts to head off yet another argument between the LaChances. We sounded like bad actors in a bad movie who didn't know their lines very well and were trying to wing it.

Our efforts were in vain. A whispered and largely ignored lecture to Persis was going on at the same time.

Persis had found the box of Cheerios in a cabinet and had begun her search for a bowl.

Ab and I silently finished and I rinsed our dishes and Ab dried them.

"Is it okay if I use some of your milk?" Persis asked me while her mother's diatribe continued.

"Of course," I told her and smiled. She looked like she needed someone to smile at her.

Ab and I couldn't get out of the house fast

enough. The van was already loaded. All we had to do was climb in and head for the venue. Once in the passenger seat, I released a sigh.

"I feel so sorry for that little girl," Ab said, turning onto the main street.

"It'll be a few years before she's old enough to leave," I said. "She's only fourteen."

After a few minutes, I said, "I don't think I've ever seen you react the way you did to Carson. Is my paranoia starting to wear off onto you?"

He glanced at me and smiled. "Don't worry, babe. There's just something about that guy that rubs me the wrong way."

"I thought you got along with everyone!" I said.

"There's something about him..."

He didn't elaborate and we rode in silence for a few minutes. I thought I understood what he meant, though. Carson seemed to do the very thing that would ignite Cassandra's anger. Either that or he was remarkably stupid. I didn't have the sense that his cluelessness was an act, though I had only just met him.

When we passed Black Lake on the left, I again noticed there were no visitors even though the day looked like it would be perfect for a picnic or a cool dip. But, obviously, no one thought Black Lake was that kind of a lake.

The venue was about a mile from our "home". We

parked and went around to the front to check in. It turned out that our booth was toward the back so load-in wouldn't be difficult from our parking spot as there were two large doors at either end of the immense hall, both propped open with bricks.

I used the hand truck to bring in the larger pieces while Ab constructed the wooden framework of our booth. He had long ago worked out an intricate frame and lighting system so that, even though the booth was against a wall, the stained glass pieces would hang from the structure allowing light to shine through them. Plus, the venue's windows provided ample opportunity for sunshine to reach from three of the four outside walls.

All around us, the huge arena was noisy with the sounds of chatter, laughter, hammering and the clatter of carts and dollies. The air was alive with anticipation as the vendors called to each other.

I was unwrapping some of the smaller windows and ornaments and attaching fishing line for hanging when I spotted a familiar face. Kirk Neilsson's red moustache and beard framed his grin as he approached.

"Looking good!" he said, inspecting Ab's work. The framework was complete and Ab was setting up the spotlights that would accent each piece. He turned to me, "We're glad you're here, Cheyenne," he said. "The board members feel a lot more comfortable knowing you'll be keeping an eye out."

"They would be even *more* comfortable if you'd let me warn the artists," I said. I saw Ab smile behind Kirk. "It would be a wise precaution. Three is a few too many dead people for comfort."

"No, no," he said. "Can't do that." He looked at the floor and kicked a small piece of wood to the side. He seemed to be hesitating. "As a matter of fact," he began finally. "And I don't want you to take this the wrong way or put any meaning into it that doesn't exist." He eyed me and I waited, silent, for him to continue. "It turns out that there has been another death. It has nothing to do with the show, though. Absolutely nothing."

"Another one?" I stopped in the act of hanging a small window. "What happened?"

"One of the artists died just a few days ago. But no one murdered her. It was suicide, plain and simple. No question about it." He looked around and spotted one of the vendors headed our way.

I wanted to ask him more questions. A lot more questions, but the vendor had reached us and had pulled Kirk away with a problem for him to tackle. I got the impression that he had been glad to be able to escape. I made a mental note to have a more uninterrupted talk with him later.

"Almost looked like it was planned that way," Ab said, smiling.

"I was thinking the same," I said. "Very convenient." He chuckled and stood back to view his work.

I saw Dak Washington arrive with a dolly loaded with plastic bins. He waved and stopped two booths away. He was one of the board members too. I finished hanging the window I was holding, spoke to Ab and went over to Dak's booth.

"Hi Dak," I said, grabbing hold of the table he was trying to maneuver into position at the front of his booth. "Let me give you a hand." I knew Dak would be an even better person to talk to. As the President of the board, he would know the scoop.

"Hey, thanks!" He gave the table a last nudge and stopped. "I saw you talking to Kirk. He tell you about Attley Silverwood?"

"I don't know any of the details. Is that the person who died?"

"Yup. She was a great artist." He shook his head. "Terrible thing. I *never* could understand why people would do a thing like that."

"Kirk did say it was suicide," I said. "What else do you know about it?"

"Not much." Dak began to unlatch the lids from the plastic bins. He lifted out a stack of tablecloths and began to toss them onto each of his four tables. "She's...or she *was* a local gal. Lived just outside of Oceanside. Not far from here. She ran her car into a seawall or a bulkhead or something." He shook his head again. "Her partner is going to do the show anyway, I guess. That's what I heard."

"Who is her partner? Is he here?" I looked around.

Dak shrugged. "She," he said. "I doubt it. I haven't seen her anyway. Name is Bliss Monahan."

"What kind of art did Attley do?"

"She painted. Mostly farm animals and signs and stuff. She put everything on barn board. I bought one of her paintings a couple of years ago. Three chickens. They hang in my kitchen."

"Dak, don't you think that, in view of a fourth death, that the other artists should at least be informed of them? Seriously, four artists dying is a bit suspect, don't you agree?"

"Four deaths?"

I enumerated on my fingers. "There was a woman in Everett and one in Ballard. You know about those. But there was one on the Oregon coast too. And now this one. That's four."

"What happened to the one in Oregon?" He asked. He ballooned one of the cloths over a table and began to straighten it.

"Car accident," I said.

He brushed my words aside. "An accident. The rest were either suicide or accident. You can't put any meaning into that. There's no reason for the artists to be alarmed, maybe drop out of the show because four people died. People die every day.

Artists die every day. None of those people died under mysterious circumstances and none were related in any way."

I could tell that he and Kirk and possibly the other board members had discussed the subject at length. They were all convinced. I knew that no matter what I said, I wouldn't be changing any of their minds. Yet I was determined to plow ahead.

I took one of the cloths and draped a table with it. "Nevertheless," I said. "I'm going to have to question the artists and the staff. I'll need a list of the volunteers." I knew that I could get a list of the artists from the show program.

"Are you sure that you aren't trying to manufacture a mystery where none exists?" he asked with a smile.

"Yes, I'm sure. Why would I want to do that?" I stopped arranging the cloth and stood up straight.

"It's your job, isn't it?"

"Actually, my job is to discover secrets and unravel unknowns, not create them. There are enough mysteries that I don't have to go around inventing them." I felt myself getting a little hot. "I can't seem to get any information from anyone so I guess I'll have to wait until Bliss Monahan gets here and talk to her." I looked around again as if I could spot her somewhere with a sign over her head showing her name.

"She probably won't be here until tomorrow morning," he said. "Seriously, Cheyenne. I wouldn't read anything into this. It's a coincidence. That's all it is. That," he smiled again. "That *and* your imagination."

I knew he was trying to lighten up the situation but I didn't want to let it go that easily. I thought something was going on and I didn't want any more deaths to occur. Nevertheless, I forced myself to smile. I didn't trust myself to say anything further, so I nodded to Dak and turned to go back to Ab. I thought I heard Dak say, "Thanks for the help," and should have acknowledged that. Instead, I pretended not to hear him. I was too angry. I hoped that the board's blindness would not cause anyone else to lose their life. Why was the board being so obstinate? Didn't they realize, as I did, that the safety of the artists was far more important than anything else? On the other hand, as I looked around at the huge venue, the staff had their hands full. Especially Kirk who was the event coordinator. If I did my job well, everyone would stay safe. And, of course, there was always the chance that I could be wrong. Unfortunately, I had a nagging suspicion that I was right.

NINE

Thursday, July 19, 1984

It took us several hours to set up the booth. When we had finished, I was impressed. It looked great. The venue was large and well-lit, so, along with the lights Ab had installed, the glass glowed with rich color.

As the place filled, the huge conference hall transformed from an empty, echoing drabness into a hive of activity. Colors, textures and fragrances mixed with the sounds of busy people as it buzzed into life.

I went around the outside of our ten by ten space to make sure everything was in place. I glanced up to see Carson's, Cassandra's and Persis' booth on the other side of the aisle and down a few spaces. Carson and Cassandra were busy unwrapping and arranging and didn't see me, but Persis looked up. I waved at her and was surprised when she gave me one of her rare smiles back.

"I'm going to saunter over there to the LaChance

booth for a few minutes and get a look at Persis' art," I told Ab when I had finished. "Then I'm going to take a walk around the hall, see where everyone is and try to introduce myself to some of the artists."

"Good idea," he said. "I can introduce you to some of them, too. Come back after you've looked at Persis' stuff and I'll go with you. Right now, most of them are busy setting up, but we can at least take a minute of their time."

I headed toward Persis and her parents, continuing to look around and keeping my eyes open for anything out of the ordinary. Of course, at the time, how would I know what was ordinary or not, since I had never done an art show in my life?

When I reached Persis' table, she was sliding a plastic bin underneath it and straightened up. She looked startled to see me.

"Hi," I said to her. "I came to take a look at what you've been doing."

She didn't say anything, but looked around to where her parents had been moments before. There were still half-emptied boxes and crates littering their tables and the floor, but the couple had disappeared and Persis seemed to relax a bit.

Persis had a small curtained off area attached to her parents' double corner booth. She had hung the curtain behind her and to the sides with small framed drawings hung from wires of differing lengths. On a table she had set small wire easels with matted but unframed drawings and she had a box of greeting cards printed with her art too.

Her work was detailed drawings of ordinary subjects with extraordinary additions. She had a small drawing of an adorable puppy sporting gigantic bat wings. There was another of a flower garden, each bloom intricately drawn, even the ones that had skulls and bats' heads instead of blossoms. Many of her works were done with pen and ink but some had touches and even splashes of vivid color. Altogether, they were fascinating and each one demanded close attention. I believed Persis to be very talented considering her age. I picked up a drawing of a dark lake surrounded by tall pines. The trees had been lightly washed with a deep green but there was no other color. The water looked gloomy and forbidding.

"Black Lake?" I asked.

She looked down and muttered something that sounded like "Not really."

"It looks like it to me. The only thing missing is a little sign right here that says 'Black Lake'." I put it down again.

"I did it before I ever saw Black Lake," she said, her low voice barely audible.

"These are quite wonderful, Persis. I'm impressed!" I said. She looked startled again as if she didn't hear compliments very often. "You have real talent!"

She mumbled a shy, "Thank you."

"I mean it," I said. "I like these very much. I'm sure they sell well."

"This is the first time they've let me share the booth," she said, giving a glance to the door where Cassandra was trundling a balky hand truck and Carson was following with a large cardboard box.

I nodded, thinking that her first show must be terrifying to her. "I don't think you'll have any trouble selling these," I said.

"My mom says that I shouldn't be disappointed if I don't sell very many."

That sounded like Cassandra to me. "She meant that it takes a little while for an artist to get attention. After you've done a few shows, I would bet that these drawings will be quite popular."

By then Cassandra and Carson had returned. Cassandra shoved some hair out of her face and pulled the hand truck from under the crate she had hauled. "Persis," she said. "Will you take this back to the trailer? It's unlocked. Lock it up when you're done." She handed the keys to the girl.

Persis looked aggrieved but took the keys. She threw me a very small, half-smile and a little wave and left.

"You set up already?" Carson asked, peering in the direction of our booth. Ab was in the act of folding up the step stool and stashing it behind the curtain.

I nodded. Cassandra was unwrapping a ceramic rabbit that was done in such fine detail it almost looked real. I glanced over her other works and saw that her trademark appeared to be realism and she did it very well. It appeared, too, that she focused on animals. Each one of the figures was represented in perfect detail and I imagined that she spent many hours on each piece.

"These are beautiful," I said. I picked up a fox and gazed at its intelligent looking eyes then carefully set it back on the table.

"Thank you," she said and turned toward Carson. "Didn't you bring the three tiered stand? I specifically asked you to."

"I did," he said, looking around and not sounding very sure about it. "I did. It's here somewhere."

I gave them a wave and moved away from the booth. I thought that if the LaChances would work together instead of bickering constantly, they would get more done.

I only had a brief glance at Carson's work but I knew I would want to come back and see it later. He did sculptures too, though from what I could see, he combined wood and clay and I thought I saw a bit of glass besides. I would have to find time to take a better look but for now I wanted to get away from the inevitable battle.

* * *

"I think I might buy one of Persis' drawings at some point," I told Ab when I returned to the booth.

He looked up. "She draw or paint or what?" he asked.

"It looks like pen and ink with a bit of watercolor. Mostly black drawings. They're very good, I think. She has lots of pictures of crows, uh, or maybe they're ravens. Her subjects seem to be pretty dark."

"Dark?" Ab was fiddling with one of the lights.

"Oh, you know, her subjects are dark. Death, fear, things like that." I smiled. "It's a teenage thing, probably."

"I don't blame her for having 'dark' thoughts," he said, winding up a cord and stashing it behind the wall curtain. "With those parents, I don't know who wouldn't think about death and destruction. Ready to go meet the crowd?"

We walked around the venue and Ab introduced me to the artists that he knew. I carried my casebook with me and made notes as I discovered who were veterans of the shows and who were the newbies. It was with the old timers I wanted to speak in more depth. I wanted to question those who had mentioned having had pieces stolen from their booths. We made two circuits of the venue and I ended with an exhaustive list.

"Okay," I said, lowering my voice when we had arrived back at our booth. "Who is the guy next door who makes those puzzles?" I gestured with my thumb. We had stopped and spoken to the middle aged man who made jigsaw-like puzzles out of glass and polished wood and stones. They were gorgeous and utterly baffling. I longed to buy one. "The man with the accent."

"That's Oskar Brandweis," Ab said also keeping his voice low. "If you ask me, that guy is a genius. Not only does he dream up those beautiful works, but he makes them into puzzles." He shook his head. "He's up for an award. If his work was in the glass category, I don't think I would stand a chance."

"Don't be so sure," I told him. "That piece you did is spectacular. I patted him on the arm and discovered that he was more nervous about the contest than he let on. I wondered why. He was an excellent artist and my intuition told me that he was going to win, even if he didn't believe me. "Okay, who is that woman who paints the pictures that end up looking like photographs?"

"That's Josette Kelleher."

"I was surprised to see what gorgeous work Julia Johnston does," I told him, straightening and re-straightening a small ornament that insisted on turning the wrong direction. I had met Julia already at the board meeting, and had known that she was one of the artists and that she made "bags" but that was all. It turned out she made fabulous purses out of her hand embroidery work. I loved the way they looked, but I never carried a handbag. Even if I did, I wasn't sure I would want one that cost more than all of my clothing put together, plus my month's rent.

"Why?"

"She's so unpleasant," I confessed. "Somehow it doesn't seem like someone with so much negativity could create such lovely things."

He nodded and laughed.

We worked in silence for a little while. I adjusted the angle of some of the pieces while Ab continued to fidget with the lights. I began to suspect that he never got them to what he considered the perfect configuration.

While we worked, I studied Ab, trying to see him from Easy's point of view. Personally, I thought Easy was a fool for being jealous. Ab was a great guy —generous, friendly, hardworking—everything that Easy himself was. But Ab had maybe twenty years on Easy and, while that wouldn't have mattered to me in the slightest if I had been so inclined, he didn't seem like the romantic partner type. Not that Easy was either, but I had had my share of lustful thoughts about Easy. Never about Ab, consciously anyway. It wasn't that Easy and I didn't have chemistry together. At least I thought we had. I knew he wanted to marry me. He knew that I didn't want to get married. I also knew that he would not, under pain of being sent to hell for eternity, enter into a sexual relationship with me prior to marriage. He had been raised by strict Catholics and he had entrenched beliefs. I could respect them even if I didn't agree with them. I probably had plenty of entrenchment myself. Again, the thought of Easy made me sad. I wondered if he would like one of those mystical puzzles that Oskar Brandweis sold, and then resolved to quit thinking about Easy and Ab both.

"Did you know Attley Silverwood?" I asked.

Ab shook his head. "I heard about that. No, I never met her that I know of. I might have known her by sight." He looked at me. "This is adding fuel to your idea that someone is stalking artists, isn't it?"

"I'm trying to keep an open mind," I told him. But I wasn't. I was pretty sure that there was something going on that I thought all of the artists should be aware of. "I'm going to walk around by myself for a while. If you want, go ahead and take the van back to the house. I can either catch a ride with the LaChances or Ayubu or walk. It isn't that far."

Ab looked skeptical. "I want to fiddle around with this lighting. I'm not happy with the way that magnolia window is looking. I'll meet you back here in a half hour."

I agreed even though I knew that he was only making work. He did not want me wandering around on my own. When Easy acted that way, it irritated me like crazy. I wondered why Ab could get away with it while Easy could not. Again, I determined to quit thinking about them both.

I set off again. This time I tried to remember the artist's name as I passed each booth. I wanted to familiarize myself with them all plus I wanted to make a quick tour to make sure everything looked like it should, whatever that was. Perhaps there would be one or two who would be able to spare a few moments for questions as well.

As I passed Julia Johnston's booth, I paused to admire one of the purses she had hanging against a purple backdrop. It had a gorgeous, intricate design depicting Alphonse Mucha's Amethyst on the front, surrounded by thin strips of some fabric, probably silk that matched some of the colors she had used. It was way beyond beautiful. I took a peek at the price tag and it was all I could do not to gasp. Of course, it had taken her months to make and it was all hand done, but I couldn't imagine anyone spending that amount of money on a purse.

"This is beautiful," I told her as I tentatively ran a finger over the stitching.

"Thanks," she said, not looking up from where she was setting up a shelf for more purses.

"It looks like you put quite a bit of time into these. They're all gorgeous."

She looked at me as though she was surprised to see someone looking at her wares. She didn't look welcoming and she said nothing else, so I wandered over to another booth. I could save questioning her for another time, although her attitude told me there may never be a good time.

I was in Luke Jeffries' booth running my hand over some satiny cutting boards that I would never use a knife on when he peeked around the curtain in the back.

"Oh, sorry!" he said. "I didn't know I had a visitor. You're Cheyenne, right?" His welcoming smile was just what I needed.

"I stopped by a little while ago with Ab Eberstein," I told him. "Thank you for remembering my name. I'm not very good at that. Your work is stunning," I added. Somehow, he had brought out a wonderful visual texture to the wood while the surface remained as smooth as glass.

"Thanks!" he said. "I remember you all right. Everyone is talking about you. The rumor is that you're a private investigator working to find out about the thefts. Is that true?"

I laughed. "It's true. I guess it's a good thing I'm not under cover on this."

"You found out anything so far?"

I shook my head. "Not a thing." I liked the way his eyes looked like he was laughing even when his mouth wasn't. He did have a kind of half smile on all the time though. I liked the man. "I will be wanting to ask you some questions over the next few days, if you don't mind."

He nodded.

"And I'll let you know if I hear anything. Meanwhile, don't hesitate to tell me if you notice anything suspicious." I hesitated. "And, do be careful, will you? Someone who would steal might be dangerous. Be aware when you're out alone and when you're driving." The board may have been reluctant to warn the artists about possible danger but I never said that I wouldn't do it.

He looked surprised. "I will," he said. "Do you think there's more to it than simple theft?"

"I don't know." I was unsure how much more I should say. I was more than tempted to tell him about the "accidents" which had taken artists' lives, but I didn't. There were already enough rumors floating around and rumors tend to get distorted fast. "Just don't take any chances," I said finally.

"I'm intrigued now," he said, looking delighted. "If there's a real mystery going on, I want in on it."

I laughed. "I'll let you know what I find out." I waved at him as I left his booth and headed over to Ayubu's space around the corner. He didn't seem to be there. Perhaps he had gone back to Beachhouse. At any rate, I looked over the artwork he had hung. He used lots of bright primary colors often with a spot of black somewhere in the picture. I noticed that several of his paintings featured crows, or perhaps they were ravens. Persis' art had lots of ravens too. I wondered if they were going to become popular like Rubik's Cubes and Swatches.

By the time I got back to the booth, Ab was chatting with the artist across the aisle, a jeweler whose name I thought was Gregor. Ab was laughing at something Gregor had said. He turned and his gaze caught mine. His grin widened and he gave Gregor a wave and started toward me. I was surprised at the little surge of pleasure I felt at his warm smile.

TEN

Thursday, July 19, 1984

We had just arrived back at Beachhouse when a VW van came down the narrow street and wedged itself into the last remaining parking space on the block.

A petite woman with gray streaked dark hair climbed down from the driver's seat. She was wearing simple attire, but I got the impression her clothes were *tres* expensive. The pants looked like designer jeans and I knew right off that her magenta shirt was silk. I could tell that her short, attractive pixie hair style wasn't a cheap cut either. It was too flattering and too perfect.

She said her name was Jade Lem. We introduced ourselves and led her into the house. She put down her bag, looked around and pronounced the house filthy. "I cannot stay in a house this dirty. It must be cleaned up at once."

Ab and I looked at each other and he gave me a slight shrug and proceeded toward the hall stairs. I glanced at Ayubu who had been reading a newspaper. He put it down and gazed at Jade as though she were an interesting but possibly dangerous animal. I was glad the LaChances hadn't returned. I could imagine Cassandra agreeing with Jade and both of them entering into a cleaning frenzy. I didn't think the house was dirty, I thought it was simply old. But if Jade wanted to clean, as far as I was concerned, she could have at it.

"Where is my room"? Jade asked.

I offered to show her the two remaining available rooms. All the way up the stairs she muttered about making a schedule of chores and something about taking turns cooking. I said nothing. That seemed the safest route. I suspected she wouldn't find too many of us willing to cooperate with her plans.

I showed her the last room upstairs and she said that it was unacceptable without giving it more than a glance. *Fine*, I thought, and led her back downstairs to show her the room next to Persis'.

While Jade was mumbling about the uncomfortable accommodations, someone else arrived and in a few minutes, Ayubu had ushered another woman upstairs. I left Jade to complain to herself and followed them up.

Skylar Tarte was a breath of fresh air in comparison to Jade. She smiled broadly and I heard a laugh from her within moments after her arrival. *Good,* I thought. It would be nice to have another friendly face in the house. She looked young, about Persis' age, but I got the feeling that she was older than she looked. She had chin length reddish hair with bangs that came down almost to her eyelashes, blue eyes and her skin was pale and lightly freckled. She was of medium height and slender with no figure which was probably why she seemed to look so young. Without so much as giving it a glance, she accepted the last room available, and put her bag inside.

I knocked on Ab's door and he accompanied us as we all trooped downstairs, joining Jade in the living room.

Jade redoubled her demands for organization and schedules. Skylar nodded at her and seemed willing to go along with whatever she said. Ayubu, though, told her she should let us make our own mistakes or it would ruin our fun.

"Is everyone here?" Jade asked and looked around her as though for allies. "I thought there would be more than this."

"There's a family, too," Ab said, as though he didn't want to reveal too much information. "As soon as they arrive, we can see about getting some dinner together."

"A family!? Children?" Jade's eyes went round and I swear she seemed alarmed.

Ayubu spoke up in his rich deep voice. "One child only," he said. "A teenager."

Jade muttered something to herself.

Ayubu turned away from Jade. "Skylar," he asked. "What is your art?" Ayubu had a careful way of speaking as though he was trying very hard to cover an accent. It was a deliberate yet charming way of talking.

"I'm staff, I'm afraid," Skylar said. "Not an artist. I always wanted to be one, but..." her voice trailed off and she shrugged.

"You should go ahead with what you want to do and not worry about what others think," Ayubu said.

"Well," she said with another shrug and a little deprecating laugh. "I've tried, but I'm just not very good. I wish I were."

I was about to ask her what art she had tried but just then the LaChances came through the front door and there were even more introductions to be made.

Jade began again on her plans for careful schedules but one look from Ayubu made her stop after a few words.

Ab was asking Skylar how long she had been on the staff. He told her he thought he recognized her from previous shows.

"I've seen you, too," Cassandra said while Carson nodded.

"Several years," she said. "I've volunteered all over

the northwest. I work for four other organizations and that covers art shows as far away as Montana and California." she said.

"You must know lots of the artists, then," I said.

"I know them all," she said. "Or, I guess most of them."

"At the risk of ruining everything," Jade said with a pointed look at Ayubu. "It's time for us to think about dinner. I suggest we take turns making meals."

"In that case, I'll be the first to volunteer," Carson said. Cassandra stopped looking at her nails, raised her head and gave him a sharp, surprised look.

"Come on, Ab," he said. "I'm thinking fish and chips would suit me. Want to tag along?"

Before they left, I had a quick word with Ab and asked him to try to get a look at Skylar's car. We knew that Jade's van was not the one which had followed us, but Skylar's may be nondescript enough to fill the bill. She must have parked around the corner, since there was no more space in front of the house.

In a moment they had headed out the door leaving Jade talking about her views that home cooked meals were the best and that she would be unable to eat anything that came from a place where she could not see the kitchen.

* * *

Skylar, Persis and I had put plates out on the table when the men came back with bags of hot fish and chips that they declared to be "the best on the coast!"

"How do you know that?" Cassandra demanded.

"It says so right on the bag!" Carson said, looking pleased with himself.

It smelled wonderful and I was starved.

Cassandra had made coffee and Jade had made "tea". It was a black looking mixture that gave off a toxic smell. I had no immediate plans to try it.

I cornered Ab in the hall. "Did you look at her car?" I asked, keeping my voice low.

He shrugged. "It's impossible to tell which is hers or if she even came in one," he whispered. "There's a tan sedan parked around the corner but..." he shrugged again. "I couldn't see any scratches on the front bumper or anything." He shook his head. "It may not have been hers anyway. I think we're going to have to accept the fact that it was either kids or some random maniac who likes to terrify people."

We headed into the dining room and found places at the table. I was still focused on the car incident. I wasn't convinced that it was a random act. It was too deliberate. Someone had targeted us on purpose. Otherwise, why us? Any cars which happened by would have been just as easy to tail as ours. Whoever it was had waited for us, more than once. And I couldn't get over the fact that three of the four deaths which had occurred had been traffic accidents; a one car fatality, purported to be suicide, hit and run and a drunk driver. It was far too much of a coincidence to me.

The fish was hot and delicious and the chips were crisp and delicately salted. I was tending to agree that it was close to the best I had ever had, but since moving to West Seattle, I had gotten to know Spud on Alki. Nowhere in the world could you find fish and chips better than that.

"We should try to get to know each other a little," Carson said after the appreciative murmurs and comments had settled down. "Maybe say where we come from and what we do." He looked around the table with a hopeful grin.

"Oh, Carson, for heaven's sake," Cassandra said. She looked tired and bored.

"I must agree with Carson," Ayubu said. "We are going to be house-mates, we should know each other. What better way than when we are all together?" He looked around with his agreeable, open smile. "You start, Skylar. Tell us something about yourself."

"Well," Skylar said tentatively. "Like I said, I've

volunteered for several years. I like to spend time with artists and art." She laughed. "Since I have no talent of my own, I get vicarious thrills that way." Her voice was high and breathy, making everything she said sound interesting.

"And what do you like to do when you're not volunteering?" Ab asked her.

She looked around the table at each of us. "I study people," she said and laughed again. "I like people. They're sort of a hobby of mine. I like to know where they come from, what they do. Everyone has an interesting story. When I meet someone, I always think about what their name means." She stopped and looked at us again with a youthful little grin that was hard to resist. "If people don't know what their own name means, I have a book where I can look it up. And I already know lots of them. Names are very important. They are symbols of who we are. It's the one thing that belongs to us."

I didn't agree with that but kept my mouth shut.

She looked around at us all again then focused on Persis. "Did you know that Persis means 'woman of Persia?'"

Persis laughed and looked pleased. "But I'm not from Persia," she said and looked at her mother.

"She was named after her great aunt Persis who came from some middle-eastern country," Cassandra said, looking displeased for some reason. "She was born in Tacoma."

"So your ancestors are from the Middle East. Then you *are* a woman of Persia," Skylar said. "And are you an artist as well?"

Persis blushed from the roots of her hair to her shoulders. "I'm not really an artist, but I draw pictures," she said.

"That's the definition of an artist as far as I'm concerned," Ab said. Persis gave him a wistful, grateful look.

Skylar turned to Cassandra. "Cassandra is a seer."

Persis made a little *snork* noise that I don't think anyone heard but me. I looked at her and winked.

Cassandra preened as though she had just learned about some wonderful yet hidden personality trait. "Well," she said," I like to play with clay, so I don't need to make any profit from being a prophetess."

"That's good because Cassandra," Skylar continued, "was a prophetess that no one believed."

Persis' laugh was squelched by a glance from her mother.

Cassandra went on as though there had been no interruption. "I like animals." She looked around the table. "That's why most of my sculptures are of wildlife. I try very hard to capture their true essence."

"What about Carson?" Carson himself asked Skylar. "What does Carson mean?"

"I believe that means 'son of a marsh dweller'," Skylar said, looking at him.

I thought I heard another snort from Persis, but she had been more discreet that time and I wasn't sure.

Carson laughed. "I'm definitely not that. My dad was an accountant, not a marsh dweller. I'm an accountant too. I'm just a regular guy who likes to play with clay. And I like to play jokes on people."

Persis groaned. "Not now, dad," she said.

He lifted his eyebrows in an "I'm innocent" gesture.

Skylar turned to Ab. "Is Ab short for something?"

Ab nodded. "My name is Absalom. I believe it means 'father of peace'."

Skylar nodded but I got the impression that she hadn't known the meaning.

"I run a stained glass shop in Seattle," he continued.

"Please tell me what Ayubu means," Ayubu said when it became evident that Ab had finished.

"Ayubu means one who perseveres and Jade is a green gemstone," Skylar said after a moment of thought.

Jade looked disgusted and began to rummage in the bag she had not let go of since arriving.

Ayubu laughed. "I am a painter who perseveres,"

he said. "I've been drawing and painting since I was seven years old and living in my native village."

"Do you live off of your art work, Mr... uh... Ayubu," Cassandra asked.

Ayubu nodded. "I do. I am very fortunate to be able to do that."

"What do you do, Jade?" I asked.

"I make clothing," she said. "I design it, weave the fabric and construct garments." She had pulled a small mirror from her bag and was examining her front teeth. She had taken only one piece of the fish and half of it remained on the paper tray in front of her.

There were some murmurs around the table. Even I was impressed until Jade added, "I am descended from emperors."

Again, there were a few startled, polite murmurs.

"So what does Cheyenne mean?" I asked rather than asking Jade what her royal family had to do with weaving.

"Cheyenne means unintelligible speaker," Skylar said.

I burst out laughing along with the others. "That's appropriate, I think," I said.

"What do you like to do, when you are not helping out in art shows?" Skylar asked.

"I work in Ab's shop," I said, nodding toward

Ab, "making stained glass. I try to help with the students and sell to customers. Sometimes, even *I* don't know what I'm talking about."

"Being unintelligible is not necessarily a bad thing!" Skylar hastened to say as though I had protested the meaning. "It could mean that you are so intelligent that no one understands you. Or that no one believes you."

"Like Cassandra," Persis said, looking pleased. Her mother frowned.

"In your work you must have to tell..." She hesitated and seemed to search for the right word. "Tell small untruths from time to time." She looked at me again, her eyes large and round. "To convince the customers to buy things and to tell the students that their work is good when it isn't."

I mulled that over for a moment and decided it was true enough. Truer, in fact, than she knew.

"What does Skylar mean?" Persis asked with a shy half-smile.

"It means one who is learned," Skylar said. "A scholar."

I stood and began to gather up the emptied paper trays and abandoned napkins. Carson stood too and joined me.

"I think we should discuss household chores and cooking tasks," Jade said. "I will write it all down, make a schedule. Vacuuming, dusting, dishes and cleaning will have to be done. Cleanup after cooking. Now, who will do what?" She looked at the faces expectantly and her gaze swept up to Carson and me. "Cheyenne, I'll put you down for cleaning the bathrooms, Cassandra—"

"No," I interrupted. Jade stopped speaking and everyone looked at me. "We will all be busy every day working at the show. When we get back here, we will be tired. I will not be cleaning bathrooms after a long day working."

"I agree," said Ab. "We're only here for four or five nights. There is no need to dust and vacuum and clean. If you want to do it, fine."

Jade looked affronted and started to say something but Ab cut in. "We can share cooking duties if you want. Those of us who don't cook can go get take out for everyone. And we can take turns cleaning up the kitchen. How does that work with you all?"

Everyone nodded except Jade.

"Feel free to do all the cleaning you like," Ab said to her.

"I cannot clean," Jade said. "I have a heart condition that prevents me from doing hard, physical labor. It's a genetic condition."

I wanted to mention that those emperor ancestors hadn't been very hardy, but I restrained myself once again.

Carson and I made short work of throwing away the detritus from the fish and chips and straightening the kitchen. When we returned, the group was still sitting around the table chatting but then they scattered. Some went into the living room to watch the small portable TV while the rest of us went to our rooms.

My room was warm and I opened the window to allow the ocean breeze to waft in.

I wanted to go over my notes such as they were. I spread out the pictures I had taken of the dead artists' studios and pored over them. I was particularly focused on the watercolors done by Barbara Robertson. I looked carefully at each of her paintings trying to find motif or pattern. She had painted beautifully rendered scenes of Seattle as well as alleys and underpasses where graffiti had been painted and repainted. I focused on those, using my magnifying glass. Some of them featured people and I thought that Barbara had taken photos to work from. As I searched, I did find the same "handles" repeated; those word pictures that graffiti artists use to sign their work without leaving too much of a clue as to who they are. I noticed similar designs and got so that I could almost identify the style of the taggers. But maybe I was wasting my time as well as fooling myself.

I looked over the list of artists and their stolen property that Gale Jens had given me. As I compared the list with the program from the PCAC show, I saw many names of artists who appeared on both.

At last, I added the rest of the housemates' names to my list. I put down my first impressions and anything that I had learned about them, which I had to admit to myself, wasn't much.

Skylar seemed affable and I liked her. I still couldn't determine her age. She intrigued me. I felt that she was skilled at dodging questions, though I could think of no examples of it when I gave it some thought. There seemed to be much more to her than what she was giving away. True enough for most of us but I thought that she, in particular, had secrets. Well, didn't we all?

Jade was another enigma. I didn't know what to make of her either. When we had been seated next to each other at the table, I had felt a great hostility from her.

That was nothing momentous, though, as the others had probably felt the same thing. I hadn't touched her and it would take that for me to see more deeply into who she was. Sometimes people use hostility as a cover for something else. She may have a great sadness, or she may be insecure, even frightened.

Cassandra and Carson seemed more of an open book to me. Cassandra ran the family while Carson did his own thing, his own way and didn't seem to care much what others thought. It wasn't hard to find out what was going on in that family at any given moment since they managed to broadcast every disagreement. I wondered what it was about Carson that Ab didn't like. I sensed a lack of self-esteem in him but that would be no reason to dislike him. He seemed pleasant enough, if a bit juvenile.

Cassandra, of course, was overbearing. In my opinion, she was the driving force behind Persis' rebellion. You push too hard and the people you're pushing against will almost always push back.

I had gotten the impression that Ayubu thought of himself as an observer; an outsider, looking in. He seemed to study us all carefully. He was pleasant and, for some reason, I felt that he was intelligent. But, in truth, I knew very little about him. I meant to find out much more about him and, in fact, all of the people with whom I was living.

The house quieted around me. It was our second night there and I was disappointed that I had not yet begun to feel its personality. It was almost as if the house brooded, waiting for us to leave before it came alive again.

There was a nightlight in the hall when I went out to the bathroom prior to going to bed. I was grateful for it. The house was very dark. Light shone from under the door of the room that Skylar had chosen but the others had apparently gone to sleep after an exhausting day.

In my room I opened the armoire and once again it made the e-e-e-e-e cry. I hung up my clothes then shut the door quickly hoping to minimize the sound. That time it made a short, interrogatory squeak which sounded almost friendly.

I was tired and fell asleep almost at once.

Late in the night I awakened, for a moment unaware of where I was. Something, a noise I thought, had awakened me. It was dark and silent in my room and the ocean air had turned chilly for a summer night. I snuggled farther down among the blankets but the sound that I had heard nagged at me enough to make sleep impossible. Had it been a bump or a bang? Someone closing a door, perhaps?

I didn't want to but I climbed out of bed and pattered across the floor on bare feet to peer out the door. The hall was dark. The nightlight had gone out. I listened for a moment, then, hearing nothing, went back to bed.

ELEVEN

Friday, July 20, 1984

I woke early the next morning. My watch said it was five-thirty. I didn't want to, but I got up. My room was still cool but the rising sun was already lightening the summer morning. I stepped into the hall, hoping to grab the first shower. Perhaps I could get breakfast started before anyone else was up. In the hall, I noticed that the nightlight was once again lit. I also smelled the faint aroma of coffee on the air.

After my shower, I dressed and, feeling awkward in the unfamiliar new clothes, headed for the stairs.

When I got to the kitchen, Ab was at the table.

"Couldn't sleep?" I asked him.

He shrugged. "I like my own bed," he said. "You look nice."

I smiled my thanks and reached for the tea kettle. I had worn one of the jackets that I had bought with Molly. The lavender silk had seemed more appropriate for a summer day. My pants were black and my shoes were, for once, not athletic shoes but had actual heels and shine. I wasn't at all sure that I would be able to stand in them all day much less walk. I had also gathered my hair onto the top of my head. That always made me feel a bit elegant if not a little ridiculous.

Ab continued to appraise me while I made tea and put bread in the toaster. I felt my face growing warm and hoped it wasn't becoming red.

"Did you change the bulb in the hall night light?" I asked him.

He looked blank.

"I didn't know there *was* a night light in the hall," he said. "Why?"

"Nothing, really. It was on when I went to bed, off when I got up in the night then on again this morning." I shrugged.

"The electricity is faulty in these old houses," he said. He took the last swallow of his coffee. "You going to have anything more than toast? I'd like to get over to the venue before the others start to stir around." He glanced over his shoulder, then leaned toward me. "Namely Jade," he said, then headed for the hall. "I'll be right back and when you're through, we can get started."

I laughed and agreed. "She should be up soon. She hasn't set up yet."

I heard Ab greet someone in the hall and before

I even had a chance to hope it wasn't Jade, Skylar came into the kitchen.

She looked startled when she saw me but smiled. "Morning," she said. Her hair was combed and her make-up was perfect, yet her voice sounded sleepy. I was always a little puzzled by women who felt they couldn't be seen by anyone unless they were at their best. Of course, I had done the same myself, that morning. Maybe that was what Ab's long looks had been—amazement that I could clean up so well.

"All ready for the show?" I asked her as she pulled a mug from the cabinet and headed for the coffee pot.

She shrugged. "I don't have to do anything to 'get ready,'" she said. "I'll help some of the artists who haven't checked in yet."

"What else does your job entail?" I asked.

"Mostly I booth-sit. I work half days. One day, morning, another, afternoon. That leaves me lots of time to enjoy the beach. Like a little mini vacation every day."

"Booth-sit?" I asked.

"If someone needs a break and they don't have anyone with them, I can come and watch their booth while they get a bathroom break, a meal or a coffee."

My first thought was that a booth sitter would have excellent opportunity to steal small items from any artist's booth, but then was ashamed of myself. I was sure that the PCAC had vetted the booth sitters and other volunteers that they employed. Nevertheless, I intended to question them all and Skylar would be included.

"What happens when a customer comes in and wants to buy something?" I asked.

She shrugged again. "It depends. Some of the artists don't bother collecting taxes and, in that case, I'll just take cash for their purchase. If it's a large item or it requires packing or processing a credit card, the artist will have to do that. I just tell the customer that the artist has stepped away from the booth for a moment and tell them to come back. The artist tells me what they want me to do. Artists get a booth sitter so the customers don't arrive at an abandoned booth. It looks better if someone is there."

"Good to know," I said. Ab appeared in the doorway and I swallowed the last of my tea and waved to Skylar. She returned a friendly wave to me and turned back to her coffee.

* * *

The conference hall was already buzzing when we got there. The customers wouldn't arrive for another few minutes so everyone was putting the finishing touches on their booths. Most of the artists who had set up the day before were putting out their wares, uncovering cases or stealing furtive bites of take out breakfasts. I saw Jade. She had gotten an even earlier start than Ab and I had. She was surrounded by half unpacked plastic bins and clothing racks and seemed in no rush to get her inventory organized.

I learned that day that art shows can be long stretches of sheer boredom punctuated by bursts of frantic activity. It didn't take long, however, before I found out just how busy a good art show could get. A mass of wall to wall people moved in slow motion along the aisles, peering at paintings, ceramics, turned wood, glass, paper, canvases, carvings and everything in between.

During the lulls, I would choose an aisle and walk first one way then turn and come back the other, making sure that I saw every booth. I stopped and talked to artists here and there and, if they weren't already chatting with patrons, I asked them some of my list of questions. I made sure to tell them to let me know at once if they noticed anything missing.

I saw Skylar booth-sitting for Jade Lem and took the opportunity to stop in and look at her work. She had told us that she did hand weaving, then designed and constructed the fabric she made into clothing. The results were gorgeous, I had to admit. The colors she used were rich and lent depth and interest to the already wonderfully textured fabrics.

I eyed a jacket that was priced way out of my league, but was such a luscious blend of turquoise and shades of purple that I almost couldn't take my eyes off of it.

"These are beautiful," I told Skylar.

She nodded. "I wish I could afford one," she said with a little regretful laugh. I tried once again to guess her age. She could have passed for anything between twenty and fifty, though I thought she was closer to twenty five.

"Me too," I said. "Which one would you buy if you had loads of money?"

She headed for one of the racks. "This one for sure," she said and stroked the sleeve of a rich deep pumpkin jacket.

"Good choice," I told her. "With your hair color, it would be perfect!"

"Well, they *all* are fabulous," she said with a sigh. "I'm afraid there's no hope of *my* ever owning one."

"Me either," I said, though I was more than a little tempted.

Even though Skylar had agreed with me, I got the feeling that she was leaving something unsaid. She wasn't lying. She did love the jacket. It was something else. A negative feeling directed not toward the clothing around us, but rather the artist. I didn't believe that she disliked Jade because of her attitude of the night before. Rather, I felt that Skylar was extremely jealous of Jade.

Again, I felt that my psychic ability was off kilter, out of balance. I didn't like the sensation. I hoped that my own dislike for Jade wasn't shading my sense of her and coloring my perception of others' feelings toward her as well.

I left Skylar in Jade's booth and wandered down the other side of the wide aisle.

At one of the booths, I encountered a beautiful woman with long, auburn hair and large eyes the color of blue glass. I introduced myself and realized that the booth was Attley Silverwood's.

"Are you Bliss?" I asked the woman when a browser had left her booth.

She nodded and looked at me with curiosity and expectance.

"I'm Cheyenne Bruce," I said. "I think you know that I'm here to investigate the thefts that have been going on."

She nodded. "Kirk told me that you would probably be by."

"He told me what happened," I said. "I'm so very sorry for your loss, Bliss."

She bowed her head, half a gesture of defeat and half a nod.

"I have to admire you for going ahead with the show anyway," I said. "I'm not sure that I could do that."

"I almost didn't," she admitted. "But it seemed like a way that I could honor Attley's memory. We both do what you might call 'street art' but Attley was the real artist. She had much more talent than I do. She's up for an award."

"I hadn't realized she was one of the finalists in the contest," I said. I thought that fact alone made one more reason to question Attley's death being due to suicide.

As if reading my mind, Bliss nodded. "I just can't believe she did it." She waved her hand in front of her face as if she could ward off tears that way. "I *know* it was suicide, but at the same time, I know it couldn't be. It doesn't seem true. It isn't like her at all. I just can't fathom why she would do it."

I hesitated, then decided to plunge ahead. "Bliss," I said. "I'm making an informal investigation into the deaths of a couple of artists. Would you mind if I looked into Attley's a little further? I'll certainly understand if you don't want me to."

Her startling blue gaze flew to mine. "Oh, no, I would appreciate it!" She said and looked relieved. "What do you want to know?"

"I don't think this is the place to discuss it," I said. "We'll keep getting interrupted."

She nodded but seemed at a loss.

"Would you mind if I took a look at Attley's

studio?" I asked her. "I might see something that was overlooked. And then we could talk."

I thought for a moment that she might turn me down. After all, why would she want to let a stranger into her home to pry into the worst time of her life? She looked tired and defeated, but after a second, she nodded again.

"Yes, I could do that. How about after the show is over today? We live in Oceanside. It isn't too far away."

"Good," I said. "I'll meet you right here after the show and we can go on over."

* * *

In my intermittent wanderings, I gradually spoke to most of the artists who were veterans at shows. They let me know that theft was all too common. Some of them took pains with security measures they thought would work, such as covering their displays or putting their wares away overnight. Some seemed to take it in stride as normal. I spoke to them about how well they knew the board members, staff and other artists. It seemed that almost everyone knew everyone else. They were familiar with the volunteers and had their preferences. Skylar was a favorite among the artists. She was always smiling, they said, as well as prompt and capable. Only one artist, a woman named Charleena, who made ceramic tiles, had anything negative to say about any of them. She told me that she would rather have Skylar than Jim French.

"What in particular don't you like about Jim?" I asked her.

"I don't dislike him!" she said. "I don't mean that. He's a fine volunteer. I just don't like the way he looks at me." Her face reddened.

"How does he look at you?" I asked.

She waved away the question. "Oh, you know how guys look at you," she said. "Like they're sizing you up."

That had been all I could get out of her. But it was interesting that she had singled out one of the volunteers. I promised myself to keep an eye out for him so we could chat.

I made it a point to warn each of the artists to keep their wits about them when they were alone, particularly when driving. I received puzzled looks, knowing stares and bewilderment. By the afternoon, I estimated I had spoken to three-fourths of the artists in attendance.

It was about three-thirty when I saw the young man I knew to be Lagan, one of the board members I had met a few days before. He was booth-sitting in the booth across the aisle from us.

I walked over and stopped to look at the shining wood pepper mills set up on a table. As I ran my hand over the satiny finish, I took a look at Lagan. He was a young Indian man who looked about twenty.

"Are you having a good day?" I asked him. "How long of a shift do you have?"

"I work from two until six today," he said. His voice was soft and his slight accent was lyrical and charming. He had a slow, deliberate way of speaking, much like Ayubu did, as though he was not comfortable with the language. His brown skin was flawless. His dark hair was tousled and a bit long, his brown eyes large and warm as he looked me in the eye. For a split second, I felt that he was challenging me to something but the feeling disappeared instantly. I also had a fleeting feeling that I knew him from somewhere. Of course, I had already met him at the board meeting. But that wasn't it. There was something about him that I knew. In a way he reminded me of someone I had met in Hawaii the previous winter. The same dark hair and eyes, the same calm, self-effacing manner. I smiled to myself. Willis would have been amused to be compared, even favorably to a very young man who looked nothing at all like him. The thought of Willis brought the thought of Easy and once more I felt a vague sadness.

"Are you an artist yourself?" I asked Lagan, determining to put both men out of my mind.

He gave a soft laugh. "No," he said "I wish I was. I think that is why people volunteer for arts organizations, though, so they can mingle with artists and get to know them. It is as close to being an artist as they will ever get."

"Do you have any particular interests?" I held up one of the pepper mills made of some rosy red wood. "Such as woodworking or painting?"

He shook his head. "I tried painting once." He laughed and shook his head again.

"Didn't work out?" I asked.

"I was using oil paints. I overworked the blending so much that I started to notice all of my 'paintings'" – he made finger quotes around the word – "*all* of them looked like they were painted in mud. It was not a good experience."

"You could try another medium," I said. "You never know what hidden talents you have. You could take a class. I never knew I would love doing stained glass until I took a class in it."

"I am afraid I am too lazy to do that," he said and sighed. "So, I hang around art shows, volunteer, work as a board member. It is a good way to soak up culture."

I laughed. "Do you have a paying job too?" I picked up a small bowl. It looked like it was made of different kinds of wood, layered to make luminous bands of color.

"Oh, yes," he said, sighing again. "I work for my father in his restaurant." Then he switched gears. "Have you discovered anything about the thefts?" He looked around as if he were hoping to catch someone in the act, or perhaps he was making sure he wasn't overheard.

I shook my head. "Not much, I'm afraid. Please do keep your eyes open and tell me if you notice anything unusual."

He nodded. The artist returned then and Lagan began to speak to him about an inquiry a customer had made. I gave them both a wave and moved on.

TWELVE

Friday, July 20, 1984

It was six-thirty when I met Bliss in front of her booth. She was gathering up the things she was taking home and giving the space one last look-over.

"I'm not used to this," she said. "Usually, Attley was the one who did the shows. I would come around to help her with the load-in and load-out but..." Her voice trailed off as though the subject was too sad to think about.

"If you would rather not do this tonight, I will understand," I told her.

"No," she said with a deep sigh. "I want to. I think that the more I face it, the easier it will be."

I looked at her a moment. I could tell that none of this was easy for her. "In the long run, yes," I said, "it may be easier. But you don't have to push yourself."

She laughed sadly. "Unfortunately, I *do* have to push myself. If I don't, I would never do anything again." She gave her booth one more glance. "Come on. Let's go."

We pushed through the door into the balmy July evening. The venue was air conditioned and I had been glad for my jacket all day but outdoors I was becoming uncomfortable.

"I guess I feel that keeping to our regular routine is something I can do for Attley." She gave me a glance.

I nodded. I understood. "It must have been terrible having to pack the items to bring to the show."

"They were already packed, thank God," she said. "What was hard was the unpacking." She shook her head. "I sometimes still can't believe she's gone. Every once in a while, it hits me again."

We climbed into her truck and after we had passed Black Lake, we had gone only a short distance before Bliss stopped in front of a modest, one story house. The front of it was weathered but the garden was beautiful.

"Are you the gardener or was that Attley?" I asked her.

"That would be me," she said when we were on the stone walkway to the front door. "And thank heavens for it. I would have gone crazy without my garden."

"It's lovely," I said and stopped to sniff the flowers of a climbing plant next to the door.

"That's jasmine," she said. "I planted that the day after we moved into this place." She shook her head again. "I used to love the fragrance of it but now, to me, it just smells sad. Everything I look at, do, smell, eat seems to bring a fresh pain."

"I'm afraid you'll be experiencing that quite a lot during the first year," I told her. "Once all the 'firsts' are over, it may get a little easier."

She looked the question at me, then asked, "Firsts?"

"The first of everything; the first Saturday afternoon, the first time you eat salmon, the first birthday. Firsts. They are the hardest things to deal with after you've lost someone."

"You sound like you've had your own loss," she said.

"My mother," I told her, although it had, by then, been several years since she had passed. I didn't mention the twenty years I had thought the love of my life was dead. I didn't want to get into that story. She didn't need it and neither did I.

We went through the comfortable looking living room and into a warm, inviting kitchen then through the back door.

Bliss unlocked a small building hidden among what looked like hundreds of climbing roses. "What things are left out here are either unfinished or else Attley didn't consider them good enough to take to the show. I haven't been in here since…it happened."

"Would you rather stay outside? Maybe go back into the house while I look around?"

Poor Bliss looked flummoxed so I decided for her. "This is a time when you don't have to push yourself. Go on into the house. I'll knock on the back door when I'm finished." I put my hand on her arm. "I promise that I won't move anything."

"Move all you want," she said, appearing grateful. "I don't mind that you're looking. I just wasn't looking forward to doing it myself."

"Do you mind if I take pictures?" I asked.

She shook her head. "Take all you like."

* * *

As soon as I stepped into the studio, I thought, in spite of what Bliss or I had said before, it might have been therapeutic for her to come in. The strong feeling of Attley's presence might be comforting to someone who had loved her. She seemed to be all around me. I got the impression that she had been contented in her studio, that she had been doing what she wanted to do and living how she wanted to live. She had found her joy in the small, cluttered space. The studio itself had a comfortable, well used aura. It had an air of pleasure. I could also feel the deep affection Attley had had for Bliss. It hung in the air like a sparkling, gossamer curtain, almost tangible. The sensations I was getting were in direct opposition to the feelings of someone who had committed suicide.

There were jars and cans of paint on a low shelf and spray equipment, pieces of metal, wood and glass everywhere. There were also many, many pieces of art sitting, leaning, hanging, piled.

I started at the wall nearest the door and began to snap pictures. I wasn't looking for anything in particular. I wouldn't have known what to look for anyway.

I moved over to the wall where the paints and equipment were stored. Much of the paint was common house paint in a huge variety of colors. On one of the shelves was a wooden crate full of found objects; rocks, glass, wires, string, shells, hunks of wood that she used in her art.

When I reached the far wall, I began to look through the stacks and piles of finished and unfinished pieces. Attley and Bliss called their work "street art" and I could see why. Sometimes an interesting chunk of driftwood was painted with what looked like a combination of graffiti and hieroglyphs. Sometimes, bits of glass were artfully attached, giving the piece a shine or an energy. Some were scenes of rainy streets or city life, some the beach in every kind of weather, all painted in a crude, primitive style. There were animals too; dogs, cats, chickens, cows and birds of all kinds. All were appealing. I took shot after shot, loaded in more film and shot some more.

I found a square piece of barnboard with a symbol painted on it with a brush. A red circle with a capital R in the middle. It triggered something in my mind but it was gone before I could figure out what it was. The red paint against the silvery wood was striking. It reminded me of an anarchy symbol only it was an R and not an A. I wondered what it stood for and set it aside so I could ask Bliss if it had significance or if it was just a bit of graffiti. It didn't seem to belong among Attley's other works. I thought maybe Bliss had done it.

* * *

"I have no idea," Bliss said when I showed her the piece. "Attley must have made this. All of the stuff in the studio is hers. I work in the garage. Believe me, I have nowhere near the talent that Attley has...had." She looked at it longer. "I like it. It has something like magnetism."

I didn't say so, but I didn't like it. To me, it didn't have the magnetism that Bliss saw in it at all. It had the opposite effect on me and I felt slightly repelled.

I wondered why.

She poured two cups of tea and we sat down at the table.

"Can you talk about what happened?" I asked her. "I know some people wouldn't be comfortable discussing it this soon."

"I'm not comfortable," Bliss said, "but I will talk about it. I think talking helps. I have no idea why." She looked at her cup for a long moment.

"When the police told me that there was no doubt that it was suicide, I wanted them to look a little deeper. I think they thought I was having trouble accepting it and maybe I was...am." She turned her head to stare out the window, then faced me again. "I'm very grateful that you are willing to look into it. If you find out that she *did* do it to herself, then I think I would be able to accept it. I thought the police had jumped to the easiest conclusion." She stopped and I couldn't begin to divine her thoughts.

"I know that probably is a normal reaction when something like this happens, isn't it? Denying that the person you love did such a thing?"

I nodded. "Kirk Neilsson told me it was a single car auto accident," I said.

"She ran her car into the seawall down at Beach Access Road. They found a note on the seat next to her."

"A note?" I asked. "Was it in her own

handwriting?"

Bliss shook her head. "It was typed."

"Did you find that peculiar at all?" I asked. "Is that why you suspected that there was more to it?"

Bliss shook her head again and swallowed as if trying to keep back tears. "Attley used to say that even she couldn't read her handwriting. If she needed to write something, she always typed it. She said that she might be able to paint but writing she couldn't do." Bliss was sobbing by then and I gave her a minute to calm down.

"Do you have the note, Bliss?" I asked.

She shook her head again. "No, I told the police to destroy it when they were finished with it. It was horrible!"

"Then you know what it said."

"Yes. They told me that it was 'undeniably suicide'. She wrote that things could not go on the way they were and that she had been feeling hopeless for a long time. Had been trying hard to fake being happy but it wasn't working." She swallowed again and sobbed once. "There were some other things but it didn't sound like her at all. Not at all. I just don't see her doing that. If she had wanted to die..." She looked at me. "She *didn't* want to die. I can tell you that for sure. And a car crash?" She shook her head.

"Was she having any anxiety? Maybe caused by

stress because of the show?" I ventured. "Was she taking any medications?"

Bliss shook her head. "Not Attley. She didn't even like to take Tylenol. She wasn't stressed either. She loved doing shows. She thought it was fun getting paid doing the stuff we do. It is." She blew her nose. "Or, at least, it was."

She was silent a moment, then asked, "Did you find what you were looking for?" I thought she was hoping that Attley had left some sort of clue behind that would somehow explain her death.

"Not really," I said and sighed. "I don't think I was looking for anything. I was hoping to get a read on Attley herself."

Bliss gave me a glance. "In what way?"

"Part of my job is to look at everything. Sometimes, something turns up that no one noticed that will lead to something else. You never know." I gave her a long glance. "Maybe you could tell me more about her," I said.

"I've known Attley since we were in high school. She was a happy person." She looked at me with pleading in her eyes. I nodded. "She loved life. She loved puttering around in her studio. She loved people. She once told me that every night she went to bed mentally listing all the things she was thankful for."

"She sounds like the kind of person I would like," I

told her.

She nodded. "Everyone loved Attley. She was excited about the show and about the contest. She said she didn't think she would win but she was thrilled just to be a finalist." She squeezed her eyes shut and when she opened them, they were red and teary. "Does that sound to you like someone who would...do what she did...what they said she did?"

I had to admit that it didn't. But people do inexplicable things all the time.

"When I was going through Attley's studio," I said. "I could feel the love that Attley had for you."

She looked at me with an expression of such heartrending appeal that I knew she had been starving for just such a validation.

"Her studio has an aura of contentment and comfort. I don't think you need to be afraid to go out there. It may comfort you," I told her. "She was happy. I have to agree with you that suicide doesn't seem plausible."

It took her a moment to collect herself. I put my hand onto hers.

"Thank you," she whispered.

In my contact with her, I felt her pain lessen. Not much. It was still deep and searing, but a little less so than it had been. I thought that, someday, she would be okay.

"You know," she said finally, sounding tentative.

"I hate to admit this, but you might understand since you've been through your mother's death." She stopped then swallowed as if deciding whether or not to continue. "I'm sometimes angry at Attley for leaving me like she did."

With Bliss' hand in mine, I felt nothing that I didn't understand. "That's a normal reaction, Bliss," I told her. "I remember feeling the same and then feeling guilty about it."

The relief on her face was heartbreaking.

I told her it was time for me to go.

We were silent on the way to her truck, but she stopped me before I climbed into the passenger side and gave me a hug. "Thank you," she said again. "Thank you for everything."

On the way back, it flashed through my mind where I had seen the symbol of the red circled R before. It was in one of Barbara Robertson's watercolors. I was almost sure of it. I thought I remembered seeing it in a scene of Seattle graffiti. So, after all, it was just a piece of random street art that both Barbara and Attley had stumbled upon. Or so I thought at the time.

THIRTEEN

Friday, July 20, 1984

I t was almost seven before we were on our way back to Beachhouse. I was exhausted and I think Bliss was too. I had to remind myself that doing shows was all new to her as it was to me. The whole world would seem new to her now.

As we passed Black Lake, I looked out the window at its dark glassiness.

"They could have named it something more cheerful," I muttered.

"You have to admit that they called it like it is," Bliss said.

"If they wanted people to enjoy it, they didn't do a very convincing job of making it seem pleasant. That sign is downright creepy," I said, gesturing to the forlorn, cracked wooden sign. "Is the city discouraging people from using it?" I asked, half kidding.

"They don't need to," she said. "Most of the locals stay away anyhow. The tourists come here for the ocean beaches. Besides, swimming is forbidden at Black Lake. There's another sign, nearer the water with a warning on it. There is no gradual shoreline, you know. At the shore there is a deep drop off. There are some stories about the place that would curl your hair."

"Really?" I asked, interested.

"Oh, sure. There's supposed to be a monster living in it." She looked at me and smiled. I was glad to see it. "Like Nessie, or the Sasquatch. Only not as famous."

"Parents probably made it up to keep the kids away," I said.

"I always thought that too. But we *have* had a couple of people go missing in the area and they've never been found. I always thought it was fun having a creature from Black Lake to talk about. It makes the place sound more interesting."

* * *

After Bliss dropped me off at Beachhouse, I went up to my room to add to my notes. On an impulse, I used the hall phone to call the Hagler County Sheriff's office and asked about Attley Silverwood's death. Suicide was always a possibility, no matter what Bliss said about it, but there had been four deaths and what *was* unusual was that they were all artists. And all women.

I got nothing from the Sheriff's office. When I mentioned the four deaths the officer laughed and said that was nothing but a coincidence. "The case," he said, "has been closed."

Just as I hung up, I could hear voices rising. It sounded like Skylar and Persis.

"I *saw* you," I heard Persis say in a vicious hiss as I reached the bottom of the stairs.

When I entered the hall, I saw Skylar shaking her head. "I never went near your room. I was in the kitchen."

"I saw you coming from my room. It's past the kitchen," Persis said and started to reach for Skylar.

Skylar backed up. "I have no reason to go down there." She turned and when Persis grabbed her arm, she wrenched it away and went upstairs.

I heard someone in the kitchen and a moment later, Ayubu stuck his head around the door.

"Everything all right out here?" he asked.

I nodded and he ducked back into the kitchen.

"She's such a bitch!" Persis said.

"What did she do?" I asked, though they had drawn a pretty clear picture.

"She went into my room," Persis said. I could almost see the smoke coming out of her ears. Her face was red and she was shaking with rage.

"What for? Do you know?"

"She's a lying, spying bitch!" Persis spit out in the general direction Skylar had gone.

I put my hand on her arm and almost yanked it back from the heat of her anger, but it seemed to calm her a little so I left it there. From contact with her I knew what had happened.

"Do you know for *sure* that she went into your room?" I asked again.

She turned to me. What calm she had gained disappeared.

"Do you think I'm a liar?"

"No, I don't," I said. "Did you see her come out of your room or was she just in the general direction of it?"

She shrugged, still furious, but said nothing.

"Why would she go in there?"

Persis shook her head. "To snoop or steal something."

I didn't think Persis had seen Skylar come out of the room. "Did you see her go in?" I asked again.

Persis was silent and I thought she was not going to answer. At last, though, she said, "No."

"Did you see her come out?"

Persis shook her head. "What was she doing in the hall if not looking in my room? Her room is upstairs."

She seemed to be calming a bit and I waited a few seconds for her to calm a little more then said, "Let's go in and see what Ayubu is making for dinner."

Persis followed me still wearing her scowl.

"Groundnut stew and biscuits," Ayubu told us when we found him at the stove. He was stirring a pot of something that smelled wonderful.

"What's in it?" Persis asked, eyeing the mixture as if she expected insects to float to the surface.

"Sweet peppers, peanuts, onions, sweet potato, garlic and other things," Ayubu said. "The biscuits are Pillsbury."

That's just the kind of thing I love," I said. "How about you, Persis?"

She shrugged.

"Let's set the table for Ayubu, shall we?"

She gave the stew one last look then took the stack of plates from me and pushed into the dining room.

❊   ❊   ❊

The stew *was* delicious. There were flavors in it I recognized and some that I didn't. I would have to ask Ayubu for the recipe. Though I knew that Easy would balk at trying anything new, I thought it was something he might like. As I thought of him, I felt that sudden heaviness that was becoming familiar. It had been more than a week since I had spoken to him, when, normally, I spoke to him every one or two days. I made myself a promise to call him that night.

"Delicious!" Carson proclaimed and Ab nodded.

Skylar took a bite and looked up at the ceiling in apparent bliss. "This is wonderful!" she said and shoveled in another mouthful.

Cassandra took a tentative bite, then another with more enthusiasm. "It *is* good," she said as if she were astounded that an unfamiliar dish could be so palatable. "Persis won't like it though," she said.

"I like it," Persis said. And, indeed, she was eating with some gusto, although I suspected it was more to defy her mother than because she loved the food.

Jade took a small bite and put down her fork. She picked up a biscuit from the plate and took a nibble of that too.

"Something wrong with the dinner, Jade?" I asked. The woman pushed my buttons and I knew I wasn't the only one.

"The biscuits taste like dirt and this—" She gestured at the groundnut stew and made a face to indicate that nothing further needed to be said. "I can't eat anything that is so spicy." She stood then and left the dining room. In a moment, we could hear the door to her room slam.

"Did I put in too much spice?" Ayubu asked. His eyes were round in surprise.

"No," said Ab. "It's perfect." He took another bite as if to punctuate his words.

"I can't eat anything spicy either," Cassandra said. "But this doesn't seem spicy to me at all."

Skylar said nothing but she seemed to be enjoying the dinner as we all were.

"I am sorry that Jade does not like my cooking," Ayubu said. "Perhaps she is not used to eating foods that are unfamiliar to her."

"You're a lot more patient than I am," Cassandra said. "That was downright rude!"

"We must be patient with those who do not behave as we do," Ayubu said.

"Everybody's different," Carson commented and took a huge bite of gravy laden biscuit.

Cassandra looked toward the hall where Jade had disappeared. "Some people are more different than others," she said. "She didn't have to be rude."

"Did everyone have a good day at the show?" Ab asked before Carson could respond.

There were a few nods but no one said anything.

"Persis," I asked. "Did you?"

She looked up as though she had just then realized

that there was anyone else at the table.

"Sure, I guess," she said and shrugged.

"Did you sell anything?" Carson asked. It was hard to believe that he was just now getting around to asking her.

"Yes, she did," Cassandra said. "I saw someone buying something."

"Good for you!" Skylar said, looking pleased for Persis.

Persis gave her a glance but stayed silent. I had seen a few people buying from her. Knowing the pleasure of selling a piece that I had made, I thought Persis was probably thrilled with the successes she'd had. It was unfortunate that she was so accustomed to avoiding her parents and anyone else that she felt she had to keep the good things to herself.

* * *

After dinner I began to clear the table. I was exhausted from the day of work but was eager to get my turn at clean-up over.

I glanced at Persis who was playing with what looked like a deck of cards. Her mother whispered, "Put those away," but Persis was having none of it. She fiddled with the cards, flipping one or two over in her hands. It was a moment before I realized they were a Tarot deck.

"Come on, Persis," I said. "Let's get this cleaned up."

Cassandra laughed out loud then. "Good luck! Persis does not do housework. She wouldn't dream of it. There is no way you can get Persis to help."

Persis threw a disgusted look at her mother, shoved the cards into her back pocket and followed me into the kitchen.

I ran hot water into the sink to tackle the pot that refused to fit into the dishwasher while Persis brought in the remaining dishes. "When we're done, we can play around with your Tarot deck if you want," I said when she had made her final trip.

We packed everything into the dishwasher and started it. It gave a somewhat alarming growl but, nevertheless, seemed to work.

"Do you know the meanings of the cards or how to do a reading?" I asked her.

"No, not really," she said.

"Well, I can show you. I used to do readings at the Pike Place Market."

She sat down at the kitchen table and looked at me with her eyes wide. "For real!? Did people pay you to do that?" she asked. She looked truly interested.

"They did," I told her. "But I don't do it anymore."

"Why not!? If people paid me to do readings for

them, I'd do it all the time." She continued to look at me as though she were seeing me in a new light. For the first time she looked like what she was, a young woman who was interested in something other than herself. It made her look pretty and eager and I wished that she could see herself then.

I thumbed through the cards and realized they weren't the standard Universal Waite deck, but rather hand drawn and painted cards.

"Persis," I said. "Did you make these? They're beautiful!"

She blushed scarlet and nodded. "They aren't very good. I made them about three years ago."

"They *are* good. Especially when you consider that an eleven year old drew them." I picked up one of the cards that, in a standard deck would depict a lion and a woman as its centerpieces. Persis' lion looked more like a saber-toothed tiger. "This one, for instance." I held up the card. "You didn't try to copy the original artwork, but instead made it your own while still keeping the essence of the original intent. Do you know what this card means?"

She muttered something and shook her head.

"This is Strength. When it lies this way, it means that whoever is asking the question—we call that the querent—possesses inner strength. Enough to conquer his or her fears. If it falls reversed," I moved the card so it was upside down—"it means that his or her fear is out of control and they must try to conquer it."

She picked up another card showing a bearded man in dark robes holding a lantern made out of a skull. "What about this one?"

"That one is The Hermit. He's about looking for ways to help others. And he listens to his own inner counsel. Tell you what. You think of a question you have, then shuffle those cards thoroughly, thinking of that question. Then divide them into three piles. You pick out three cards and we'll see what they say."

She squeezed her eyes shut, trying to think of something to ask. At last she opened them and smiled.

"Got it?"

She nodded. "I want to know if this house is haunted."

"Good one!" I said. "Okay, keep shuffling, thinking about that."

Persis' eyes almost sparkled with anticipation as she gathered the cards and began to shuffle. As she handled the cards, her forehead was wrinkled into a frown as if she were concentrating hard.

As she worked the cards, I could see the small anarchy sign she had on the inside of her wrist. It reminded me of the graffiti symbol I had seen on Attley's work and Barbara Robertson's.

"May I look at your tattoo again?" I asked when she was dividing the cards.

A becoming flush of pink flooded her face. "Sure," she said and pushed up her sleeve a little so I could get a better look. It was very similar to the symbol I had seen except for the color and that the anarchy sign was an "A" and the other was an "R".

"Skylar has a tattoo," Persis said suddenly. I wondered if Persis' dislike of Skylar could be stemming from simple old fashioned jealousy. Skylar was older than Persis and could do what she wanted to do. Persis would not be independent for several more years.

"Really?" I said. "What is hers?"

Persis shrugged. "I couldn't really see it very well. I just caught a glimpse. It's on the inside of her arm, like mine."

"Another anarchy sign?"

"I don't know." She looked at me with just a breath of suspicion on her face. "I said I didn't really see it. But I know she has one."

I thought she was lying. I got the distinct feeling that she knew exactly what Skylar's tattoo depicted but that she was so envious of it that she didn't want to acknowledge it. Or, perhaps Persis had not seen a tattoo at all. Her having admitted knowing about it had been something she hadn't meant to do. I decided then not to ask if Persis had ever seen the symbol with the R before. She appeared to be retreating again and I didn't want her to leave.

"Now," I said. "Pick three cards. They can be one from each pile, three from one pile or whatever you want. They don't have to be the top card. Just select three and give them to me."

She did as I asked, taking some time to deliberate over which cards to pick, though they were all lying face down and she had no way of seeing which ones they were.

At last she had chosen the three cards and I turned over the first one.

It was the Page of Swords in the reversed position. Unpredictable behavior. *Interesting*, I thought.

The second card was The Moon which can indicate unforeseen events and heightened emotions as well as psychic ability and dreams.

The third card was The High Priestess, a card signifying the importance of trusting one's own intuition to uncover that which is hidden.

As I explained the meanings of the cards to Persis and their possible interpretations, I tried to get her to relate them to her own life.

"Do you think any of these cards could represent you?" I asked her.

She picked up the Page of Swords. "I think this one does," she said. "He's unpredictable, you said."

I nodded. "What else do you find in these cards, now that I've told you what they can represent?"

She looked them over and picked up the Moon card. "I think this one represents the house." She flushed. "I mean, the spirits in the house. You said it represents psychic stuff. Like ghosts." She looked both pleased and hopeful.

At last, she picked up The High Priestess. "If I use my own intuition, I think the house *is* haunted," she said at last, sounding triumphant.

"Very good!" I said. "That's what the cards are for, to help you to figure out your own answers to your questions and problems. "You're a natural!"

It was right then that Skylar pushed open the door and entered the kitchen.

"I don't want to interrupt," she said, smiling. "I just wanted to get a soda." She went to the refrigerator and peered in.

"You aren't interrupting," I said. I almost invited her to join us but I saw Persis' scowl and kept my mouth shut.

In a moment, Skylar had gone. I got up and fetched a soda from the refrigerator. I raised it and looked a question at Persis. She nodded so I opened two and brought them back to the table. I don't normally drink it, but I wanted to get Persis back into her sharing mood again. It would have been better if Skylar could have joined us and I could have gotten to know her better too but I knew that Persis would have shut down if she had.

"Something wrong?" I asked Persis, handing her one of the bottles. She had gathered up her cards and was shuffling them again.

"I don't like Skylar at all," she said, sullen.

"Why not? She seems friendly to me," I said.

Persis didn't say anything.

"I know that you think Skylar went into your room, but you have to admit that you could be wrong about that. You didn't see her do it." I waited for Persis' reluctant nod.

"I hate that way she talks, like she's all out of breath all the time. It sounds fake."

I laughed. I had noticed the breezy, breathy way that Skylar spoke too, but I liked it. "I think it's kind of charming," I said.

She scowled harder and took a drink of her soda.

"So, you like everyone else here except Skylar?" I asked, already knowing what the answer would be.

"Well, I don't like Jade either," Persis said, the corners of her mouth turning down.

"She isn't the easiest person to get along with, is she?" I said.

"She hates me." Persis turned over one of the cards. The Ten of Wands. She took a long swallow of her drink.

"Oh, I don't think so, Persis," I said. "She's probably an unhappy person and it's her habit to complain about things. She doesn't seem to like any of us in particular."

Persis shrugged, buying none of it.

"She makes beautiful clothing," I said.

She shrugged again. "I like Ayubu," she said. "And Ab. They're both really nice."

"You must know a lot of the artists from having come to shows with your parents since you were quite small."

"Yeah," she said, sounding very young. "They were always nice to me. They would give me things."

"Oh? Like what?"

She gathered up the cards again and gave them another shuffle. "Luke Jeffries gave me a really pretty little wooden box that he made. Sandra Scollcroft gave me a tiny dish to keep rings and stuff in. I have a little picture of a bunny and a flower made with paper quilling and, oh, lots of things."

I was reminded of the small items that were taken from the artists' booths. But Persis had been just a little girl when she had acquired these pieces and it was easy to see an artist giving a small gift to a cute child who spent the weekend in the booth next door or across the aisle.

"How long have you been doing your own drawings, Persis?" I asked when she had finished.

"Most of my life," she said, turning over card after

card. The Six of Cups, the Queen of Wands, the Two of Pentacles. "I draw all the time. When I go to my room at night, my parents think I go to bed but I usually stay up pretty late drawing or something."

"I have to say, you're very talented."

Her face turned red and she shrugged again. It was unfortunate, I thought, that she was so insecure about her work. I put my hand on her arm.

"Don't sell yourself short, Persis. You *are* talented."

I was surprised by the degree of envy that emanated from her. I could feel that she did like the people she had spoken about and loved their art, but it troubled me that I could sense how deeply jealous she was of them too.

FOURTEEN

Friday, July 20, 1984

Cassandra pushed open the kitchen door and glanced around. If she had planned an offer of help, she was far too late. In a second, she had spotted Persis' Tarot cards.

"Put those away," she said, and picked up the soda bottle. "I don't want you drinking this stuff either." She carried the bottle to the sink and dumped the contents down the drain.

Persis glanced at her, looked at me and whispered, "Thank you." She stood and shoved the cards into her hip pocket and left. In a moment, we could hear her bedroom door close across the hall.

Cassandra still stood by the sink. I started to get up. I thought I would rather go to my room and read than sit around with the other tenants. Besides, I was tired all the way down to the bone.

"Could I speak with you a moment?" Cassandra asked. She had put her hand on my arm and I felt worry and some defiance coming from her.

"Of course," I said and sat back down. Cassandra stood for another second, looking uncertain, then she pulled out the chair Persis had recently occupied and sat.

"I don't want Persis to continue playing with those Tarot cards," she said. "Or, for that matter, any of the other things she seems to be into these days."

"What other things is she into?" I asked, though I thought I already knew.

"She has a Ouija board and I don't know what all. She's fascinated with those fortune telling cards and I don't want her to persist in that."

"Tarot isn't about fortune telling," I told her. "It's much more about *self*-discovery than discovering anything from the future."

Cassandra shook her head. "That stuff frightens me." She laughed uncomfortably. "Call me an overprotective mother if you want to, but I don't understand Persis' preoccupation with...with dark things." She stared at her clasped hands. She looked like she was praying. "Death and darkness and magic." Her face was beginning to pink and I thought she was embarrassed. "She's fascinated by Black Lake." She shuddered. "Ugh! Did you see that lake? It's... She wants to go swimming there, of all places. Fortunately, she doesn't know how to swim. That place is horrible!"

I laughed and agreed with her.

"Persis is at the age where she's trying to figure things out about herself," I said. "There's nothing harmful about learning about the Tarot. It can show people why they act and think the way they do because it uses the subconscious mind. It will help to get Persis thinking about who she is and what she wants to be." I put my hand on hers. The woman *was* frightened. "She probably won't go swimming in Black Lake. For one thing, swimming is forbidden there. For another, if she doesn't know how to swim, she isn't likely to try it on her own. As for Ouija boards," I shrugged. "Consider that a game. Kids play with them all the time. There's nothing magical about those either."

"I just don't know what the attraction to Tarot is," she mused.

"Like I said, you can find your personal meaning in the cards just as you can in art or music," I said. "The only thing it may say about the future is that you have choice in what you do with it."

"What if she finds out something she doesn't want to know?"

I laughed. "That would be a risk, wouldn't it? If the Tarot was about telling the future, that is. But it isn't." I stood. I needed to get to my room and get a little sleep. We had a big day tomorrow. "The more she knows, and the more you know, the more she will find out about herself and the more she will mature. The external things, the candles, the black clothing, the Ouija board and cards will no longer be important to her. Tarot can give her self-knowledge and that will lead to self-esteem and confidence in the future. The cards aren't magic. The magic comes from within the person who is using them."

"I'm still not comfortable with it," Cassandra said, standing too.

"I won't encourage her, then," I said. "But if she asks me questions or seeks my help, I won't turn her down."

She thought for a moment. "That's fair. What you say makes me feel better," she said. "You seem to know what you're talking about. If you say you won't encourage her, that's fine."

I smiled at her as she headed for the kitchen door. She turned back. "I don't want Persis to find out I've been talking to you about this, if you don't mind."

"Don't worry," I told her and she gave me a faint smile. She pushed open the door and I could hear the television in the living room.

As I crossed the hall, I caught a glimpse of Jade standing near the bathroom door. She stared at me a moment before going in. I wondered if she had been listening and had heard Cassandra's and my conversation.

I climbed the stairs to my room and left the chatter from the living room behind. My feet and calf muscles were smoldering with a slow burn from wearing unfamiliar shoes all day and my back was all but screaming out loud.

I got out my notes and all of the pictures I had taken over the past week. I spread the photos of Barbara Robertson's watercolors out onto the desk and looked at them with the magnifying glass from my bag. At last, I located the painting which had the R symbol on it. Since I was looking at a photo of a painting, the symbol was very small and difficult to see. It blended into the other graffiti in the picture and yet it stood out on its own. I wondered who the graffiti artist was who had painted it and what it represented.

As I arranged the photos, I was fascinated by the "Skedaddle Seattle Series." For the most part they were the worst of Seattle; Skid Road, cheap hotels, bawdy clubs, derelicts, graffiti. Still, I thought, Skedaddle Seattle was a great name for the series. I imagined telling Easy that it would have made a good rock band name too, but then, once more, that blanket of sadness and unease fell over me and I vowed not to think about him.

I pored over the photos trying to find just one clue, just a single justification for my suspicions. Maybe I was overthinking. Perhaps it was overreaction to what I did every day; look for details that fit with the puzzle I was trying to put together. I didn't know if a puzzle even existed. As a child, my friend, Linda and I used to read Nancy Drew mysteries and look for sinister goings on everywhere. Was that what I was doing now? Fabricating a problem? I decided to give up for the night and go to bed. Things would look different in the morning.

The armoire squeaked when I opened it and squeaked again when I shut it. I opened it once more and found that I could make it sound like it was almost speaking with a careful opening and closing at different speeds. I laughed, thinking that Easy would have found it funny too. Then, again, I remembered that Easy and I were so out of sympathy with each other that it hurt my heart. I wondered if our friendship could ever get back to the way it had been.

It occurred to me that I had promised myself to call him that night. I glanced at my watch. It was too late, I told myself. Maybe in more ways than one.

Just as I started to close it for the last time, I spotted something on the floor of the armoire and bent to pick it up. It was an earring. It was a fake pierced earring like the kind that Persis wore. Had she been in my room?

I glanced around. There was nothing that Persis shouldn't see. I kept my case notebook locked into my bag when I wasn't in the room and didn't have the bag with me.

Persis had accused Skylar of snooping in her room. I wondered if Persis was trying to cast blame onto Skylar away from herself. I set the earring on the desk and was a bit surprised that I hadn't gotten any feeling from it at all. Normally, I get some kind of emotion, or feeling from any tangible object, even if it's just a trace. But the earring gave me nothing. It was a small flower. Quite pretty but seemingly dead.

* * *

I t was still dark when I awoke and I knew that I had not been asleep long. I thought I had heard the armoire door open. Perhaps my playing with it earlier had put the sound into my subconscious mind, ready for a later dream. I sat up. It was dark but I could see that the armoire door was indeed open.

I got up and closed it, hoping to make sure it was securely shut but, since it had no latch, the best I could do was shut it all the way. After I had climbed back into bed, I listened to soft voices. I didn't know if any of the other residents of the house were still awake or if it was, at last, the voices of those who had once lived in Beachhouse. Before I could figure it out, I had drifted to sleep again.

FIFTEEN

Saturday, July 21, 1984

I saw Lagan again the next morning. Ab had wanted to go in early to do a bit of rearranging. I left him to it and wandered the venue, looking at booths and talking to the other artists who had come in to reorganize too.

"Scoping out the good stuff?" I asked him as I passed a booth with fused glass tiles lining the walls. Lagan had been leaning in, unwilling to encroach on the floor space since the artist wasn't there. I didn't have any such reservations. If the artist wasn't in evidence, I walked in anyhow and looked around.

He turned and managed to look guilty and defiant at the same time.

"I like to check out the booths where I am scheduled to booth-sit later," he said, with a trace of apology. He spoke with hesitant deliberation as though to think through his answer before voicing it.

I nodded. "I didn't realize people signed up ahead

of time. How do they know when they'll need a bathroom break?"

"Most of them sign up for lunch breaks and breaks midway through the morning and afternoon," he said.

I nodded and picked up one of the tiles and held it to the light. The colors, rich and deep, glowed.

"I saw your booth with the stained glass," he said. He was watching me handle the tile. I got the feeling that he disapproved. "It's beautiful. I would love to be able to do that."

"As I said before, you could take a class, like I did," I told him.

He chuckled. I saw that he was missing one of his upper bicuspids. "No," he said, shaking his head. "I can only dream."

He seemed in a hurry to get away but not eager to be rude, so I moved on and gave him a parting wave.

I had spotted Josette Kelleher, whom I had not yet had a chance to question. Her artwork was so realistic that it was difficult to tell if it was a photograph or a painting. She was a heavily built woman in her mid-fifties or early sixties. She had bright orange hair and wore it in a disordered mess on the top of her head. She had the sweetest face of anyone I had ever seen. Her eyes almost disappeared when she smiled. Even when she wasn't smiling, and that was seldom, they were full of merriment.

In a way, she reminded me of my neighbor, Mrs. Graft, but younger. Josette had moved a stepstool to one side of her booth and was eyeing a spot above her head.

She turned to look at me when I arrived. "Hey," she said. "Want to do me the biggest favor in the universe and earn yourself some karma?"

"Sure," I told her.

"Mind climbing this ladder here and hanging this painting up there?" She pointed to the empty area.

"I don't mind at all." I positioned the painting, a gorgeous small work of a red rose bud with perfect dew drops on one of the leaves and one of the petals.

"You are a treasure," she said when I had stepped down again. "We short people are at such a disadvantage. Are you having fun at the show? You guys selling much?"

"Yes, we've sold some things and yes, it's been great fun," I told her. "Mostly, it's humbling. I'm astounded at the talent that's here right now and half of the artists haven't arrived yet."

Josette eyed me for a moment, then said, "I heard that you're here to keep an eye on things. That you're a detective. Is that true?"

I nodded. "The PCAC has noticed an increase in the number of thefts. They asked me to look into it for them." I glanced around. "Have you experienced any thefts?"

She shrugged. "Sure. We all have. I had a small painting go missing at a show in Idaho last year. I think some cards have been lifted, but it's hard to tell with them. I don't mind losing them so much. They're relatively inexpensive. But the painting that was stolen was an original. Whoever took it didn't bother with any of the prints. Whoever it was seemed to know which ones were the good stuff."

"How many of these are originals?" I asked her, looking around again.

"Only four or five of them. I don't put out more than a few originals at a time. Whoever took that painting, they knew what they were doing." She sighed. "I hate to say this, but it's almost expected at a big show like this one and the Idaho show. There are lots of people around and it's pretty much impossible to keep your eye on everything all the time. I'd say everyone here has had something stolen at one show or another. Especially if they've been doing this for years."

"You probably get to know the artists and the show staff pretty well," I said.

She nodded. "You do. It's lots of fun when you get someone you know well as a neighbor." She hung another small, matted picture of a daisy. I would have sworn it was a photo, but knew it wasn't.

"What about the staff? The volunteers who booth-sit and do the clean-up and general helping out?"

"Oh, sure. Some of them are artists who got tired of doing shows or quit for some reason. Some of them are people who just love art."

"Have you done shows with the volunteers who are here this weekend?"

She thought for a moment, then nodded. "Yep. All of them."

"So you've gotten to know them. Any preferences?"

She shook her head slowly then leaned over toward me. "Personally, I'd rather not have Jim booth-sit for me, but that's just me."

"Why?" I swear I felt my ears swivel.

She shrugged. "I don't know. He's always rushing. He rushes in, late, when you've asked for a, say, noon volunteer, and then when you come back, he rushes away again. He never sells anything." She laughed. "That isn't fair," she said. "The volunteers don't like to sell things while you're away from the booth but they do it if it's just a cash deal." She thought for a moment. "I get the feeling he... No! No, he's okay. I just would rather have one of the others. I like all of them."

"You don't have any specific reason for not trusting Jim?" I persisted.

"No..." she said, hesitating. She leaned over again and sighed. "That Idaho show I mentioned? Jim was working that one. He booth-sat for me a couple of times. I noticed that painting—the original I told you about?—was missing. I'm sure it was there when I left, because I had to move it a little. It was too close to the edge of the table. Later that day, it was gone. I didn't notice right away but I knew that I hadn't sold it. When I came back to the booth, Jim didn't say that he had sold anything. He just rushed away like he always does." She shook her head again. "It could have been taken by one of the customers walking by. I don't necessarily think it was Jim. I learned that day to hang the originals and not leave them on the tables."

Jim, I noted on my mental checklist. *I have to have a chat with him for sure.*

"What about the other volunteers? You said you know them all. What do you think of them?"

She shrugged. "Like I said, I like them all. That Skylar is a fun one. But then, so is Rhonda. Well, they all are. I don't want you to think that Jim isn't a good person. I'm sure he is, but you know how some people just don't click with you?"

I nodded. "You can do me a favor, if you would."

"Of course! I owe you," she said.

"Let me know if you notice anyone hanging around. Especially if they come around more than once."

She looked doubtful. "Sometimes buyers come back two or three times before they decide to buy. It would be hard to know."

"If you see anything that looks suspicious, then," I said. "You know where my booth is. Let me know."

She nodded and I started out on my way to look around for another few minutes before the show opened.

"Cheyenne," Josette called before I had gone more than a couple of steps. She came over to me and looked around. "There *was* something funny that's happened a few times. I don't know if it has anything to do with the shows or..." She gave a big sigh. "It probably doesn't mean anything but I've gotten phone calls."

I waited for a moment, then said, "What kind? You mean threats?"

"No, no!" She gave a dismissive laugh. "Nothing like that. They're hang-ups. Someone calls and I answer but no one's there." She laughed again. "Not even heavy breathing. Not so strange, really. Things like that happen all the time."

"When did this happen?" I asked. "Was it once or several times or what?"

"Well, a couple of times. Once just after I did the Cannon Beach show. There were several hang-ups on my answering machine when I got home from that. 'Course, those are par for the course. But later, when I was home, it happened maybe three times."

"Any other times?"

"Once, right before a show I did in Bend. I didn't pay any attention to it, but now that I'm looking for things that are odd..."

"Thanks, Josette," I told her and laid my hand on her arm. She was frightened, despite her smile and her assurances. "Do you check your answering machine when you're away?"

"Yeah," she said, then added, "sometimes."

"Maybe you should do that while you're in Oceanside," I told her. "If you get any more calls or if something else goes missing, please let me know."

"I'm getting a little freaked," she said. She looked it, too.

I patted her arm. "I doubt that you are in danger, Josette," I said, hoping I was right. "I'm trying to follow up on anything that seems unusual."

She nodded and I turned to continue on my way but turned back to her. "And be careful driving. Be especially watchful. Will you do that?"

She *did* look scared then, but I thought that was a much healthier attitude than the board's dismissive one.

❄ ❄ ❄

I caught up with Kirk Nielsson at the check-in desk. He seemed a tireless, personable guy who never stopped moving. Even sitting at the desk, he looked like he was ready to leap up and rush away to clear up a problem. I could see he was antsy for the doors to open so he would have something to do.

"Caught any thieves yet?" he asked when he saw me coming.

I looked around, wondering if anyone had heard him. What did it matter, after all? I wasn't under cover, and, according to Josette, everyone was talking about it anyway.

"Not yet," I told him. "I'm interested in the volunteer staff. Do you know them all or can anyone sign up to help?"

"What? You think the thief is one of our volunteers?"

"No," I said, trying to be patient and wishing he would calm down. He was making me antsy too. "The volunteers know the artists and are all over the venue. They probably know more about what goes on at the show than you do. I was interested in knowing how well you know them."

"Well, we have a pretty big pool of volunteers. There are the ones who do the preliminary work, like marking the booth spaces, organizing the electrical. Then there are the ones who do the behind the scenes stuff."

"I'm interested in the volunteers who work at the show, here, in the venue."

"Well, let's see," he mused. "Skylar, Jake and Rhonda have been volunteering for a couple of years. Maybe more. Lagan too. And, you know he's on the board of directors now. Uh, Jim, though, I don't know *real* well. I know he's been doing shows for a while but until I became the Event Director, I'd never run into him. I never met him until a few months ago. He seems nice. Hard working, for sure."

"But he had volunteered for PCAC before? Has he done other shows for other organizations?"

"Oh, yeah. He's a veteran." He looked up at me. "Why?"

I ignored his question. "Do you often get people who spontaneously sign up? People who aren't artists and people you don't know?"

"Oh, sure! It's a great way to get to see the show for free and to meet the artists. Sometimes artists who've quit doing shows volunteer because they still want to be part of it without having to sell at it."

"When I was talking to Dak, he said he could get me a list of the volunteers, but he hasn't had time to do that yet."

"I can do that," he said. "Give me one second." He ducked into the makeshift office curtained off behind him. In a moment he was back and handed me a list.

"Thanks," I said. "So, you pretty much know all of the volunteers," I mused and gave the door a glance.

It was almost ten o'clock. I saw Rhonda and Jake at another table also waiting for the doors to open.

He shrugged. "Yeah."

"Did anyone on the board discuss with the volunteers my purpose for being here?"

He looked blank. "I don't know," he said. "I can try to find out..."

"Thanks," I said and started to turn away. "Oh," I said, turning back. "Have you ever had any complaints about any of them?"

He shook his head. "No. If we ever did, depending on the complaint and how serious it was, they wouldn't be allowed back. What makes you ask?"

The doors opened then and I was able to escape answering him. I thanked him again and he turned to checking lists and taking tickets. I thought I had better get back to Ab, but first I wanted to see Bliss.

* * *

"T he horde is on the way," I told her when I stopped by her booth. "They were lined up outside the door, apparently."

"Well, I was nervous yesterday," she said. "Now, I'm terrified. Today is supposed to be busier, according to all the neighbors." Her already large eyes looked huge and she did look like she would prefer to crawl under one of the tables.

"Don't worry," I told her. "You did fine yesterday." Of course, I knew no such thing. I had never done a show either and had no idea about how the second or third day would go, but at least I was with Ab who had done so many of them that he couldn't remember them all.

I glanced toward the doors. "Bliss, do you know if Attley knew Barbara Robertson?"

Bliss frowned, her mind off her current worries for the moment. "Tall and blonde?" she asked.

"I don't know how tall she was but I do know she was blonde," I said, remembering the pictures I had seen in her home when I had visited with Tyler. "She lived in Seattle and painted watercolors of Seattle scenes."

"Oh, yes! She's the Skedaddle Seattle lady. I remember her. She and Attley had neighboring booths somewhere. I think it might have been Vancouver. Why?" She started to look worried again.

"One of her street scenes has that same red circle with the R in it that Attley had in her studio and I wondered if they knew each other."

Bliss nodded. "They did. Maybe Attley saw the painting with that sign. Was it one of her graffiti pieces? Either Barbara picked it up from Attley or Attley picked it up from her." She shrugged. "Does that mean something?"

"I have no idea. Perhaps not." I suspected that Bliss did not know that Barbara was dead even though I had been referring to her in the past tense. In her current state of mind, though, I was reluctant to tell her.

"I suppose it could be a common graffiti symbol," I said. "And it could be a coincidence that they both used it." Was I again inventing meaning where none existed?

Two women had just turned the corner and were headed down Bliss' aisle.

"One more thing," I said. "Have you ever gotten hang-up phone calls before or after a show?"

She shook her head. "No, not me." She looked at the women who had stopped at a booth near the corner. "But Attley got a couple of those right after her last show."

"When was that?"

She shrugged. "Let's see, it was the Newport Summer Festival, I think. That was the beginning of June." She looked at me. "Is that important?"

"I don't know. One of the other artists was saying the same happened to her. I just wondered."

The women had started on their trek again and several more people were heading the other way.

"I'd better be getting back to our booth," I told her.

I started off toward Ab. I had said that it could

have been a coincidence that the two artists had used the same obscure little sign in their work and it probably was. But what of the hang-up phone calls? Was that coincidence too? It kept nagging at me and I wondered if it *was* a coincidence. For some reason I didn't think so.

When I got back to the booth, Ab was deep in conversation with the artist next door. He was Oskar Brandweis, the puzzle maker whose work fascinated me. I had thought one of his intricate jigsaw-like puzzles made of wood and glass would make a perfect gift for Easy. Before they were assembled, in a pile, the pieces were beautiful chaos; bits of color and texture that somehow complimented each other. When they were put together, they formed gorgeous pieces of art in their own right. Glowing sections of glass and polished wood representing flowers, trees, ponds or all three. I greeted the men and got to work dusting the glass in our own booth.

So far, the crowd had not made it to that point but the noise level was getting louder and I didn't think it would be long.

Sure enough, we were kept busy for the rest of the morning. It wasn't all selling. We had scores of people stop and ask questions, run their fingers over the glass and move on. Some didn't even give us a glance as they walked by. I wondered why they took the trouble to attend an art show if they weren't going to take the time to look at the art.

Ab was in the middle of a sale when I saw Jim stop by Oskar's booth next door and, in another moment, Oskar was heading toward the food trucks in front of the building. I stepped around the corner after making sure that Ab didn't need me.

"Well, hel-lo!" Jim said when he saw me.

I smiled, thinking that Charleena's description of Jim's demeanor was right on target. He looked me over thoroughly.

I held out my hand and introduced myself to him. I refrained from wiping my hand on my pants leg after he had held onto it a shade too long. During that not brief enough physical encounter I had learned that he was there to have fun, that he had something to hide and that he didn't trust me. None of what I discovered about him came as a shock. People almost always have something they keep to themselves and they don't trust at first meeting. Nevertheless, I segued into my questions, trying to learn as much as I could about him in the short space of time available.

He told me that he "loved" volunteering, that it was "a riot" to follow the shows around the Pacific Northwest and that if the job paid, he would do it for a living.

"What is it you particularly like?" I asked him.

"Meeting women, hanging out with people who have money and class," he said, with a wink.

"Are you an artist yourself?"

He took a deep breath and I had a strong feeling that he was going to lie.

"I do metal etching," he said.

"And do you, yourself, participate in shows?"

"Yup!" he said. "I do real well," he added and I knew that, for some reason only he knew, that he was not being honest.

When Oskar returned, Jim hurried away and I felt like I had learned nothing. The man was full of bluster, hubris and himself. Not only had I gained nothing from my questions, it was difficult to "read" him as well. I would make a point of having a much more in-depth discussion with him.

* * *

It was not much later that I glanced over to the LaChance booth and saw Persis talking to Lagan, who had volunteered all morning, booth-sitting and running errands.

Since there was a lull right then, I went over to Persis' booth, hoping to engage the both of them at once.

As soon as I came close, Persis said something to Lagan and he glanced at his watch then walked away as though he had a pressing appointment.

"I'm sorry," I said. "Did I interrupt something?"

I knew the answer to that when Persis' face turned bright pink and she looked down to straighten a small pile of cards.

"No," she said.

I was not sorry. I felt protective of Persis. I could tell that she was attracted to Lagan and I suspected that he was to her. At any rate, that was highly inappropriate, given her age.

"Did he have anything to say about your artwork?"

"He says he likes it."

"Of course, he does," I said. "It's quite wonderful."

Her face went even redder, if that was possible, and she mumbled something.

"Maybe he'll buy one," I said, and picked up a small drawing of a woman with bat wings. It was sensuous and ethereal and seemed almost too adult for someone Persis' age to have done.

"Maybe I'll give him one," she said in a low voice that I thought I was not meant to hear. A moment later a potential customer caught her attention and I drifted away.

I felt none of the camaraderie I had felt with Persis the night before. Perhaps she had heard me talking to her mother and thought I had betrayed her in some way. Or maybe she had been embarrassed at my catching her showing interest in something.

I glanced over to Ab's booth and there were no customers. Ab was looking over the morning's receipts. I took a moment to stop by Jade's booth and look through the hand-woven garments she had on display. She had several jackets hung on a rack to the side. The other side had plastic models draped with sumptuous scarves in jewel colors. Her booth would have looked quite elegant but for the two plastic bins which had not yet been unpacked.

The turquoise and purple jacket still hung in its place. I fingered the sleeve. Next to it was a similar jacket of sea green. The buttons were drilled seashells and it was lined with a gorgeous apricot silk. I took a quick look at the price tag. It was priced the same as the turquoise and I wanted both of them. Jade glanced up at me, then went back to whatever she had been doing. It looked like a crossword puzzle.

I decided that, big ticket or not, I needed one of those jackets. I could wear it to the show the next day and it would definitely jazz up my wardrobe in the future.

"May I try this on?" I asked Jade, selecting the green one at random.

She said nothing, just gestured toward a floor length mirror she had in the corner of her booth.

The jacket was silky and wonderful. It was unfathomable to me how such an unpleasant person could make such exquisite items. She and Julia Johnston, I thought, should team up. Sort of concentrate all the negative vibes into one area.

"This is beautiful," I said, turning to get a good side look then turning to the other.

Jade nodded as though she heard compliments every day.

"And these are all woven by you?" I knew they were, but I wanted to get her to thaw a little.

No soap. She nodded again.

"Well, I'll take this one if you'll accept a check."

She stared at me for a moment as though she couldn't understand why I didn't have wads of cash in my pocket. Then she nodded. She folded the garment and slid it into a bag. She still had said nothing. As I handed her the check, our fingers touched and from her I felt nothing but hostility and suspicion. I wondered if I should be more curious about her too. I would need to question her about thefts and about the phone calls as well, but it might be easier to do when we were back at the house.

Just before I left her booth, Jade said, "I heard you are here to watch us all. That you think we are all thieves."

I turned toward her. "No, Jade, I don't think that at all. The board hired me to make sure that no one steals from you."

"That isn't what I heard," she said.

"What did you hear?" I asked, trying to look reassuring while I fake-smiled at her.

"That you are watching us all and saying that we should all be careful. That sounds threatening to me."

"No, no," I said, still smiling and trying to look as genuine as I could, which wasn't much. "The board hired me because the artists have been getting their work stolen and I'm here to find out who is doing the stealing. Or at least prevent it from happening."

She muttered and seemed to give up. Or maybe she had run out of her quota of words for the day. I stood for a moment to see if she had anything to add then went on my way.

So far, no one had reported any thefts to me but I didn't think that I was doing any prevention. I had noticed, too, that there had been no uniformed guard in evidence. I knew that the board had voted to hire one, but I was somehow not surprised to discover that they had not.

* * *

That afternoon I saw Skylar. She waved at me from a booth across the aisle, where she was booth-sitting for Gregor who was taking a late lunch. She was sitting behind a glass case filled with jewelry. Next to it was a table covered with ring trays and racks to hold necklaces and bracelets.

"I'll be nearby," I said to Ab and he nodded.

"Are you having fun?" she asked as I came nearer.

"I am," I said. "Just when you think there's nothing happening, people suddenly swarm the booth and you don't have a second to think." I bent to look at one of the intricate glass necklaces displayed on the table covered with others in a prism of color.

She nodded. "I would love to be able to do a show," she said, sounding wistful. "Unfortunately, performance art doesn't cut it with the PCAC."

"How do you know? Maybe you should suggest it. You never know."

"I know," she said, frowning. I think it was the first time I had seen her when she wasn't smiling. "I tried. They acted like performance art was some sort of aberration."

"I don't know anything about performance art at all." I slipped a ring onto my finger then put it back on the table. After buying the jacket, I couldn't afford anything else. "I don't think I've ever seen any."

"Of course you have," she said. "Singers are performance artists. Dancers. Even cheerleaders. And there are some very well-known ones, like

Marina Abramovic and John Lennon and Yoko Ono."

"I wasn't aware that John Lennon was," I said, surprised.

"Sure. The 'bed-in' that he and Yoko Ono did is a famous performance art piece."

"If the PCAC decided to admit performance artists, what would you do?" It was hard to imagine a booth with an artist doing nothing but ballet poses or cheers.

"They won't. But if they did, I would work up a piece that portrayed sexism maybe. Marina Abramovic is so good at that. I'd love to have her talent. She once sat in a chair for six hours and the audience could do whatever they liked to her."

"Yikes!" I said. My imagination balked. "I don't even want to think about that."

She laughed. "It was pretty rough, I guess. But she got famous."

"Fame isn't everything," I told her. I could see that Ab was becoming inundated with customers again so I headed back his way. "See you later," I said and gave Skylar a parting wave.

The rest of the afternoon, I kept an eye out for Jim French, but didn't see him again. It wasn't just Josette's words that had piqued my interest in him, it was the strange way he had of answering my questions and, at the same time, not giving me any information.

Josette had admitted that she hadn't noticed the missing painting until long after Jim was gone from her booth. There had been ample time for someone else to have taken it. I wasn't going to assume that Jim had stolen the painting, nor was I going to assume that he had sold it and pocketed the money. But Josette's words continued to play in my mind. At the very least, I wanted to have a deeper discussion with him.

SIXTEEN

Saturday, July 21, 1984

I was exhausted when we got back to Beachhouse that evening. Ab was quiet, so I thought he was tired too, though I had always thought of him as a man with an unlimited amount of energy.

We had had what I considered a good sales day. Ab agreed when I asked him about it in the car.

"Oh, sure. It was great! Better than I had expected. But then, it's Saturday. That's always the best day of a weekend show for me. Some people will say that Sunday is better, but you'll see. It'll be quieter."

"Quieter would be nice," I said with a sigh. "Oh, God, it's my turn to cook."

We climbed out of the van. "Want me to run down town for fish and chips again?"

"No. I'm going to use up those two packages of chicken breasts Carson bought yesterday. I had him add those and some other things to the list for me when he went to the store. I can't get out of it now."

Once in the house, I headed upstairs to change my clothes and hang my new jacket in the armoire. I checked to be sure my case was still there and locked. Normally, I take it wherever I go, but after the first day I began leaving it in my room. Space in the booth was at a premium and there just wasn't room for that bulky bag.

* * *

Skylar was not at the table along with everyone else. My inquiry got nothing but shrugs from the rest of the group.

Altogether the Chicken Cheyenne I made was a hit. The one person who complained about the delicious yogurt based sauce was Jade. No surprise there. She said it was too spicy for her. Since there was no pepper in it, I wondered what it was she didn't like. She took another grudging bite and then said she couldn't eat any more. She excused herself and went down the hall to her room.

"What do you suppose she lives on?" Carson asked when she had gone. "I don't think I've ever seen her take more than two bites of anything."

"She did not like my cooking either," Ayubu said. He shrugged. "It was her idea for us to all take turns cooking."

"Maybe we should all go get our own food," Ab

said.

"You're just saying that because it will soon be your turn to cook," I said. I didn't know if Ab could cook or not.

"That won't be hard," he said. "I'll be bringing home pizza."

There was a chorus of approval from the rest of the diners.

"I don't like Jade, anyway," Persis said. "I'm glad she's not here."

"Hush, Persis!" Cassandra cut in. "That's very rude of you. I taught you better than that."

"What?" Persis said. "She's not here. She doesn't like me either." She looked unruffled by her mother's reprimand.

Cassandra laughed. "How could you possibly know that? She doesn't talk to anyone. Certainly not to you." She chewed for a moment, then said, "Persis *always* thinks people don't like her. How *do* you know, Persis?" I wondered why she would deliberately bait her own daughter.

"She called me a witch," Persis said before putting her last forkful of rice into her mouth.

"What? When?" Cassandra's face became red but Persis only shrugged.

"I'm sure you must have misunderstood, baby girl," Carson said.

"You don't have to look so happy about it," Cassandra said to Persis who was sopping up sauce with a corner of bread. "I want to know. When did she say that?"

"Last night. In the hall. She said I was evil and a witch."

"Well, I'm going to speak to her about that," Cassandra said, pushing her plate aside and getting up from her place. "I will not stand for that." We continued to hear Cassandra mutter as she went to Jade's door.

"Great!" Persis grumbled. "Now she'll go make a huge deal out of it." She picked an olive out of the salad bowl with her fingers and bit it in half. I knew that if her mother had seen that she would have had even more to say.

Ab stood. "If everyone is finished, "I'll take kitchen duty tonight. Ayubu, how about you and I take this stuff in?"

I knew that Jade's meticulous schedule was hanging in the kitchen. That night, Jade had scheduled Cassandra, Carson and Persis to clean up after dinner, but so far, most of what Jade had decreed had been ignored.

"I think I'll go in and rescue Jade from my wife," Carson said and left Persis and me still sitting at the table.

"Wow, Dad," Persis muttered after he had gone.

"Way to stand up for your family."

I rummaged in my pocket and located the earring I had found in my armoire. "Persis, is this yours?"

She looked at it with distaste. "God, no! It's a flower. I have standards, you know."

I laughed. "I didn't think it was your style. It doesn't seem to have a post, but I can tell that it's an earring," I said.

She plucked it from my palm. "This is a fake pierced earring. I do the same thing to mine. I cut off the post then use a magnet to hold it on. But, no, it isn't mine. I wouldn't be caught dead wearing earrings as ugly as this."

"Who does it belong to then?" I asked her. "I found it in the armoire in my room. I'm quite sure it wasn't there yesterday."

"Well, I wasn't in your room, if that's what you think!" she said, standing.

"I don't know if you were in my room or not," I said, "but I think you may have been in Skylar's room." I gestured to the bracelet Persis had on her wrist. "Isn't that Skylar's?"

Persis put her hand over the POW/MIA bracelet. "It's mine," she said. Even if the timbre of her voice had not broadcast her guilt, I knew she was lying. I had seen Skylar's bracelet and I remembered the name on it. Sgt. Michael Bartell was similar enough to my uncle Mitch's name, Mitchell Bartelli, that I had made particular note of it.

Persis shoved back her chair and gave me a glance so disdainful I would have shriveled under it if it had been a heat ray. Then she turned and stalked into the hall.

"Persis, wait," I called to her but I heard the door to her bedroom slam.

I followed her and tapped on it.

"What!?" she said from within.

"I'm coming in," I told her. She said nothing so I stepped inside and shut the door behind me. She had flung herself onto the bed and was glowering at the ceiling.

The room was in teenager-ish disorder. Clothes were hung on the back of the chair, draped across the foot of the bed and on the floor. I stepped over a t-shirt and sat down next to her. She didn't protest.

I could feel Persis' deep insecurity filling the room like a vapor. Besides that confused uncertainty, I could feel something of the deep dislike and envy she had for Jade as well as Skylar.

"I know you think the world is against you," I told her. For a moment, she looked surprised before she put the scowl back onto her face. "But it isn't. I also know that the bracelet belongs to Skylar. I saw it the day she arrived."

"So?" she said. "Maybe she gave it to me."

"If that's true," I said, "then why are you so angry?"

"Because you accused me of going into your room. Then you accused me of stealing." She sounded like a frightened little girl.

"I asked you if the earring was yours. You said it wasn't and I believe you. But the bracelet *is* Skylar's. I think you should return it."

"First you tell me that I shouldn't go into other people's rooms, then you say that I should put the bracelet back," she said as if she were making the most rational of all arguments. She looked at me in utter fourteen-year-old defiance for a moment. "Fine," she said and sat up to swing her legs off the bed. "I'll return it."

She headed for the door and I stood to follow her.

Neither of us said anything as she marched down the hall and climbed the stairs. The fact that she went unerringly to Skylar's door told me that she had been there before. She flung it open then pulled the bracelet off her wrist and gave it a healthy pitch into the room. It made a metallic clunking sound as it hit the opposite wall and fell to the floor.

"Now are you satisfied?" she asked as we headed back to the stairs.

"Yes," I said. "You didn't do that with much grace, but I have to admit, I admire your style."

I thought I saw the smallest smile hit her face for

a split second. It was so fast I don't think even she knew she had done it. From that, I believed that the budding relationship between Persis and me may not have become permanently damaged after all.

Just as we reached the foot of the stairs, Skylar came in through the front door. She was wearing her traditional jersey dress with a flowered jacket. She looked trim and neat as usual, except she was carrying a gym bag.

"Oh, did I miss dinner?" she said. "I needed a little work out before I got too tired to do it."

I felt that something about her words did not ring true. Maybe because I had seen no gyms in town or maybe it was the neat, put-together way she looked. In all fairness, she could have gone for a run, but in that case, how did she get her clothes changed? And, too, for all I knew there was a YMCA in town that I was unaware of. I felt guilty for my thoughts. I liked Skylar. I told myself not to be so suspicious of everyone.

"I left some dinner for you in the oven," I told her.

"Thanks, Cheyenne," she said. "I'll eat it later." She headed for the stairs.

"Well," I said when she was gone, "I'm going to go for a walk. Want to come with me, Persis?"

She shook her head. She wouldn't look at me.

I could hear the men clattering dishes and pans in the kitchen and I could hear nothing coming from

Jade's room so I let myself out, grateful to have some time on my own to concentrate.

One thing I knew I had to do was to try to get into each room in the house. I didn't like to snoop in people's private spaces if I didn't have to, and knew I could get into big trouble by doing it. Unfortunately, in order to eliminate my housemates from my suspicions, which I admit had grown a bit out of proportion, it was becoming a necessity. At that point, I wasn't at all sure how I was going to accomplish it. They were all out during the day at the convention center but so was I. They were home when I was. Living in such close quarters with them, it seemed ironic that I couldn't find a way to get to know them better. I was glad I had had a chance to get a look into Persis' room. Her belongings had been strewn everywhere so I doubted she even used the armoire or the chest of drawers. I had learned something more of her simply from being there. The insecurity, I had already discerned. But the feelings of envy and jealousy, even dislike to the point of hatred she felt for Jade and Skylar had been so strong they were almost palpable. For all she tried to hide, everything that was Persis seemed to be out in the open in her bedroom. To me, her life was entirely visible.

I walked through the town and noted how small it was. I spotted a variety store that looked like it had come from the 1950s. Back then it would have been known as the "Five and Dime". The place looked like it was barely holding on to the corner of downtown. In the window were faded cardboard cutouts of smiling women wearing aprons and holding utensils. A stack of dusty straw hats leaned in a precarious heap against the glass and nearby were dingy plush toys and boxes of puzzles.

Nearby, there was a large building that looked abandoned. I saw a woman carrying a gym bag come out and lock the door. A makeshift gym. I gave myself a little kick in the butt and told myself not to be so quick to jump to conclusions.

In a few moments I happened upon Black Lake. It was forbidding and dark even in the late July evening. There were no picnic tables, no swings, nothing that would invite recreation or leisure. There was, as Bliss had said, a sign warning that swimming was forbidden and that there were dangerous drop-offs close to shore. I shivered in the evening heat. I thought this cold and menacing looking lake would have made a much better place for the Green River Killer to dump his victims than in and alongside the Green River.

As I walked, I thought of the red circle with the R in the center. Was it a common graffiti motif and what did it signify? Both Barbara Robertson and Attley Silverwood had incorporated it into their work. It had captured my attention for some reason and, while I wanted to trust my instincts, I thought my imagination was working overtime and had gotten out of control. Was I beginning to see mysteries where none existed as Dak had suggested? I decided to ask Skylar—and Persis, if she was still speaking to me—about it when I got back. If anyone would know what it stood for, they would.

On impulse, I stopped at the phone booth outside the pharmacy that was close to Beachhouse. The minute I turned the corner and saw it, I knew that I was going to call Easy. I both did and didn't want to. If he was still jealous and angry at me, I didn't need the aggravation. If he wasn't, then great! I would be delighted as well as relieved to talk to him. Besides, he always seemed to bring me back down to earth.

I didn't find out if he was still angry. He didn't answer his phone. With disappointment mixed with relief, I hung up just as his answering machine clicked on.

Next, I called my own answering machine. By punching in a code, I could access my messages. There were none from Easy which was the real reason I had for retrieving them, but there was one that put me on the alert.

Brynn Jagger's husband had left me a message saying that he had remembered something that I might be interested in. I was astounded. The man had almost hung up on me and he had been unwilling to discuss his wife's accident at all. Whatever he had discovered must have made him either alarmed or uneasy. I didn't have anything to write with so I saved the message, then turned back to Beachhouse knowing I could call him from there.

The light was fading as I made my way back. I felt out of sorts and frustrated. I couldn't seem to make any headway. I needed to talk to the volunteers and the board members. And, again, I thought that a brief look-around in each of the tenants' rooms would help, although I wasn't likely to find stashes of stolen items or suitcases full of imaginative weapons. I didn't know what I was looking for and that was what bothered me so much. When the show was over, what would I tell the board about the investigation? "Sorry, people, can't tell ya. Didn't find out a thing."?

* * *

Rupert Jagger was just as disagreeable as he had been the first time I had spoken to him.

"I don't know why I left that message," he said. "Except that it just didn't look like something Brynn would do."

I waited but he said nothing further. "What kind of art did your wife do, Mr. Jagger?" I asked. I knew she had been a sculptor. I had seen the tiny house she had made at Pete Rainey's home, in Ramona's studio.

"She built doll houses," he said, sounding uncertain. "Well, not doll houses exactly. She did miniatures in clay. Little houses, little boats, buildings, things like that. I didn't keep much of it. I tore down her studio and gave most of the stuff to the kids and grandkids. There was one piece that I did keep, though. It was a model of our house."

I waited again, then asked, "What did you find, sir?"

"It was on the doghouse," he said.

"The doghouse?" I asked after another pause.

"We have—had—a dog. She made a model of our house and the doghouse was in the back, just like when she was...here. The sign over the doghouse says 'Trigger'. That was the name the kids gave the dog. Only she circled the 'R' in 'Trigger'. The last 'R'.

"Was the name painted in capital letters?" I asked him. "And in red?"

"How did you know that?" he asked, sounding angry again and suspicious.

"Did she take that piece to the last show she was in?"

"Yes... I think so. Why? Is this important? It doesn't mean that Brynn was killed, you know. It doesn't mean anything."

"Possibly not, sir, but I sincerely thank you for letting me know about it." He said nothing so I added, "I have one other question."

I got the usual response from him so I continued. "Did your wife get any hang-up phone calls, either before or after shows?"

"I don't know," he said, sounding, if possible, even more irritated.

I wanted to urge him to think, to remember, but I thought I had gotten all I could get.

I was wrong again. After another brief pause, he cleared his throat. "There was a call," he said. "But it wasn't a hang-up."

I waited. Finally, I said. "Oh?"

"Somebody called her right after the last show she did."

"What did the caller say, sir?" I prompted.

"They said, 'You are being watched.' That's all they said but it scared her so bad I was afraid she would be sick. I told her it was just kids. That's all it was. Just kids."

I would have been willing to bet my life savings that it wasn't "just kids" but I didn't say that to Rupert.

"Was it a man or a woman?"

"She said she couldn't tell," he said. "*I* would have been able to and I answered the phone every time for a while, but they never called again."

"Thank you, sir. I very much appreciate your talking to me."

He muttered something and hung up. No "good-bye", no "go to hell." Nothing. My heart was breaking for the man.

I hung up too, then called Ramona Rainey's husband, Pete.

After we had accomplished the initial small talk, I got right to my point. "I have a question and a favor to ask of you, if you don't mind," I said.

"Sure," he said, though he sounded unsure. "Anything I can do to help."

"Did Ramona receive any phone calls with either no one at the other end or threatening in any way? This would be either before or after shows that she did."

He thought for a moment. "I'm not sure..." he started to say. He paused, then continued, "You know, maybe she did. I don't remember if it was before or after shows, but she was complaining to me about someone calling her and not saying a word. We didn't think it meant anything. Did it?"

"I don't know. It may, but I have to look into it further," I told him. "I'll let you know. In the meantime, I need you to look over all of the remaining pieces that Ramona made and let me know if you find anything that has a red circle with an R in the center. It could be on the bottom of a piece, like a signature or it could be included in the design."

He was silent for a moment and I wondered if he had decided that he wasn't up to looking at all of his late wife's wares. Then he cleared his throat.

"I did find that," he said. "Only it wasn't on the bottom of a piece. It was on the top of a round lidded box Mona had made but hadn't yet fired. She had another whole kiln full of things that she was going to fire the next morning after she…she went."

My excitement notched up. "Do you still have it?"

"I like it," he said as if he hadn't heard me. "I fired it along with the rest of the stuff. I'll probably donate the other things but keep that box. Her first, middle and last names all began with R and it's the last thing I have left of her."

"It may not mean what you think, Pete," I said.

"What do you mean?"

"I don't know," I said, feeling the familiar wave of defeat. "I have a theory that could very well be off base. For now, will you take good care of the box?"

"Of course," he said. "Like I said, I like it. To me, it represents Mona."

I thanked him and hung up.

I had one more call to make. I had dialed my long-distance calling card number so many times that I had it all but memorized.

Tyler Robertson confirmed for me that Barbara had indeed gotten hang-up calls prior to her death. Just a few days before she died, he said, she had complained to him about what she thought were kids playing around with the telephone.

"Have you found out anything?" he asked. His tone was so eager it broke my heart. "Were those calls something more than kids?"

"I'm still gathering information," I told him. "Tyler, did Barbara do studio tours?"

"Yes, she did," he said, sounding wary now. He hesitated before asking, "You will tell me when you find out anything, won't you? These questions make me think that you're onto something. I'd like to know what."

"Like I said, I'm still gathering information and you've been very helpful. I will let you know if I learn anything meaningful."

I thanked him, sorry to leave him disappointed.

I didn't want to have to tell any of these men that their wives had been murdered. Nor did I want to have to destroy Pete Rainey's severe case of denial fever. I didn't think that the R on the box stood for Ramona at all. I hoped I was wrong but I was almost sure that the symbol was a sort of ideogram, like a logo, and that it was the signature of a killer.

SEVENTEEN

Saturday, July 21, 1984

When I got back downstairs, Ab and Ayubu were in the dining room deep into a game of checkers. Apparently, there were stakes involved because I saw small stacks of pennies in front of each man.

Persis was watching television in the living room and as I entered, she gave me a disgusted glance and looked toward her parents who were having another of their arguments. Persis rose periodically to turn the volume up on the TV as the voices raised. I thought Jade was still in her room and Skylar was either in hers or she had gone out again.

I crossed the living room, trying not to look at the arguing couple, then headed into the kitchen where it would be quieter and I could make a mug of tea to take to my room.

I saw Persis' Tarot cards on the table in disorder, as though she had abandoned them in the middle of her habitual shuffling. That was strange, since she usually kept them out of sight. I was beginning to think that she was deliberately pushing her parents, particularly her mother, as far as she could, for reasons only a fourteen year old would know.

I gathered up the cards and shuffled them, looking at them and again marveling at Persis' artwork. She must have had access to a standard Tarot deck to guide her in making a deck that was uniquely her own. Some of the royalty cards— the kings, queens, knights and pages—looked a bit familiar, as though she had made them look like various celebrities as well as herself and her parents. She had given her own spin to the deck, putting fantastic creatures in place of lions and dogs and horses. But she had followed the general original art well enough to make the cards recognizable.

I avoided doing Tarot readings for myself unless it was a "mini" reading of just three cards and it had been years since I had done even that. I thought, as I sat there shuffling that a mini reading might help me to get the lay of the land, to guide me toward some of the answers that I sought.

I cut the deck into three piles then picked the top card from the first one. It was The Tower which indicated something taking me unawares. Of course, I had already been blindsided by the invitation to attend the show, so there was no help there. I stuck the card back into the deck and shuffled again. At random, I chose a card from near the top of the deck. The Tower appeared again. Disgusted, I shuffled once more, wondering how, if having been warned of an occurrence that would surprise me, a bolt from the blue, so to speak, how shocked would I be after all?

Skylar pushed open the kitchen door then.

"Oh, sorry," she said. "I didn't know anyone was in here. I just came in to get something to eat. Didn't you say you'd left something for me?"

"I moved the leftover chicken to the fridge, if you'd like that," I said. "Why don't you heat some up and join me?"

She bustled around the kitchen for a few minutes while I shuffled the cards and watched her at the same time. She was slender. She had small breasts and her hips were as slim as a boy's. I wondered how she could stay that way in view of the gargantuan sandwich she was constructing.

At last, she came to the table with her sandwich and sat down.

"What are you doing?" She looked more interested, if possible, than Persis had been. "Those are Persis' cards, aren't they?" She looked around at the still closed door. "Could you do a reading for me?"

"Sure," I said, thinking that if Persis caught us, she would be outraged at us using her Tarot cards, but this was the perfect opportunity for me to get into Skylar's head a little bit. I thought it was worth the risk. Persis was already mad at me.

"Have you ever had the Tarot cards read for you?" I asked.

She shook her head, her gaze fixed on the cards before me. "I don't really believe in Tarot," she said. "I think they're..." She hesitated.

"Spooky? Phony?"

She nodded, looking a bit sheepish.

"Well, they're none of that."

"That's okay," she said with her slim hand in front of her full mouth. She swallowed, then said, "I want you to do it anyway."

"A reading might not answer your question since you don't believe in the power of the cards," I told her, half joking. "Think of a question you have that requires a yes or no answer."

She mused about that for a moment while she ate her sandwich. At last she said, "I've got it." She looked at me, her blue eyes were crinkled in mischief. "Do I tell you the question, or what?"

"You ask the cards as you shuffle them thoroughly," I told her and handed her the deck.

She shuffled, continuing to watch me.

"Talk to *them*," I said, gesturing to the cards, "and ask them your question."

"Hi, cards!" she said, laughing. I could tell she felt a little foolish. "I want to know if I will ever be famous."

"Interesting question," I said.

"I'd like to give that Marina Abramovic some competition," she said with a wink.

Ah! I thought. *The performance art thing.*

"As you shuffle, think about your question," I told her.

After she had shuffled five or six times, I instructed her to cut the cards into three stacks, then to select a card from each stack. She did and handed the three cards to me.

The first card she had drawn was The Magician.

"This card tells you that you have all the power, ability and the tools you need to create your own reality.

She nodded but said nothing.

I turned the next card, The Five of Swords reversed. "This card represents victory, but perhaps not the way you think. It could also mean gossip."

Her eyes brightened. "You mean like people talking about me?"

"Yes," I said, though I didn't see it that way, but the cards were representing her and her question. She had to find the answers within herself.

The third card was The Tower. I had a moment of feeling glad that Skylar had gotten it and not me this time. "This card brings something unexpected. It isn't necessarily a bad thing but it could be. It's a drastic change. A change in your lifestyle that may already have happened."

I looked at her to see if I could tell what she was thinking. She didn't look discouraged, in fact, she looked eager.

"So, this tower card could be a good thing?"

I nodded.

"A complete change in lifestyle. That could mean that I will become famous, couldn't it?"

"It could," I said, but I doubted it. "It means a drastic change of some sort."

"Well, a 'drastic change' could be going from an obscure nobody volunteer at art shows to a famous performance artist, couldn't it?" Her eyes gleamed.

"The cards are telling you that you have all the skills you need to accomplish your goal, people may talk about you and that a drastic change can or has come into your life. You have to decide for yourself what they mean to you."

"Whoa! I guess I do believe in Tarot after all!"

"Keep in mind that what these cards tell you is dependent upon what you make of yourself. They aren't telling your future. They are a guide."

She stood and put her plate into the sink. "I don't mind working hard to achieve my goals," she said, running water and then wiping the dish.

"Well," I said, pushing myself up from the table.

"I'm going to bed."

"Thanks again, Cheyenne," she said, turning to me. "That was great!"

I waved at her and, leaving the cards on the table for Persis to find in the morning, headed upstairs.

* * *

L ate in the night—I don't know what time it was but I thought I had been asleep for a while—I awoke to an eerie sound. At first, I wasn't sure that I had not dreamed it but then it came again. A long, deep "crooooaaak".

I got out of bed and put my feet on the cool floor then went into the hall where I found Carson and Cassandra. Carson was trying to persuade his wife to return to bed but Cassandra was shaking, either with cold or with fright. Since it wasn't that chilly in the house on that July night, I guessed it was fear.

"What if it's Persis?" Cassandra asked. "I need to go down to her." She pulled her arm from Carson's grasp and headed for the stairs just as Jade came up from below. In a moment, Ab, Ayubu and Skylar had joined us. Cassandra and Persis came up the stairs not long afterward.

We all listened to the eerie croak again. Cassandra, her face white, cowered against her daughter but I saw Persis shrug away. She was doing her best to appear unconcerned although I saw terror in her eyes too.

"What is it?" Skylar asked, her eyes huge and round.

Ab shook his head and turned to go back into his room. "Whatever it is, I hope it stops soon."

"It is *bahari*," Ayubu said, as we heard the mournful sound once more. "The raven."

"The ravens that hang around outside don't sound like that," I said.

"Ravens have different calls, like many birds. That is a raven." Ayubu nodded along with his own words. I would have to take his word for it.

Cassandra now looked even more terrified. She was crowding up against Carson and trying to draw Persis into the group but Persis was having none of it. She stood alone with her arms crossed over her chest. I saw that she was trembling too.

Skylar looked as frightened as Cassandra. "A raven is a symbol for death and disaster," she whispered.

"It's a ghost!" Jade said

"Don't be ridiculous," Carson said. "It's only a raven. There are lots of them around here. And they don't portend death and disaster either."

Skylar didn't look convinced.

"In the middle of the night?" Jade said, almost spitting out the words. "Why is a raven in the house?

In the middle of the night?"

I have to admit I was wondering the same thing. And, if a bird had gotten into the house, where was it? In the attic? I had seen from the outside that the attic windows were covered so how could a bird have entered?

Ayubu smiled at Jade. He told her that ravens often are seen in the evening and at night whereas crows are more likely to be around in the daytime, but Jade was not believing him.

I looked at Persis. Her eyes were wide with fright but she was still doing her best to appear unconcerned. It wasn't working.

Suddenly, Cassandra didn't look terrified anymore. She looked pissed. "Carson, this isn't one of your asinine jokes, is it? If it is, I swear..."

Carson threw his hands up in a gesture that seemed to ward off his wife. "I didn't do anything!" he said, now looking frightened himself, although I thought his fear was more of Cassandra than of the sound we had all heard.

"Well, raven or not, I'm going back to bed," I said.

Everyone else turned then and headed back to their own rooms. Persis looked doubtful but even she headed downstairs, keeping as far away from Jade as she could.

But I didn't go to bed. I went into my room, yes, but after a half hour of listening to the faint sounds of the others settling in their rooms, I thought I heard something else. To me, it sounded as though someone had walked across the attic. Someone trying to be stealthy.

I went to my door and cracked it open just wide enough to see into the hall. All was dark and quiet. The nightlight was out again. I could have sworn it was lit when we had gathered in the hall, but there had been light spilling from the open rooms and I could have been mistaken. I was about to shut my door again when I thought I heard or perhaps sensed movement at the end of the hall. I closed the door even more so all that remained was a slit big enough for me to peer through. In a moment, someone passed the door.

I drew back. Whoever it was, it was no one who was staying in the house. I had gotten one swift glimpse, but what I had seen had started my heart thumping. It was someone small and hairless, with an almost skeleton-like appearance. I took a deep breath and peeked out again just in time to see a flash of—not white because it was so dark in the hall—but a lighter shade of black. It seemed to be a garment of some sort but what or who I had seen, I couldn't begin to guess.

It took me seconds to grab my flashlight and I was out the door. Whatever had been there had disappeared. No one was lingering in the hall. I had heard no doors open nor close, I had heard nothing at all. I crept down the hall to where I had seen—or thought I had—the figure. As I passed each door, I hesitated close to it listening for any sound from within the room. Nothing moved. I went downstairs, my bare feet making no noise on the steps. The house was silent and seemed to be waiting for me to complete my search. I didn't switch on my flashlight, but peered into the darkness and saw nothing but the hulking black shapes of the furniture lit only by the ambient window light.

At last, I returned to the second floor and headed toward the attic stairs at the other end of the hall.

The house was old and made plenty of creaks and groans as it cooled off during the night. Even so, I was careful to climb the stairs along the edges so I wouldn't alert anyone as to what I was doing. I would feel foolish if someone caught me. Not that there was anything wrong with checking out the attic, it was just that I wasn't doing it out of fear, I was doing it out of habitual snoopiness. At least, that's what I told myself.

I opened the door onto a dark, musty attic. I shone the light around and saw no evidence at all of a bird, though I did see the leavings of mice and lots and lots of dust.

There was the usual detritus; the sort of stuff that people consider too good to get rid of but don't want to keep either. Whatever furnishings the owners of the house had wanted to keep away from the summer renters stood around me like soldiers guarding secrets. There were plenty of trunks and boxes pushed here and there in no particular order. I played the light around and again saw no evidence of a bird. I shone the light on each of the walls. The windows on the third floor had been covered with boards on the inside. My flashlight showed no gaps between wood and frame. No way for a bird to enter.

At the door, ready to return to my room, I noticed a dusty hand print on the edge of the door frame. I knew it wasn't mine. I was always careful to touch as little as possible when I was snooping. I gave the room another sweep with the flashlight and saw that the dust around one of the trunks had been disturbed too. It looked as though it had been moved recently and the dust on top had been disarranged as well. By whom or by what, I didn't know. I knew that any of us could have come up stairs. The attic wasn't locked. But, why, I wondered, would someone have gone to the trouble to create a sound for the sole purpose of scaring us? To give us a little excitement? Who, besides Carson would want to do that? He had insisted it wasn't his doing. Persis then? But she had looked terrified.

Of course, foremost in my mind was the identity of the figure I had seen in the hall. I had the impression of a boney, pale creature, without hair and rail thin. Without warning, I was reminded of that very old film, *Nosferatu*. I had seen it as a child and it had scared the senses out of me and ruined my sleep for a long, long time. Though what I had seen was indeed the stuff of horror movies and nightmares, I knew it had been no dream.

EIGHTEEN

Sunday, July 22, 1984

I had just sold a sun catcher to a lady who seemed more than thrilled with it before I had a chance to sit down for the first time the next morning.

I could understand how small items could go missing from a booth, especially if it was crammed with shoppers and the artist was distracted with a couple of buyers at the same time. The booths were ten feet square and there was comfortable room for maybe three people. At any given time that morning, I wouldn't have been surprised to find that there were seven or eight people trying to look at our wares. The other artists were having the same success.

I glanced around, spotting Ab's business cards in the stained glass card holder he had made. I knew there were other, similar holders in all the booths. It would be easy for a killer who was eager to torment an artist to pick up business cards. Then, after having stolen a piece from the artists booth, he could call them and hang up, again and again.

It would, at the very least, annoy, at most, terrify the recipient. Next, a car chase on a deserted coastal road, a little nudge to send the car ahead off the cliff and it would be ruled an accident. A jogger on a deserted early morning street in Seattle, hit by a speeding car then left to die was an obvious hit and run. The auto accidents were easier for me to accept as deliberate murder, but what about Ramona Rainey's death by faulty space heater? Was her death a terrible coincidence? Maybe. Or had the killer found a way to accomplish that one too? I could see it happening. I believed I knew the *what*. I didn't know the *how*, the *why* nor the *who*.

The question of *who* was my greatest and most urgent puzzle and, after the strange events of the previous night, I was coming to the reluctant conclusion that the perpetrator may well be someone who lived in Beachhouse. Each one of them was a veteran artist who had done multiple shows. Even Persis, a relative newbie in the arts, had been to many shows and had gotten to know the artists. I felt I could eliminate Ab and me, but I had learned in my long years as an investigator, that I couldn't discount anyone.

I stayed in the booth, helping Ab even though he knew that I was eager to continue with my interrogations. I needed to question the remainder of the artists and I still had to find an opportunity to investigate the rooms of the inhabitants of Beachhouse.

"I can handle this," he said at one point, indicating that I should go ahead and roam the venue again and ask the questions I needed answers to.

"Everyone else is just as busy as we are," I told him. "They won't have time to talk anyway."

I saw Kirk hurrying by on his way to some crisis or another. Later, I saw Lagan helping an artist who had sold a large painting. Another time, he brought a Styrofoam box of lunch to Gregor, the jeweler across the aisle.

*　*　*

By early afternoon, the crowds had thinned a bit and Ab left in order to deliver a large window that we had sold that morning. It left a sizeable blank spot in our display so I was trying to fill it up with smaller pieces and man the booth until he returned.

I hadn't had anything to eat since breakfast and had asked Ab to notify the desk that I would need a volunteer when one was available so I could get a lunch break.

About one-thirty, Skylar turned up in front of my booth. I had been hoping to score Jim since I had had so little chance to talk to him but he didn't seem to be anywhere around.

"Busy morning?" she asked.

"Very," I said, at last feeling like I could catch my breath. "How about you?"

"Not me! I just started my shift. And we don't have the pressure you artists have," she said. "All I have to do is sit here and look at all the gorgeous stuff." She scanned the booth. "Wow! These things are beautiful. I would love to know how to do this."

"We have classes at our shop in Seattle. If you're ever around there, you should come in and check us out. I just realized I have no idea where you live, Skylar," I said.

"Oh, I'm a wanderer," she said breezily. "I was born in Tacoma and I've lived in Seattle, the Tri-Cities, Portland when I was in college. All over the place. But, hey," she continued without pause, "maybe I'll do that sometime. I'm not very artistic, but this looks like something even I could do."

While I was still wondering what she had meant by that, she asked, "What do you want me to do if a customer wants to buy something?"

I told her how to handle a sale then left for a hurried trip to one of the food trucks in front of the building.

I didn't make it all the way to the front before I was waylaid by one of the ceramic artists whose name I had forgotten. I was trying to think of it when she told me that she thought someone had made off with one of her small dishes. I went to her booth with her. She seemed to think that it had just occurred. I was about to ask her if she had left one of the volunteers in charge at any point when she laughed. Her face had gone as pink as the small ceramic bowl she held up for me to see.

"Here it is," she said. "Someone must have moved it. I'm so sorry. After all the talk going around about thefts and killings, I guess I'm a bit paranoid."

"Killings?" I said. "What did you hear about that?" *So,* I thought, *the board's hopes of keeping the deaths a secret were dashed.*

She shrugged. "Isn't that part of what you're investigating?"

"I was hired to find out about the thefts," I said. That was true enough. "Do you remember who it was that mentioned deaths?"

"I think it was one of the volunteers," she said. "I don't know their names. A man, anyway."

"Jim? Jake? Lagan?" I pressed. I saw a group of five or six people headed our way.

"One of the Js. Not Lagan. I know which one he is. He's a cutie pie if you ask me." She turned to her customers and I went on my way, inexplicably feeling like I had taken care of her original problem.

When I returned to the booth, Ab was just back and had dismissed Skylar who had gone on to her next job. I scanned the pieces we had hanging and didn't see anything amiss.

I saw Ab watching me. "Did you think she was

going to steal something?" he asked me, just before biting into the sandwich I had brought him.

"Not exactly," I said. "I feel like I don't trust anyone right now. I feel a bit guilty for suspecting her but I think we are not the only ones who are getting a little paranoid." I told him about the dish which had not been missing after all.

I did have a chance to talk to more of the artists and even some of the volunteers, but, again, I couldn't manage to reconnect with Jim.

Through the afternoon, I could not stop my mind from stirring the pot where my suspicions were cooking. I returned again and again to the phone calls, the accidents, the stolen items.

* * *

It was later in the afternoon when we heard a commotion coming from an aisle toward the front. Customers walking by were glancing in the direction of the noise and whispering among themselves. In a moment, Kirk Nielsson had hurried over and asked me to accompany him.

"It's a theft," he said, pushing through the crowds and pulling me behind him. I followed him to Jade's booth.

"Someone stole it!" She was insisting. "It was a shawl. Very expensive!" Her voice carried over several aisles and I knew that trying to shush her would be impossible. I had only lived with the woman for a couple of days, but already I knew that much.

"Very, very expensive!" she said again. She was standing in the middle of the aisle and peering at each patron who walked by. "Her!" she suddenly shrieked. "She was in my booth when that shawl went missing. It was her!"

The poor woman looked at her friend and spread her hands out to me in that classic "I'm innocent!" gesture.

"I demand you arrest her!" Jade was saying.

"Jade," I said. "Will you please go back to your booth and I will take care of this." I was relieved when Kirk pulled Jade away so that I could speak to the woman in relative quiet.

"I didn't steal anything from her," she said. She looked like she was about to cry. "Her things are very lovely but they're way too expensive for me. But I didn't take anything."

"No," her friend said. "She wouldn't do that."

"She didn't take anything. I saw her in the booth," another woman said. "I was there too."

"You can look in my bag if you want," the accused woman said, crying now. She held open a cloth bag with nothing more than a package of notecards and a small polished wood cutting board in it.

I glanced at them and put my hand on her arm.

"It's okay," I said. "I know you didn't take anything." Even without my lie detecting ability, I could tell that she wasn't the culprit but my brief touch had told me that she had not even given stealing a thought.

"I'm so sorry for the trouble," I told her. "Kirk," I called to him and he seemed grateful to be pulled away from Jade who was continuing her loud commentary.

"Do you think we could refund this lady's ticket fee or something?"

He nodded and steered her toward the front of the venue where I knew the artists' lounge was.

"That shawl was the most expensive item I had!" Jade was insisting when I returned to her booth. I doubted that it cost more than the jackets or one of the long coats, but I held my tongue. I knew not to fan the flames of her dramatics. "I made it out of some very important blue wool that I spun myself. I can never replace it! I am losing hundreds of dollars because someone stole it! This is terrible! I am not—"

I could see that customers were giving her booth a wide berth, but I turned back to her after her abrupt halt. She glanced at me then quickly pushed something under a pile of items she had pulled from their hangers.

I went to her and pushed aside the pile then brought a brilliant blue shawl to the surface.

"Is this the shawl?" I asked, keeping my gaze on her.

She shook her head, but said nothing.

"This *is* the shawl, isn't it?" I pressed. I knew that Jade had never unpacked it.

"While I was busy trying to find it, the thief brought it back," she said.

I spotted Kirk and the accused customer at the end of the aisle. She had stopped crying and was smiling. I wondered what Kirk had told her.

"Are you going to apologize to the customer?"

Jade looked outraged. She glanced at the woman and Kirk. "No! She stole it. Why should I apologize to her when she brought it back? She should apologize to me!"

I turned my back on her and left her talking to no one.

❊ ❊ ❊

"So, I notice that the commotion settled down," Ab said when I returned. "Whose ass did you have to kick?"

"I would have been glad to kick Jade's but that would have been unproductive as well as unprofessional," I said.

"Things are never dull at the art show," he said, shaking his head.

It was at that moment that a gong sounded throughout the venue and over the loudspeaker I could hear Dak announce that the contest winners had been determined.

Back at the shop I had told Ab that he was going to win the contest in his category. Once in a while —certainly not always—I "know" things. It isn't from physical contact or watching body language or listening to the faint voices I hear in buildings. It's just plain, old fashioned intuition. I "knew" that Ab was going to win the prize in the glass category.

We had hung the immense window with the wisteria and peacock that was Ab's entry in the back of the booth. It took up most of the back wall. Ab had arranged the lights so that the purples, golds, blues and greens showed to perfection. It was magnificent and customers and artists alike stopped by often just to look at it.

When the winners began to be announced, I looked at Ab. He didn't appear to be listening, but I knew he was. Instead, he was making a show of chatting with Oskar next door.

When his name was announced, he was far more surprised than I was. His eyes went round and his face flushed. I was surprised that he was so astonished. Did he think that gorgeous window would fail to get notice?

Oskar grabbed Ab's hand and gave it a hearty pump. I went over to the two men and gave Ab a hug and said, "I told you so!".

He put his hands on my shoulders and his eyes narrowed in mock suspicion. "How did you know?" he asked. "What did you do, bribe the judges?"

I laughed and said, "Oh, I don't know. Call me psychic."

Oskar laughed and, shaking his head, went back to his own booth.

In a moment Ab was surrounded again when several of the nearby artists came by to congratulate him as well.

I was more than pleased to hear Persis' name announced as the winner of the Outstanding Emerging Artist Prize. When I had asked Ab if they had made up the category just for her, since she was so young, he said that PCAC had been awarding the Emerging Artist Prize for several years.

I went over to Persis' part of the LaChance booth and saw a small group of people pressed against her table. Customers and artists both had gathered there to congratulate her and be among those owning a piece of the contest winner's art. She glanced up and saw me and I gave her a smile and a victory sign. I knew that she had not been hopeful about winning and had entered the contest only after her mother had badgered her into it.

She gave me a small grin in return, but I could see that her eyes were sparkling with pleasure and her face had flushed. I was glad to see it and grateful for the smile. I had gotten the impression that she had been even more stand-offish to me since I had asked her about the earring I had found and made her return the bracelet. I left her with her public and headed over to Bliss' booth.

There was a crowd there as well. Attley Silverwood had won the Multi-Media category and Bliss had all she could do. I waited for a few minutes until the buzz had subsided then reached out to Bliss.

"I'm so glad you decided to do the show for Attley," I told her.

"I don't feel anything but sad right now," she said.

"You'll be glad you did it, nevertheless," I told her and gave her a hug. I could feel her sadness and her deep grief over the loss of her partner. I could also feel a fresh healthiness within her that let me know that she would, one day, heal.

When I passed the LaChance booth on the way back, Cassandra called out to me. "Cheyenne!" she said. "What do you think of my little girl getting an award?"

"I think it was well deserved," I said.

Persis looked at me then looked down again, arranging and rearranging a stack of cards on her table.

"You are very talented, you know," I said, looking through a small pile of drawings.

"Thanks," she mumbled. "But I was the only emerging artist."

"No, you weren't! Patricia Shipley has never done a show before at all and Leland Canfield hasn't either. This contest wasn't for being the youngest. It was for being the best."

She looked up at me again as if to discern if I was telling the truth or not. I had been right. She had been avoiding me. I smiled at her and selected two of her drawings.

"I'd like to buy these, please," I said.

She looked so startled I was afraid that she would forget to collect the money.

"Why do you look so surprised, Persis? I admire your work very much! You know that."

She shrugged and slipped the two drawings into a paper bag.

Just as I was about to turn and go back to Ab, Persis said, "I didn't go in your room, you know? That earring isn't mine."

"I know that," I told her. "I believed you."

"Did you ask anyone else if it was theirs or just me?" She had pushed her jaw out a bit and I knew that she was still angry.

"As a matter of fact, I did," I said. "I asked Skylar but she has pierced ears. I know your mom wears those hoops all the time. Jade doesn't wear earrings at all that I can see and neither do any of the men except Ayubu and his are for pierced ears too. It could have been left there by one of the former tenants."

That seemed to satisfy her. I was pretty sure, though, that it had not been left there by accident. I was certain I would have seen it if it had been there when I first hung my clothes in the armoire. Somebody, perhaps not Persis, but someone else staying at the house, had snooped in my room.

❋ ❋ ❋

That night, we arrived back at Beachhouse in a celebratory mood. Ab was almost giddy from his contest win and I thought Persis and her family would be too.

It was Jade's turn to cook dinner and I couldn't decide if that was a good thing or not.

I glanced at my watch and saw that I had just about enough time to give Easy a quick call. I didn't want to make it one of those long, uncomfortable, awkward chats but I knew that there was every chance in the world for that unless he had come to his senses.

I had known Easy for a long time. We had been friends—the best of friends—until his unreasonable jealousy over Ab which, in my mind, had come out of nowhere. Never had he acted that way before. He was a big, easy going, affable, downright friendly guy with whom anyone, though apparently not me, could get along.

Again, he didn't answer. I considered leaving him a message this time, and telling him about the four deaths and what I had learned about them. It would have been good to hear his take about the circle with the R in it. I wanted to remind him of why I was at the show. But I hung up before his answering machine clicked on.

Not two seconds after I had ended the call, I heard Jade shriek and her shrill voice say, "Don't you touch me!"

I turned and saw Jade sitting on the floor near the top step and Ayubu was nearby.

"You pushed me!" Jade shrieked, her voice ragged. She turned and saw me. "He tried to push me down the stairs!"

"I...I..." was all that Ayubu could manage in the face of Jade's accusations. "I did not try to hurt you," he said finally. "I tried to save you."

Jade, by then, had burst into loud sobs. Carson and Cassandra came up from downstairs, Ab with them. Skylar emerged from her room and rushed to the fray as well. I didn't see Persis.

"Jade," Cassandra said, crouching near the fallen woman. "Are you all right? What happened here?"

"This man tried to kill me!" Jade wailed and pointed at Ayubu. "He waited until I was going down the stairs to cook the dinner and then he pushed me hard!"

Ayubu stood with his hands to his side, shaking his head. "No. That was not my purpose," he said. "I saw that you were about to fall and rushed to keep you safe."

"I was not about to fall!" she screamed. "I am not a fragile old woman who cannot keep her feet under her!"

Ab helped Jade to stand and talked to her in a low voice. Gradually hers lowered to a loud rant, but at least she was no longer screaming.

"What *did* happen, Ayubu?" I asked him when Ab was talking to Jade.

"I did not try to hurt her," he said. "I saw that she was about to step on the wire and pushed her to safety. If I had not pushed her, she would have fallen all the way to the bottom."

I looked toward the stairway. "Wire? What wire do you mean?"

He walked toward the top of the stairs and peered down the staircase. "It is no longer there. It was one of those..." he tried to sketch a shape in the air. "One of those things to use holding a picture."

"Do you mean that wire was stretched across the stairs?" I asked, hearing the doubt in my own voice.

"No, no! It is a wire holder. I believe that many artists use them to put pictures on. Like an easel."

I remembered seeing those on Persis' table at the show. She used them to hold her small drawings so they would be more visible. Many of the artists used them.

"There was one of them on the stairs," Ayubu continued. "In the middle of the step, right where Jade would have walked. She would have fallen. I am very sorry if she is hurt. I am very sorry that she was frightened but I did not want her to fall down the stairs and suffer broken bones or worse."

"There was no wire easel on the stairs," Jade said, her voice edging up to loud once more. "I am not blind. I can see as well as anyone! He pushed me and tried to make me fall!"

"No, no, I did not," Ayubu said with more force than was normal for him.

"All right," Ab said. "No harm was done. Jade, Ayubu did not hurt you. Ayubu, Jade is not hurt."

Jade, muttering and not mollified, went downstairs exaggerating a limp, first in one foot and then the other.

I went back to my room so I could add a few notes to my casebook. It was a few minutes before it occurred to me to wonder why Jade had been upstairs. Her room was downstairs, next to Persis'.

NINETEEN

Sunday, July 22, 1984

By the time I made it downstairs, I saw that Jade was in the kitchen making a big to-do of chopping vegetables and complaining that the right spices were not available. She also didn't like the brands of other ingredients which had been bought. She kept up a muttered running complaint as she fussed about with the "unsatisfactory" utensils.

My good mood had vaporized with the doomed phone call to Easy and was sliding into self-pity. The proximity of Jade didn't help. I asked her if there was anything I could do, but she told me that I didn't know enough about cooking to be of any use.

Fine, I thought, and headed for the living room.

Ayubu was talking in a low voice to Ab who was nodding. I heard Ab say, "No, I believe you."

Cassandra looked toward the kitchen and said, "I hope Jade doesn't try to poison us all now that her life has been threatened."

Persis snorted.

Ayubu looked at Cassandra and grimaced. "I didn't..."

"We know you didn't do anything, Ayubu," I said, but I was beginning to wonder about every one of them.

Had there been a wire easel on the stairs as Ayubu had claimed? If so, who had put it there? And why? Was it put there on purpose to make someone fall down the stairs? And where did it go during the commotion? I knew that Persis used metal stands just like that to hold her drawings upright. I didn't remember seeing any in Ayubu's booth. Ab and I did not use the easels. I didn't think Carson and Cassandra had any use for them and Skylar didn't either. The signs all pointed to Persis. I knew Persis didn't like Jade, was jealous of her but I couldn't see her trying to harm her. Of course, the question remained that, if there had not been an easel on the stairs, and Ayubu had pushed Jade, why would he do that? Granted, none of us cared for Jade's attitude, but none of us wanted to kill her. Did we? I was still puzzling over it when Jade came into the living room and called us into the dining room for dinner.

I had to admit that, once Jade had begun to cook, the scents that wafted into the living room had been tantalizing and the dinner itself turned out to be impressive.

Somehow, even without the proper cookware or

ingredients and with an (according to her) inferior stove, Jade had made a delicious meal. The dishes seemed to be a fusion of Chinese and American foods and she had made enough for twice the number of people at the table.

Jade seemed to be able to eat her own cooking because she devoured at least enough for two. The rest of us chowed down as well and I was surprised at how little of it was left. I had heard of people who eat one substantial meal during the day, but it seemed that Jade made do with one humongous meal for several days. It didn't seem like a healthy habit to me, but what did I know?

After we had finished, Cassandra and I left Jade basking in her praise and carried the dishes into the kitchen. I almost ran into Cassandra's back as she stopped in the doorway.

It looked like every dish, every pot, pan, fork, knife and spoon had been used in the making of the dinner. It was hard to believe that anything remained in the cabinets or drawers. Not only were all of the dishes dirty, but empty containers, cutting boards and mixing bowls stood about on the counters, unrinsed, unwashed and undiscarded. It looked like every cabinet door and every drawer had been left hanging open as well.

"Good heavens!" Cassandra said as she took in the mess, though there was nothing positive and nothing remotely resembling heaven about any of it.

"Damn!" I said. There wasn't even anywhere to set down the dishes we had carried in from the dining room. The sink was full of pans covered with congealing sauce, drying rice and vegetable parings.

With one hand, the other balancing the stack of plates I carried, I pulled the garbage bin from under the sink and swept an empty rice bag and a dripping Styrofoam pan that had held chicken into it so we could set down some of the dishes we carried.

Cassandra went back into the dining room to retrieve the rest of the dishes and I could hear her telling Jade that she needed to help clean up the kitchen. I couldn't hear what Jade's response was, but she did not accompany Cassandra on her return. Skylar, however, did.

"Jade was 'forced to cook the dinner in the inconvenient kitchen' so she will not be helping," Skylar said. "Should we go back out there and drag her in?"

"I would rather do it all by myself than have to work with her," I said, and Cassandra nodded.

Even with the three of us working, it took us almost an hour to set the kitchen in order again. I wondered if there was enough food left in the house for breakfast the next morning, but by that point I didn't care. Ab and I could go out for breakfast if it came to that and let the others fend for themselves.

With my hands dry, prune-y, and smelling faintly of onion, I wandered into the living room.

I had planned to go upstairs and add to my notes but the conversation piqued my interest. I sat down while Skylar sank to the floor next to Carson's chair and Cassandra took a seat near Persis.

"The Ouija board is a Chinese invention," I heard Jade say.

"I do not think so," Ayubu said in a voice that perhaps he had not meant anyone to hear.

Jade glared at him. "It is." She said it in the tone she used when she meant that the end of the discussion had arrived. I had heard that tone way more than I had ever wanted to.

"I understand the name of it is the French and the German words for 'yes'," Ab said, no doubt hoping to divert Jade.

"I heard that wasn't true," Cassandra said. "Although, frankly, I don't know anything about it." She laughed.

"I heard that the inventor asked a ghost to name it and 'Ouija' was what was spelled out," Persis said, her voice tentative. I was surprised. She didn't usually join into the group conversation.

"You don't know anything about it, of course," Jade said, "because none of you are Chinese."

"Let's try it and ask it how it got its name," Carson said. He had that "I'd like to stir up a bit of trouble" gleam in his eyes again.

"No!" Jade said. She looked alarmed. "It's too

dangerous! Absolutely not! You will be inviting evil into this house with us." She gave a glance toward Ayubu and I heard her mutter, "There is enough here already."

"I think we should," Persis said. I could see a mischievous sparkle in her eyes too. It told me she was persisting because she knew as well as I did that we didn't have a Ouija board to play with, even if we had wanted to.

Jade shook her head and Cassandra frowned at Persis.

"Cheyenne can read Tarot cards," Persis said.

"That is dangerous too!" Jade said and stood. "I do not want to sit here and watch evil come into the house to inhabit the souls here. Next, I suppose you will be wanting to tell ghost stories."

"Yes, let's!" Persis said.

Skylar seconded her with joyful enthusiasm.

"There is the very old story of the demon called Zozo, an African spirit who is very evil," Ayubu said.

I glanced at him trying to determine if he was being serious or baiting Jade. He looked as mischievous as Carson.

Jade, however made a hasty retreat to her room, leaving the rest of us more relieved than sorry.

"Well," Carson said, "Tomorrow is the last day of the show. I have to admit, I'm glad. I look forward to it but I'm always happy to have it over."

"Jade said she's going to break down right after the show and leave," Ab said. "How about you, Ayubu?"

Ayubu nodded. "I will do the same."

"Yes, I think we will too," Cassandra said. "I need to get back and start work on that India series. There's an art gallery in Bellevue that has asked me to display some of my pieces. I'm going to put together a collection of the indigenous animals of India."

"I think we should stay here tomorrow night, Cass," Carson said. "I don't want to drive all that way back at night."

"Oh, for gosh sakes, Carson," Cassandra said, giving him a disdainful look.

"I agree," Ab said. "We'll be going the next morning. After the show, I'll be too wiped out to drive back. We have the house until the day after tomorrow and I'm going to use it."

Ab hadn't mentioned his plan to me, but I was glad to hear it. I believe he was thinking, as I was, of the harrowing encounter we had had on our trip to the coast. Driving in the daytime was hazardous enough without navigating those winding roads in the dark.

I felt that I had done next to nothing toward finding out about the thefts and the deaths, though.

On one hand, I wanted to leave. Wanted to get back home, iron things out with Easy, if possible, and go back to my regular life. On the other, I wanted to hang around until I had figured out who the thief was how he or she was connected to the killings. There were still too many questions and too few answers. Something didn't seem right and I didn't feel much closer to finding out what it was than I had in Seattle.

Carson and Cassandra continued to spar despite the attempts to steer them off the course.

At last, I went into the kitchen to make myself a last cup of tea before going up to bed.

I had just put the kettle on when Persis pushed through the door. She gave a quick glance at the living room where her parents' voices could be heard getting louder by the second.

"Escaping the fireworks?" I asked her.

She nodded. She pulled her Tarot cards from her back pocket and sat down at the table to shuffle them. I had noticed that she used her cards as a kind of security blanket. When she was uncomfortable or uneasy, she often took them out and shuffled through them, turning up a card here and there.

"Would you like me to do another reading for you?" I asked her.

Persis looked up at me with such hope on her face that it was heartbreaking. I wondered how much positive attention the girl ever got.

"Do you have a particular question you would like answered?"

She looked embarrassed and said, "No, that's okay."

"Because your mother doesn't want you to use the cards?" I asked. I shouldn't have offered, I realized. If that wasn't encouraging her, I didn't know what was.

"No!" she said with an uncomfortable laugh. "I have a question, I just...It's kind of private."

I nodded. "Okay, then. Let's just do a general reading and see what comes up." I nodded at the cards. "Shuffle them well while you're thinking of your question. Then cut them into three stacks and put them back together again."

She did as she was told and when I took the cards, I began to lay out a Celtic Cross.

"This card represents you," I told her as I set down the first one. It was The Fool. Apt, I thought. It was a card that was all about new beginnings.

I caught her frown.

"It does not mean that you are a fool," I told her. "This means that you are still at the beginning of your life, with everything yet ahead of you. What you do with your life is up to you. It's a fresh start. The beginning of a wonderful adventure."

"This card represents someone either supporting or opposing your energies," I said as I turned over the next card and set it down beneath and slightly overlapping the first.

"That's probably my mom," she said, "with that sword and everything." I had to agree. It was the Queen of Swords.

"She is a woman of strong character," I said. "She knows how to deal with difficult situations."

Persis laughed and rolled her gaze to the ceiling.

I set down the rest of the cards explaining what each one represented to her. Of course, I didn't know what her question was but I could make a very good guess from which cards came up.

"All taken together, I will say that someone new has entered your life..."

"Is it a boy?" she asked, before her natural reticence could kick in.

"Could be," I told her. "It means that you have met someone who is important to the path your life will take. It could be a woman or it could be a man." I, in fact, didn't think that it represented someone male.

"It could be you, then," she said with a shy little smile.

"It could be," I said, but, again, I didn't think that. I thought it might be a teacher perhaps and told her so. I tapped on the Page of Wands which lay in the reversed position. "This card could represent caution. I would advise not making any hasty decisions." Silently, I thought that it did represent some kind of danger to Persis. Major or minor, I had no idea. "And this card," I continued, "The Hierophant, tells me that you should use conventional wisdom."

"You sound like my mother," she said. She seemed to think for a moment. "What do you mean, 'use conventional wisdom?'"

"I mean that in decision making, you should do what you know to be the correct thing. Nothing rash, nothing…rebellious."

She laughed. "Who me?"

I laughed too. It was good to feel that I had made a positive connection with her. "Not knowing what your question is restricts what I can tell you about the cards' meaning. You have several Cups here," I said, indicating the spread. "They represent emotions." I pointed to the Knight of Cups. "This one tells you to look at your deepest feelings. It could also indicate the beginning of a romance. Does any of this answer your question?"

She nodded.

Just then Skylar came in.

"Hi, Skylar," I said. "I've just done a Tarot reading for Persis. Would you like one too?"

"Oh, no thanks!" she said. "What did Persis' reading tell you?" Skylar asked. "Or is it a secret?"

She whispered that last part and made the word 'secret' sound eerie and mysterious.

"What do you think, Persis? Is it a secret?"

"The cards said that someone new was coming into my life," Persis said. I thought she sounded pleased. I was pleased myself that she seemed to be coming out of her shell a bit.

"What do you say?" I asked. "Would you like a reading too? I could do a mini reading for you."

Skylar shook her head. "Not tonight," she said, as though there would be hundreds of nights that might be better. She went to a cabinet, got a box of cookies and returned to the table where she sat.

"Could I see them?" she asked and smiled at Persis. With obvious reluctance, Persis handed over the cards.

Skylar looked at a few of them, making comments praising Persis' work and began to shuffle through them as if looking for something. She stopped now and again to look at the art and she seemed to be fascinated by it.

"Why don't you think of a question you have and go ahead and shuffle them," I said. I glanced at Persis and raised my eyebrows. She shrugged but didn't say anything. I took that as permission to let Skylar use the cards. I got up to take the kettle off and pour my tea. "You ladies want to join me in a cup of tea to go with those cookies?"

They both nodded. Skylar's attention was on the cards and Persis' was on Skylar. I wondered what she was thinking.

Skylar continued to shuffle while Persis sat mute. I got the impression she wasn't happy to have Skylar handling her cards.

I brought three mugs of tea to the table and sat.

"Have you found out anything about the big 'mystery'?" Skylar asked, putting finger quotes around the word mystery. She turned over one of Persis' cards. It was the High Priestess. She put it back in the deck and continued shuffling them.

"Not much," I admitted. I thought for a moment. "I'm noticing a symbol that keeps recurring. It's something I had never seen before. A red circle with an R in the middle. Do either of you know what it stands for?"

Persis stared at me.

Skylar, still shuffling the cards, was looking down at them and I couldn't see her expression.

"I've seen it a few times," I continued. "Some people are using it in their artwork. I had never heard of it before."

Persis glanced at Skylar and I thought she was going to say something, but then she shrugged. "It's probably a, you know, a young person thing."

I wondered if Persis saw me as old. My thirty-nine years suddenly seemed to have more weight than usual.

"It's the sign of the raven," Skylar said, her voice not much more than a whisper. She kept her gaze down at the cards. "I've heard of it."

"I think… I think it's like a club or something," Persis said, obviously uncertain, glancing at Skylar once more. "I've heard of it too." I wondered if she had or if she didn't like to be shown up by Skylar.

"Ravens are symbols of evil." Skylar looked up at last. Her eyes were bright. I thought it was fear but there seemed to be something else. "I told you before. Ravens are a symbol of death and disaster. That sign…" she hesitated. "That's the sign of the raven."

"So, is it a gang sign or what? I've seen it in graffiti."

Skylar took a cue from Persis and shrugged. "I guess," she said. She gathered the cards into a neat pile. "I think it's time for me to get to bed."

When she handed them back to me, our hands brushed together. I was surprised to discover through just that momentary contact, that Skylar was a hodge podge of emotions. She was scornful of almost everyone in the house. And yet they fascinated her. I felt a large, dark cloud of distrust in her as well, though for who or what I couldn't tell. It didn't seem to be for me in particular, rather for everything. It was huge and dark, like a storm cloud before a tornado. Opposing forces seemed to swirl through her. There was a mishmash of fear and bravado, shame and pride, weakness and invincibility, ambition and an almost disabling defeat all overlaid with a pall of envy so bleak that I had to stop myself from taking a step back from her. I felt so much that I knew I would have to be alone in order to dissect it further.

In a moment, Skylar had pushed out the kitchen door and, in another, we could hear her footsteps on the stairs.

Cassandra opened the door a little, glanced at us then pushed it open wider.

"Persis, I think it's time for you to get to bed," she said.

"Okay," Persis answered but made no move to go toward her room.

"Would you mind if I borrowed these for a few minutes?" I asked her, gesturing to the cards. "I promise I'll bring them back before I go to bed."

"Sure," she said. She gave her mother a quick glance. "I can get them from you in the morning," she said quietly. I gathered that Persis was in no mood for an anti-Tarot lecture from her mother that night.

When they had gone, I sat on at the table.

I felt a bit guilty with what I was about to do. Skylar had been the last person besides me to touch the cards and to shuffle them. If I put down a reading, I might be able to get something of what had been in her heart and mind as she handled the cards. This kind of snooping was similar to going into someone's home and looking through it. That was something I had done many times and I never got used to it. It's a gross invasion of privacy, but I was an investigator and snooping was one of the tools I used. Reading Tarot was a little different. I had gotten some interesting insights into Skylar when I had touched her but I was still curious about her, about the source of the overwhelming emotions I had felt in her. I, of course, did not know everything that was in her mind but I felt that I would be able to get at least some idea of who she was from doing a reading. And maybe I would be able to sift through the baffling mixed impressions I had received from her touch. I stifled my guilt and laid out the cards.

As I turned over each one, the shape of Skylar began to emerge. I was intrigued when The High Priestess came up reversed as well as the Seven of Swords. Both conveyed to me that there was more to Skylar than met the eye. Of course, that is true of many people, myself included. There are facets of ourselves that we always keep hidden. Some of us change our names or even our identities. In my last big case, I had come across a man who had invented an entirely new persona for himself. Skylar, I was beginning to think, may have done the same or at least something similar. She didn't seem to be who she said she was. I also saw danger ahead for her. Several cards came up which were signals of caution. There was loss, grief and sorrow as well and the overall negativity of the reading troubled me.

I sat at the table sipping my now cooled tea and thinking. I wondered if Skylar was in actual danger. She was an artist, of sorts. She had said that she wanted to be a performance artist and, in my mind, that qualified her. Could the killer come after her next?

In doing the reading, I had only succeeded in putting yet more questions into my mind.

I gathered the mugs and washed them in the sink. Then, still deep in thought, I sat down at the table again and gazed without seeing at Persis' cards.

What, I wondered, had the incident with Ayubu and Jade been about? Had Ayubu, or someone else put a wire easel on the stairs in order to trip up Jade? There hadn't been one in evidence. Had Ayubu made up the story to cover that he himself had tried to hurt or even kill Jade? Jade herself seemed to me the most unreliable witness I had ever come across and her take on things was not to be trusted.

That all led to the question, was the killer here in Beachhouse? The idea gave me a chill. I knew that each of the others had done shows over the years and had even known each other by sight if not by name. They had attended the same shows. Even Persis, as a little girl, had gone to the shows with her parents and had gotten to know the other artists. They all, it seemed, had ample opportunity if not motive and some may even have thought they had that.

I sat long at the table, trying to organize my thoughts and prepare my mind for the possibility that I might be living with a killer.

TWENTY

Sunday July 22, 1984

When I at last gathered up the cards and stepped into the hall, I thought about tapping on Persis' door so that I could hand them to her myself. There was no light under her door, so I headed upstairs. The cards seemed to be a source of security for her and I wondered if she would be okay without them for a night.

The house was quiet except for the typical creaks and groans that an old house makes as it settles itself. I could, at last, hear the distant voices of long ago tenants when I stood still to listen, but those were mere whispers of the past.

I added my strange encounter with Skylar's inner self to my notes and ruminated about it while I got ready for bed.

I had just settled to read for a while when I heard an urgent tapping on my door. Before I had a chance to find my slippers, Persis opened the door and, seeing me sitting up in bed, came in and closed the door behind her, then leaned on it as if to keep someone out.

I could see that she was breathing hard and that her face was pale in the light of the lamp on the bedside table.

"Persis!" I said. "What is it?"

"I'm...I... Look!" She pushed something at me and I took it. It was a Tarot card, though not from her deck. It was the standard Waite deck artwork.

"Where did you get this?"

"Someone pushed it under my door! I got up to go to the bathroom and found it on the floor." She was panting as though she had run a long distance. "It's the Death card! Someone is going to kill me!" She started sobbing then.

I got up, went to her and put my arm around her and steered her over to the bed where I sat her down then sat next to her. The fear in her was palpable. Almost a solid, dark entity lingering around her.

"Honey, the Death card doesn't mean that someone is going to die. It means that something is over and something else is about to begin."

"Yes, my life!" she said, still crying, but she was looking at me and I saw a glimmer of hope on her face.

"It means that a change is taking place, that's all. Maybe someone found it and thought it belonged to you."

"Who would do that?" she asked. "And why in the middle of the night?"

"Well, I don't know. But let's think. It isn't from your deck. This is from a very commonplace deck that you can find in almost any bookstore or even variety store. Perhaps someone was trying to scare you."

She gave a shaky laugh. "They did that, all right."

"Do you have any idea who might have done it?" I asked. If someone had found it in their room at some point, I thought it odd that they had waited until after midnight to push it under the door instead of just asking Persis if it was hers.

"I think it was either Jade or Skylar," Persis said. "They both hate me."

"Oh, Persis, I don't think…"

"Yes. They do." She was so positive about her statement that I had no answer for her.

"Why do you think that is?"

"I don't know. Jade hates everybody, I think."

"What about Skylar?"

"Skylar's just weird," she said, musing. "Who knows why she does things?"

"I don't think that Skylar is any weirder that anyone else."

Persis looked at me as if I had lost my senses. "You don't think Skylar is weird? Honestly?"

"Well, everyone is different. I'm considered weird by most of the people I know."

She looked at me for a long moment. "You told me that I should be careful." She was still balancing on the edge of tears. "I'm scared," she whispered. "Would you do another reading for me?"

I nodded and got up to get her Tarot cards off the dresser.

"What specific question did you want to ask?"

Persis didn't give it a second's thought before she said, "Is someone going to kill me?"

"Are you sure you want to know the answer to that?" I asked. "What would you do if the answer came out yes?"

"Then I *would* be careful!" Her voice rose as if she thought I was stupid. But maybe it was just panic. "I would call the police! I would run away!"

"Well, the cards don't give specific yes or no answers anyway. They offer choice while giving us information to make an informed decision."

She shuffled the cards, muttering her question under her breath. At last she cut them into three piles then looked at me.

"Go ahead and select three," I told her.

She chose three cards and I laid them out. I studied them a moment.

"What do they say?" she asked, her breath coming

a little too fast.

"Well, this one says that there is cause for celebration," I said, holding up the Four of Wands. "It also means harmony and a good life."

She smiled, but she still looked scared.

"This one warns you to be cautious," I said, "but that's always a good idea."

"This one doesn't look like it's a very good one," she said, pointing to the Five of Cups.

"That means a loss of some kind, but more like regrets, not the loss of life. Why don't you select a couple more and we'll see what they say?"

She pulled two more cards from one of the three piles and handed them to me. The first one, The Knight of Cups and the second The Page of Pentacles.

"This card," I said, pointing to the knight, could mean the beginning of a romance. You had that in your reading this evening. I think that's a clear sign, don't you?"

At last, her attention veered away from fear and she gave me a hopeful smile.

"And this one brings hope and promise of good luck. So, you see? You don't have a thing to worry about."

She nodded, looking more relieved.

"Remember, though, that the cards did tell you to exercise caution, so don't go walking across the street without looking or anything."

She smiled then. She didn't know I was being deadly serious.

As I gathered up the cards, Persis was silent. I was pretty sure I had quieted her fears. I think that she was very much in awe of the Tarot. To her, it still seemed like some kind of fortune telling device despite my assurances that it wasn't.

"It's late," I said, standing. "Maybe we should get ourselves back into bed. We have a big day tomorrow."

She seemed to snap to attention then. Her face went pink and she now seemed embarrassed.

"Thank you," she said after a moment.

"Are you okay, Persis? Will you feel safe if you go back to your room?" I asked her.

She shrugged. "I wish there was a lock on my door," she muttered.

"You could put a chair back under the doorknob," I told her. "That works pretty well." I demonstrated with the desk chair in my room.

She nodded, looking unhappy.

I put my hand on her shoulder and guided/steered her toward the door. The poor girl *was* scared. "I'll see you in the morning."

She mumbled something I didn't catch but she did give me a little smile before she disappeared in the direction of the stairs.

When I turned to shut my own door, I thought I heard another door latch click somewhere in the darkness of the hall. I peered in the general direction and saw nothing amiss, wondering if I had imagined it.

What I had not imagined was the almost overwhelming uneasiness I felt on Persis' behalf. It *was* one-thirty in the morning and she was in my room getting her Tarot read. Her mother would, without doubt, have something succinct to say about that if she ever found out. But that wasn't the cause of my persistent anxiety.

The "mini" reading I had done for her had contained cards that had reassured her but there was more to it than that. The cards she had selected had some negative aspects as well and I had tended to ignore those and stress the positive. I *did* feel that she was in danger. I felt that we all may be and that the danger may be closer than I thought.

TWENTY-ONE

Monday, July 23, 1984

The morning of the last day of the show was going to be a scorcher. The air coming in the open window felt heavy with heat as I dressed. I was achy from lack of sleep and my eyes felt full of sand. It seemed late and a glance at my watch confirmed it.

I had half hoped to get a look into Ayubu's room after he left for the venue and before Ab and I had gone.

Ab had been up early, as usual and was all finished with breakfast by the time I had made it down to the kitchen. It seemed that everyone *but* Ayubu had already headed to the venue.

"Let me just grab a piece of toast and we can be on the way," I told Ab. "I can get some tea at the show."

"No," he said, frowning. "You're going to eat something more substantial than that. Let me make you some eggs. It won't matter if we're a few minutes late."

"Yes, it will matter," I said and took the pan out of his hands. "I promise I'll get something from one of the food trucks."

He frowned even harder but allowed me to put the pan away.

"Why is he still here, do you think?" I whispered to Ab while we were going down the front steps. We had left Ayubu, who seemed in no hurry at all, sitting in the living room, reading a newspaper.

Ab shrugged. "I was wondering that myself. Maybe he doesn't expect a lot of customers until later in the morning."

I glanced at him as we climbed into the van. "Is my perpetual suspicion rubbing off onto you?"

"I don't know," he said. "I heard him talking to Carson last night. You know how Carson just kind of stares at you for a second after you've asked him a question?"

I nodded.

"I think that's kind of creepy. It's like he's thinking up a lie."

I laughed. "I think it's because he's so used to being criticized by Cassandra that he's careful to mull over everything before he says it. But what does that have to do with Ayubu?"

"Well, nothing, really," Ab said slowly. "Only, last night I heard Ayubu and Carson talking about something. I didn't hear much but I thought they might be talking about the raven we heard. Carson asked him a question and Ayubu said that yes, of course it was. He asked Carson if he thought it was something else." Ab sat behind the wheel but made no move to start the van. "Then Carson didn't answer, like he does." He turned to me. I nodded. "Finally, Carson said, 'You and I both know the answer to that.'"

"That *is* a little creepy, but you said yourself you weren't sure what they were talking about. It could have been anything. It could be perfectly innocent," I said, thinking that it may not be innocent at all. "I think you have caught my Paranoia Flu, Ab. They could have been talking about golf scores for all you know. You're one of the most trusting guys I know, and now you're suspecting two innocent men of something nefarious. You sound like me. What did Ayubu say after that?"

Ab started the van then said, "Nothing." After another moment he said, "You said they were two innocent men. I think you forgot the word 'probably.'" he said. "It's 'probably' nothing. Ayubu isn't hanging around the house planning God knows what. Carson *probably* isn't going to hit someone over the head with one of those branches that he makes. *Probably* the person who chased us on the highway was a mischievous kid. *Probably* everything is fine."

I didn't say anything for a moment. He was right, of course. There was something going on. Even Ab felt it. The night before I had felt the same sort of paranoia. I still did. Maybe the house *was* haunted after all. Maybe whatever was going on had nothing to do with the killings, maybe it did. If it did, I knew that I had to find out what it was. And soon.

"I think I'm being paranoid because I didn't sleep very well last night," Ab said. "I thought I heard someone creeping around in the hall in the middle of the night."

"You did," I told him and he turned to look at me again. "Persis came up to my room about one all freaked out because someone had slid a Tarot card under her door."

"Seriously?"

"It was nothing, really. Someone may have found it and thought it belonged to her." I didn't believe what I was telling Ab. After all, if someone had found the card, why not just ask Persis about it instead of pushing it under her door in the middle of the night? To scare her, of course. But who? And why?

"Ab, if it's okay with you, I'd like to borrow the van to go back to the house sometime during the day. There's something I have to do there and this is the last chance I'll have to do it."

"Do I want to know what you're up to?" he asked.

"No, you don't. You'll have to trust me." I stopped and waited to see if he would have anything more to say. He didn't.

We had arrived at the venue, not very late after all. After he had locked the van, Ab handed me the keys. "Just wait for a lull," he said. "That's all I'll ask of you. It's the last day so it won't be too busy."

The doors hadn't yet been opened to the patrons so I had time to make good on my promise to Ab and go find something to eat.

On the way past Persis' and the LaChance booth, I stopped. I hadn't yet taken a good look at Carson's sculptures but my conversation with Ab had put Carson into my mind. I had seen Cassandra's small, finely detailed animals but I wanted to get a better look at what Carson made.

I had to admit I was impressed. The booth was artfully arranged with the polished wood branches on which Carson displayed his work. They were both part of the presentation and part of the work itself. I saw lots of birds of all kinds but I was interested in the number of ravens that he had sculpted. They were beautiful, though not as detailed as Cassandra's birds. They were rough, primitive and, yes, a bit sinister.

Just because a man makes sculptures of ravens doesn't make him a killer, I told myself. After all, Ayubu painted many ravens into his works. There was another artist at the show who painted ravens onto maps. I had never seen ravens until coming to Oceanside for the show, now I noticed them everywhere. According to Ab and Ayubu, there was nothing untoward about hearing a raven call during the night.

There was, however, I told myself, still the question of who I had seen in the hall. And a question of what had really happened with Jade and Ayubu on the stairs. There were so many questions and I was so short on answers.

I paused at Persis' section of booth. She was sitting behind the table looking down into her lap. I suspected she had a book or a magazine there. Maybe her Tarot cards.

"I came to buy another one of your pieces," I told her and she looked up. She looked pleased to see me, but she said nothing. "But I don't see it. It was that drawing you did of Black Lake."

"That wasn't really Black Lake," she said. "I had that picture already but I darkened it up and added the sign that says it's Black Lake. Anyway, I sold it."

"Good for you!" I said, pleased for her. I bent over her other works. I did want another one, but I had liked the somber darkness of the Black Lake piece.

"I sold it to Lagan," she said. Her low voice put a very subtle emphasis on the name. She glanced at her parents' side of the booth. "Don't tell my mom that, okay?"

I touched my lips to indicate keeping my mouth shut and bent over the drawings again.

"So, have you had fun doing your first show?" I asked her when I had selected another piece, this one a pen and ink drawing of a stylized Tarot card. It was The Empress, a card that indicates good, positive things. This Empress did not look like the kindly, Mother Earth woman in the standard Tarot deck, though. She was instead, an emaciated woman wearing black with a basketful of puppies at her feet.

Persis glanced at me and looked surprised. "I did," she said, sounding surprised too.

"Did you not expect to?"

"I've been at shows before." She glanced again toward her parents. They were both talking to customers. "It's pretty boring when I'm just hanging out with them."

I laughed. "I can imagine. Did you make any money? Well, I know you did! You got the prize money from the contest."

She nodded, but looked glum. "My parents will make me put it into my savings account, though."

"You know that's the best thing to do with it, right?"

She looked startled, then sheepish. She nodded and smiled.

I paid for the small drawing and told Persis that it was my favorite Tarot card.

I gave her a wave while I resumed my path to the food trucks.

When I returned to our booth, I took a look at the few glass boxes which were left and selected one that was built to resemble a book. I remembered that when I made it, it had been a day when all had been right in my world. Easy had not been mad at me, I had finished a difficult case successfully and I had shed the depression that had plagued me most of the previous winter. The box meant something to me. I pulled my wallet from my pocket and put the requisite amount into the cash box.

The morning seemed long. There were customers wandering the aisles, but it looked like few sales were taking place.

All morning, I looked for Skylar. According to the schedule, she should have been working the morning shift. I wanted to get a look into everyone's room and I knew that Jade and the LaChances were trapped at the venue. Ayubu would be too, if he ever arrived. I had seen that he still wasn't at his booth when the doors opened and wondered what was up. Skylar wasn't in evidence either so I wasn't altogether sure that she wasn't still at Beachhouse as well.

It was somewhere around noon when a quiet seemed to drop over the venue like a blanket. The stream of customers had slowed to a trickle as patrons made their lunch plans. I peeked around the corner to see Oskar reading a newspaper.

"Is it as slow for you as it is for us?" I asked him.

"Slower," he said, watching me pore over his puzzles. He had packed them in boxes with a picture of the completed puzzle on the front. The picture itself was a work of art. If you lifted the lid from the box, you would see a glorious, glittering melee of polished wood, stones, glass and sometimes porcelain. "I'll sell you any one of those for $11.00," he said.

"Eleven?!" I said and glanced at the price tag. That was about a fourth of the cost. "In that case, I'll take this one. Why the good deal?"

"I'm $10.88 under my goal for the weekend," he said. "You'll be doing me a favor."

"I can't do that to you," I said. "I was going to buy one anyway." I held out the full amount.

He took a ten from my hand. "Got a one?"

I fished in my wallet and came up with one.

I thanked him more than once. The puzzle was to be a peace offering for Easy.

After that, I gave Ab the word then went for the van.

✳ ✳ ✳

No one was parked in front of the house. Nevertheless, I called out as soon as I entered. The last thing I needed was to be caught red handed looking into Jade's armoire or Skylar's.

I started in Jade's room which was downstairs next to Persis'. I had already been in Persis' room and, since I was pressed for time, I didn't think I needed to snoop further in it.

As soon as I opened Jade's door, I felt the residue of her typical hostility. It was faint, since the room wasn't hers and she hadn't occupied it long, but the negativity was there. Her suitcase sat next to the door. She was not the neatest person in the world, which was something I already had seen in her treatment of the kitchen. Her clothes lay draped over the chair and the bed. Shoes and discarded stockings littered the floor. I opened the armoire and gave a glance to her clothes. She had brought more than she needed, but then, didn't we all? I pushed a jacket and a dress aside to look into the bottom of the armoire.

At first, I didn't see it. The colors were dark so the card blended into the deep brown of the wood. I bent and picked up a Tarot card. The Devil. Had this card been put there on purpose, the way the earring had been dropped into my armoire and the Death card had been slipped under Persis' door? Or was this a mislaid card from a deck that belonged to Jade? She had made such a fuss over the evil purpose of Ouija boards and Tarot cards that it didn't seem like something she would own. On the other hand, she would not be the first person to feign fear of something that she herself owned and used. Had she been the one to put the card into Persis' room? Had she been upstairs yesterday in order to cook up more mischief or did she have more deadly intentions?

A quick search of the rest of the room yielded nothing else. I returned the card to where it had been. Before I left, I opened Jade's suitcase, hoping to find the remainder of the Tarot deck, only to find it empty.

A glance at my watch made me hurry upstairs to try to get a look into Carson and Cassandra's, Ayubu's and Skylar's rooms, though I knew I didn't have time for all of them.

I started with Carson and Cassandra's. It was ordinary enough. They had put their clothes away as I had and nothing seemed out of the ordinary at all. Of course, If one or the other of them was a killer, it's not as though they would hang clothing covered in blood in the armoire. I could feel the tension that always seemed to settle around the two of them. Underneath that, though, I also felt affection. The room was remarkable in its normalness.

I was just about to start for Ayubu's room when I was sure I heard someone open the front door. Its squeak was as distinct as my armoire's. I quickly headed down the hall.

I met Skylar on the stairs. She seemed taken aback at seeing me, as well she should, since she must have thought I was at the venue.

"Sorry to surprise you," I said, giving her a

cheerful smile. "I was clumsy enough to slop some coffee on my blouse this morning and had to come back and change. Aren't you working today?"

She nodded. "I did. This morning," she said. "I'll be back to help with the clean-up later." She seemed to be watching me as though she hadn't bought the story of the stained blouse.

"See you later, then!" I clattered the rest of the way down the stairs and out the door.

✵ ✵ ✵

The afternoon was no busier than the morning. Nevertheless, we did sell a few pieces. I wasn't looking forward to the breakdown of the booth and the packing of the left over works any more than Ab was. I hadn't gotten all that much sleep the night before myself. I was grateful that we were planning to leave in the morning rather than right after the show.

I saw Lagan a few times and then Rhonda, who came to booth-sit for Oskar next door. I had spoken to them both over the past few days and had been satisfied with their answers to my questions. I had also gotten the opportunity to question Jake. I discovered that he was the one who had spread the word about the alleged killings, having heard it from someone else.

It turned out that Jim was to remain a mystery to me. I never did have the chance to question him further. As it happened, he had been called away for a "family emergency" and had spent but two days at his stint volunteering. That bothered me more than I cared to admit. One of the artists had told me of an argument Jim had had with a glass blower at the Spring Art Spectacular in Bend, Oregon in April. I had wanted to find out more. I thought his sudden departure was, at the very least, suspect.

It was not yet three o'clock when I saw Josette Kelleher hurrying toward our booth. She kept looking around her. She wasn't wearing her habitual smile and I knew something was wrong.

"Cheyenne," she said. She was breathless. "I'm so glad you're here! I didn't want to leave my booth but my neighbor said he would watch it for me. I was afraid to ask for one of the volunteers!"

"Try to calm down," I told her. "And tell me what happened."

"Look!" She held up a small painting of several trees surrounding a park bench. One of the trees had a tiny red circle with an R in the center as if it had been painted there. "I did not put that there. I just noticed it today. Someone drew this on here. I don't know what to think of it. What does it mean? Do you think I should be worried?"

I did, but I didn't tell her so. I believed, then, that Josette may very well be the next artist to die. Maybe not that day. Maybe not even that week. But soon. If I had not gotten to the bottom of the murders by the end of day, I would tell her and together we would alert the police here, in Oceanside, and in her home town.

I tried to reassure her as well as I could. I impressed upon her again to be careful especially when she was driving.

She promised and, still looking scared, she went back to her booth.

I went over to the desk and asked Kirk if I could see the volunteer schedule. It confirmed that Skylar was scheduled to help with clean-up after the show. According to Kirk that would mean sweeping, gathering up evaluation sheets and offering general help to the artists. The show closed at five o'clock so I knew I would have a little wait. I very much needed to get into Skylar's room and Ayubu's as well. The surest way I had to do it, at this late date, was to wait until Skylar was performing her volunteer duties, hoof it back to Beachhouse and do a quick run through while she was otherwise occupied. Hopefully, Ayubu would also be busy breaking down his booth. That, I knew, would be my last chance.

When, at last, the doors had closed and the final few customers had straggled away, I helped Ab dismantle the booth while keeping one eye out for Skylar. I felt guilty leaving Ab to most of the work but I was there to do a different job, and that's what I would have to do.

We packed the left over, unsold pieces into the van. Jake came by our booth to collect the show evaluation sheets and I asked him about Skylar.

"Gosh, I don't know," he said. "She might have traded with Lagan. I see him, but I don't think he was scheduled for clean-up. You could ask him."

I thanked him and went to the desk to confirm what the volunteer had said. Sure enough, Skylar had traded with Lagan. Great! I thought. That was just great. There was no more time left. I was going to have to do it now or I never would get another chance. For all I knew, Skylar had packed up her stuff and left for home. Her room may be empty. Nevertheless, for Josette's sake, I felt I could leave nothing undone.

"Ab," I told him when I was back at the booth. "There's something I have to do. Will you be okay if I'm gone for a little while?"

"Sure, babe!" he said. "Do what you have to do."

"Uh, the thing is," I said. "I need to use the van again. I'll try to get it back here as fast as I can and then I can help you finish loading it."

He looked surprised but not disgruntled. "Sure. I've got to break this down anyway, but I can handle it. I've done it alone many, many times." He dug into his pocket and extracted the keys, tossing them to me.

With a deep sigh of relief, I started the van and, in a moment, I had pulled up to Beachhouse. None of the other vehicles were there.

I unlocked the door and called out. "Anybody here?" The house was silent. It felt empty and abandoned already.

As I walked through the house, I continued to call out, "Skylar? Jade? Anyone here?" But I knew that no one was.

I don't like snooping, even though I do it often. There are several ways I get the information I need to understand what is happening in any given case. I talk to people. I touch people and can get insight into them that way as well. Another way is to observe and another is to snoop. I don't take things. I don't tell other people's secrets unless their secret involves illegal activity. In order to fully understand people, I have to look at and sometimes touch their belongings. Often that is the only way I can get the information I need.

I headed into Ayubu's room. It was empty. It was obvious he had packed all of his things that morning and had them in his car, ready to leave the moment he had his booth broken down. So much for that, I thought. I felt a ripple of guilt. If he was the killer, I had let him go, free to kill again.

Skylar's room was two doors from Ayubu's.

When I opened the door, I almost backed up. The emotions were thick, heavy and almost tangible.

Instead of leaving, I forged ahead and shut the door behind me.

What first hit me was that veritable fog of despair and insecurity that Skylar carried with her. Again, I got the impression that she was much more than what she appeared to be, almost that she was two people. Once more, I was reminded of my last case where I had run into a man who had created his whole persona. I never did know what his real name was, nor anything about him. I had the same kind of feeling about Skylar. It was as though she had two separate and distinct personalities. The man in my last case had only been one man—his invented self. Nothing of who he had been before remained. But Skylar's essence was confusing. I couldn't pin down who she was. Did she have a split personality? I didn't think so. To be honest, I didn't know enough about that phenomenon to even guess at what that felt like. She had me utterly baffled.

The room was neat but Skylar had not yet packed up to leave.

She had a book on the nightstand, *The Stranger Beside Me* by Ann Rule.

I opened the armoire door and noticed that it did not squeak the way the one in my room did. The few articles of clothing she had brought hung on the pole in a neat row. I recognized the two multicolored jackets and their coordinated dresses I had seen her wear. Besides that, there were a couple of plain white shirts, a pair of navy slacks and a pair of blue jeans.

After the experience in Jade's room, I pushed aside the clothes to see if anything was on the floor. She must have brought two pair of shoes; an unworn pair was to one side, but I noticed a shoe box pushed toward the back. I pulled it out and lifted the lid. Inside were several small, unlabeled jars filled with something that had the consistency of thick mayonnaise. I unscrewed one and brought it to my nose. It smelled like cold cream. Another jar held something that was tinged with green and had a minty smell. One was half full of a dark brownish substance. Some sort of make-up, I thought. I touched some of the dark cream, then smoothed it onto the back of my hand. Make-up, yes, but not a commercial brand, though there were jars of traditional foundation and eye make-up too.

While I was pondering the creams, I looked further into the armoire and found a black plastic bag which I believed at the time to be a bag meant to hold Skylar's dirty laundry. Before I could unfasten the twist tie, though, I spotted another shoe box. This one was larger, meant for boots according to the picture on the side of the box. Inside, I found a treasure trove.

Of course, the pieces of artwork that I saw could have been something Skylar had bought for herself. I had noticed that she revered art in most of its forms. In fact, I had felt extreme envy from her when she was looking at or touching art or talking to artists. It wouldn't be difficult to believe that she bought as many pieces as she could find and afford.

And yet... The pieces in the box didn't feel right to me. I lifted a small ornately decorated plate from the box and turned it over. I found the name of one of the artists at the show. Indeed, I recognized her style and had spoken to the woman more than once. Another was a small finely finished pair of wood salt and pepper shakers. I wondered if they were the work of Luke Jeffries. I had seen the same depth in his pieces.

Okay, I tried to concede that Skylar had bought the things she had placed in the box. There were a few other items to which I gave a quick look, but I had to move on. Then I noticed the small painting that Persis had made. It was lying on the bottom of the shoebox so that it wouldn't be bent. I looked at it, puzzled. Persis had sold it to Lagan. So, why did Skylar have it? Maybe Lagan had given it to her. From what I had seen when Lagan was talking to Persis, he was interested in her art no less than he was interested in her, in spite of her youth. And so, why would he give away the drawing?

I picked up the plastic bag and saw yet another box under it. But it turned out to be not a box at all. It was a very small tape recorder. I pressed the play button and the deep, rasping sound of a raven filled the room. I switched it off.

I opened the plastic bag and dumped the contents onto the floor. At first, I didn't recognize what I was seeing, but in a moment, something began to clear in my mind. It was a wig. The reddish brown, chin length hair that Skylar wore.

I shoved the wig back in the bag, put the lid back on the box and started to stand. A glance at my hand showed me that the place where I had spread the brown cream had turned my skin a shade darker. I rubbed at it and it reluctantly came off.

I jumped to my feet and got my bag from my room. In a moment, I was back and grabbed a few small glass bottles from the case. I opened one of the jars and dipped a swab into the mint-smelling cream then put it into a bottle and sealed it. I did the same with each jar.

I put everything back the way it had been and without delving further into Skylar's room, shut the door and hurried down the stairs.

* * *

The Three Stars Variety Store looked as though it had been transplanted from another generation. The floor was wood and the counters were bins holding hundreds of small items. There was a candy counter along one wall and the smell of vanilla wafted over the store.

A young woman appeared and asked me if she could help me find anything.

"Do you carry Tarot cards?" I asked.

"Right over here," she said. "We don't sell many of them, but you're the second person this week." She laughed. "Maybe they'll be the next fad."

"Can you describe the person who bought them?" I asked her.

She did and without anything more than a quick thanks, I pushed through the door onto the hot street again.

The pharmacy was just a few steps down the street and around the corner. I hoped the pharmacist was there. He was.

"I think this is wintergreen," he said and handed me back one of the bottles.

"What on earth would a jar of wintergreen cream be used for?" I asked him as he unscrewed another.

"Oh, some people, women, I guess, used to like to use it for plumping their lips. You know, to get that bee-sting effect. I didn't think women did that anymore."

"That one," I said, indicating the bottle he had just opened, "I smeared onto my hand and it seemed to turn the skin darker."

"Probably walnut. It will do that."

"Isn't it permanent?" I asked.

"Not if you use a foundation of cold cream and don't leave it on for more than a few hours," he said as he sniffed the cold cream jar.

I knew at once that my half-formed, fully incredible idea was correct. I gave him a hurried excuse then left him with a baffled expression and headed to the venue. If I was right, and I knew I was, Persis was in grave danger.

I ran in the front door and scanned the workers who were sweeping, gathering electrical cords and stacking the rented tables.

I passed Ab's booth and saw that he wasn't there. The LaChance booth was empty too and stripped of the wares they had been selling. But I caught sight of Cassandra and Carson near the door arguing, it seemed, about the proper handling of the dolly. I didn't see Persis anywhere.

I saw Rhonda sweeping the littered floor and asked her if she had seen Lagan.

"Sure," she said, looking and sounding irritated. "He's supposed to be helping me. But he told me he wasn't feeling well and that Skylar had agreed to replace him." She leaned on her broom. "But then, she didn't show up either. Frankly," she said, wiping her forearm across her forehead, "it's the perfect day for 'not feeling well'. I kind of don't blame either one of them."

"Do you know where he went?" I asked, though I was sure that I knew.

She shrugged. "Who knows? Home? The beach. That's where I'd go!" She shook her head and resumed sweeping. If she had anything else to say, I didn't hear it.

Without another word, I raced again for the exit. I had a good idea where Lagan had gone and with whom. Persis knew that she was not allowed to go anywhere without both her parents' permission. The LaChances, however, were too caught up in their own power struggle to even notice that their daughter had left the building.

As I sped past the booth, I saw that Ab had returned. He looked startled as I called to him. "Ab, get to a phone and call the sheriff. Tell them to go to Black Lake as fast as they can!"

TWENTY-TWO

Monday, July 23, 1984

I t took me just a few minutes to get to Black Lake. I hoped I was in time.

Even before I climbed from the van, I could hear screams. I rushed toward the shore and saw that Persis was floundering in the water. I saw no one else.

It seemed to take forever to reach Persis, though, in reality, she was only a few yards from land. Even so, the warnings about Black Lake had been correct. There was no gradual shore, no beach, no gentle slope into the water. When I stepped in, the ground seemed to disappear under my feet. I swam and at last reached Persis.

She was screaming something I couldn't understand and at first she tried to fight me off. I grabbed at her but she was hysterical. Frantic, I clutched a handful of the back of her shirt and pulled her slowly to the shore where I gave her a heft onto the grass. She immediately curled into a fetal position and screamed something into her hands.

"Persis!" I said, but she couldn't hear me over her own cries. "Persis! You're okay."

At last, she looked at me and seemed to realize who I was and where we were.

"He melted!" she shrieked when she saw me looking at her. "He was melting!"

"Where is he, Persis?" I asked and shook her shoulder. "Where is he?"

She pointed out to the lake and again began that horrible crying.

I scanned the surface of the water but saw no one.

"You stay right here," I told her. She didn't appear to hear me, but I didn't think she would leave and certainly not go into the water again. I hesitated a second before diving back into the dark depth of Black Lake. It was impossible to see through the murk. I found nothing. For all I knew, he could be mere feet from me but it was too dark to see.

I didn't want to leave Persis for long, especially if Lagan was somewhere nearby.

When I again climbed from the water, Persis' cries had become mournful moans but as soon as she saw me coming back, she burst out again, shrieking over and over that "he was melting!"

"Persis, stop!" I said, trying for a calm voice but she was so loud I didn't think she heard me and she kept screaming.

I could hear sirens in the distance and I knew the sheriff would be with us in a few moments.

She had heard the sirens too and, to my profound relief, began to wind down.

"Persis, can you tell me what happened?" I asked. I put my hands on both sides of her face and tried to force her to look at me but she couldn't focus. Her eyes darted back and forth in near panic. It was several seconds before I caught her attention and her gaze.

"Lagan said we could help each other to learn to swim," she said, her breath coming in exhausted pants. "And, it's so hot, I really wanted to go with him. We came down here and we were playing around trying to push each other into the water." She looked at me as though she wanted my approval. I nodded so that she would continue.

"He pushed me really hard and I was going to fall in, so I grabbed his arm and he went in too. There's no bottom to the lake!" she said, and I could hear the hysteria rising again.

"Here! Look at me!" I commanded and she did, though she was still panting in heavy, ragged breaths.

"I thought I was going to drown and he wasn't helping me. He didn't know how to swim either! He started melting!" she shrieked.

Just as I saw the red lights flashing on top of the sheriff's car, Persis seemed to calm a little. "All of a sudden, his hair started coming off and his face—" She buried her face in her hands and began much more normal sounding sobs.

"He wasn't melting, Persis," I told her. "He was wearing a wig and makeup. Those are the things you saw coming off. Just a wig and make-up."

She stared at me. "A wig? But..."

"Persis," I said. "Listen to me. Lagan was not who you think he was. He was trying to hurt you."

"No, he likes me," she said. "He likes me and I like him too. You're wrong. Just wrong!" She started crying again.

"Listen to me," I said. "Listen!" She stopped again, looking at me, anger, fear, bewilderment all over her face.

"I can't explain it to you right now. The police are on their way and I will explain to them what I know. After that, I will tell you. I promise." I gathered her into my arms. "You'll be fine now."

TWENTY-THREE

Monday, July 23, 1984

We were taken to the tiny Oceanside hospital where orderlies and nurses in black scrubs attended to us. Persis was hysterical half of the time and insistent that Lagan wouldn't hurt her the other half. She had not taken in any water, though, and was not hurt—physically, anyway.

Someone from the Hagler County Sheriff's Department went to where the show venue was just closing up and managed to notify Persis' parents what had happened. They brought Ab along with them to the hospital since I had taken the van and it had been left at Black Lake.

A sheriff talked to Ab and the LaChances who stood in a worried little huddle out in the hallway. I could hear them explaining the living arrangements at Beachhouse.

I sat on the side of the hospital bed. The hospital personnel had wanted me to lie down but there was nothing wrong with me but a little water in my ears. I didn't see Persis but I could hear her somewhere near, once more insisting that she was all right and that no one had tried to hurt her. No one wanted us to talk to anyone else until the sheriff had had a chance to find out what had happened.

A uniformed man strode into my room and introduced himself as Sheriff Gene Eckles. He looked uncomfortable, as though it was embarrassing to him to be talking to a woman sitting on the edge of a bed with bare legs and feet and a gown that opened in the back. As I talked, trying to explain in the simplest way possible what had happened, he stared at my face. He was concentrating so hard on not looking at any possible naked skin, that I doubted he even heard what I was saying.

"What is your relationship to..." he looked at his notebook. "What is your relationship to Persis?" He pronounced her name "Per-cease."

"Per-sis," I said. I was exhausted. I had already told him who I was and what I had been investigating, minus the part about the killings. "She is one of the artists. I believe that one of the show volunteers tried to kill her."

He looked doubtful, but didn't say anything. Rather he seemed to be waiting for me to continue.

I took a deep breath. "As I said, I am an investigator who was hired to look into an increase in thefts centered around art shows. In the course of my investigations, I discovered what I believe is also several murders."

"Murders?" Eckles said. His eyebrows raised. "You mean like a serial killer?" I could see that he had already slid into disbelief mode. He was ready to dismiss what I was about to say.

"Yes," I said. "It's possible that at least four people —artists—have been killed." I hoped I didn't sound defensive, but I was afraid I did.

"Well, no one has been murdered," he said, looking and sounding relieved. "The girl didn't drown. She shouldn't have been swimming in Black Lake anyway. There are penalties..."

"Look," I said. "You need to send someone out to look for the person Persis was with."

"Well, ma'am, we're not sure that there is a 'person' to look for. The girl claims that this..." Again he consulted his notebook. "This Lagan character was trying to push her into the water and she grabbed him and pulled him in with her. No one else saw him. You say you looked under the water for him and didn't see him. You didn't see him get out of the water. Are you sure that she didn't just make up this little story so she didn't get into trouble for breaking the law?"

"Lagan exists," I said, exasperated to the point where it was hard to keep my voice level. "He's a volunteer for the Pacific Coast Arts Collective. Any of the PCAC people will tell you that. He's a board member for God's sake!"

"I'm sure he exists," Eckles said, his voice dripping with condescension. "We've talked to the folks over there at the Collective. But they tell me he was sick and he was going home. Nothing unusual about that. Nothing at all."

"Did you ask them for his address at least? Did you check it against Skylar Tarte's address?" My patience had flown out the window long ago.

"It seems that the address for Lagan Irshad is false. As for Skylar, we have people working on that."

I had just about had enough of law enforcement. First the Oregon State Patrol had all but laughed at my suspicions. The Everett and Seattle Police Departments hadn't shown much interest regarding the two cases in their respective cities. And lastly, the Hagler County Sheriff had insisted that Attley Silverwood's death had been suicide and was still stonewalling me. I have the greatest respect for law enforcement, but I wondered how in the world murders ever got resolved with attitudes like that.

* * *

It wasn't until later that evening that I worked it all out in my mind by explaining what I could to

Ab and the LaChances.

Jade and Ayubu had cleared out their rooms and gone. Most of Skylar's belongings remained where I had left them, but I had moved the box of artworks to my room. I would contact each artist and ask them if the pieces I had found had been stolen. I doubted that the other items, Skylar's clothing, wig and tape recorder, would ever be claimed. Even the police were not interested. It would be left to the owners of Beachhouse to deal with them.

The house seemed quieter and somehow calmer with just the five of us there. Ab and Carson ordered a couple of pizzas and we all sat in the living room eating it and drinking beer.

At the hospital, Persis had been told that Lagan and Skylar were probably the same person, though she did not believe it. She refused also to believe that Lagan had been bent on drowning her. In her mind, Lagan had "liked" her and that was as far as it went. I thought she had blocked out the hysterical interval where she had been convinced that he was "melting," and that, in her mind, panic had made her hallucinate. She thought that he had drowned.

Cassandra had seen to it that Persis spent the evening in bed. She allowed the portable TV to be wheeled into Persis' room for the evening and she seemed happy enough with her pizza, soda and The Monday Night Movie.

"So, how did you figure this out," Cassandra asked

me when she had come back into the living room and picked up a slice of pizza.

"I was looking for Skylar in her room," I told her, even though that was not the whole truth. "I found the wig, face darkening cream, even lip enhancer. She was able to change her looks very easily apparently."

"You mean like a split personality?" Carson asked.

"No, not exactly," I said. "I think that so-called split personalities are very rare. That may have been the case, I don't know. I don't have a psychological background. She changed her look and her persona as easily as you change your clothes."

"But..." Carson wasn't getting it but I could see that Ab was.

"I've seen Lagan many times in board meetings," Ab said. "While he doesn't stand out or anything, I never once had any idea that he was a woman masquerading as a man."

"I don't know this for a fact," I said. "But I believe she had some kind of disorder that made her lose her hair."

Cassandra nodded. "Alopecia. My nephew has that. Why do you think Skylar does?"

"She had wigs, quite good ones, I think, that look natural. I saw the one that she wore as Skylar in her room. When she was Lagan, as she was this afternoon, she wore another, shorter, black wig. I think she was darkening her skin with a cream that was made from walnuts. She also plumped her lips up with some other kind of cream. She blackened one of her teeth so that it looked like it was missing. Not in the front where it could be spotted as fake, but toward the back so you got only a glimpse of it when he smiled. She could lower her voice a little and she became Lagan. He even had a slight Indian accent. When she wanted to be Skylar, she went with her regular skin color, a longer wig, fake pierce earrings, and she was a woman. I believe she had colored contact lens to make her eyes look brown when she was Lagan and then she could take them out and they would be Skylar's blue again."

"But why?" Carson asked, looking baffled. I thought he still didn't quite believe what he was hearing.

I shrugged. "Maybe at first it was just for fun. But she wanted very much to be an artist. She wanted, more than anything, to be a performance artist.

"Why didn't she do it, then?" Carson asked.

"She had applied to shows but was turned down because there is no category for performance art in PCAC shows, nor in any of the others," I said. "She could have tried some other medium, but she wasn't willing or maybe she wasn't able to become good enough to be recognized. Recognition was the main thing she wanted. Her focus was on becoming famous." I stopped for a moment, thinking. "When you think about it, she *was* a performance artist. She made herself into two different people and she did it successfully. If that isn't performance art, I don't know what is."

Ab shook his head. "Wanting to be famous is a surefire way to be disappointed," he said.

"She was extremely envious of the artists in the shows. I think there was a progression in the way she did what she did. It started with the jealousy which led her to stealing small but good pieces of art from the artist she was focused on. That led to her trying to frighten them. I think that may have been, in her mind, a way to make them notice her. She made anonymous calls and either hung up or said something that would terrify the listener. The need to frighten grew into a compulsion and when the jealousy became strong enough, she couldn't control the urge to kill."

Carson still wasn't buying it. "I think that's a little..."

"You should listen to her," Ab told him. "She usually knows what she's talking about."

"There have been four killings; one in Seattle, one in Everett, one in Oregon and one here in Oceanside," I said. "And those are just the ones we know about." I gave each of them a look in turn.

"You should have reported this," Cassandra said, sounding worried. "Maybe you could have prevented some deaths if you had let someone know."

"I called the Everett Police Department about Ramona Rainey's death. It was ruled an accident and that was that. I was told I was imagining things," I told her. "I called the Oregon Highway Patrol because Brynn Jagger was in a hit and run accident on the Oregon Coast. They all but hung up on me. I spoke to the sheriff's office here in Oceanside about Attley Silverwood's death and they insisted it was suicide. Despite her partner's saying that she would not have done such a thing, her death remains a suicide. A painter, Barbara Robertson, who lived in Ballard, died from a hit and run accident between car and pedestrian. I don't think that one will ever be solved either. We will never know." I sighed. "I *did* try."

"I didn't mean to imply that you didn't do anything, Cheyenne," Cassandra said. "I only meant that..." She stopped, then began again. "I wish *I* had known. I would have cancelled out of the show. I would not have put my daughter in danger. The artists should have been told."

Ab looked at me and gave one eyebrow a slight raise then shook his head.

"I tried to get the board to let me warn the artists but they wouldn't hear of it. They were afraid that the artists would quit the show *en masse* and it would have had to be cancelled."

Cassandra's indignation had caught fire. "They should be sued!" she said. "I'm going to see to it that they are!"

"In a way," I said, "I can see their point. There had been four deaths and all of them were ruled suicide or accident. It was only my intuition that told me they were murders. I doubt if it would have been enough. I think it would be a waste of time and money to try to sue, Cassandra."

To my amazement, Cassandra nodded. "You're right," she said with a sigh. "It just makes me so..."

"But you're still sure it was all done by Skylar?" Carson asked.

"Skylar left a sign wherever she committed one of her murders. She had left a red circle with an R in the middle on pieces of artwork in the studios of the artists she killed. I bet she left one at Black Lake."

"Her tattoo!" Persis said from the doorway, startling us all. I wondered how long she had been standing there. "That's what her tattoo was, I think. A red circle with a capital R in the middle. I thought it was some kind of a club."

"Young lady, you get back to bed immediately!" Cassandra started to rise and Persis half turned to return to her movie.

"I never saw a tattoo on her," Carson said.

"It was on the inside of her arm. I saw it once, by accident." Persis' face went rosy. I wondered if she had, like me, been snooping where she shouldn't have. I didn't even want to imagine the circumstances.

"Persis!" Cassandra's voice was strident. This time she did get up and head toward her daughter. Persis looked at us from around her mother who seemed to be trying to corral her.

"It must have been a temporary one, like Persis'," I told Carson. "Lagan didn't have one. I saw him with short sleeves several times."

At Lagan's name, Persis turned and headed back to her room. It seemed she was willing to hear dirt about Skylar, but not Lagan.

"At any rate," I said when Cassandra had returned, there have been four deaths and all of them have links to Skylar because either she or Lagan or both volunteered at the shows in which those artists had recently been participants. All of them have something marked with the sign of the raven. That's what Skylar herself told me it was called."

"There was another death a couple of years ago," Ab said, out of what looked like deep thought. "I can't believe I forgot about it until now." He nodded. "She was an artist. I was next to her at one of the shows. I noticed that little red symbol on one of the bird-houses she had made. I thought she had done it. A couple of weeks later, I heard that she'd died." He stopped and looked at me. "They said it was from natural causes. I'm sorry, babe. I should have remembered before now."

I waved off his apology. "I suppose Skylar could have somehow mimicked natural causes," I said.

"And, I guess we'll never know. At any rate, that *was* the raven's signature."

"If you don't know which one was the..." Cassandra floundered. "If you don't know which was the real 'person', why do you always refer to Skylar?

"Because it seemed she was the blank canvas. She had to do things to make herself into Lagan; wear a wig, blacken that tooth, put on make-up, wear colored contacts. To be Skylar, all she had to do was put on a wig. If Lagan's body is ever found, I would be willing to bet that *he* is a *she*."

"What about that big to-do with Ayubu and Jade?" Carson asked. "Do you think she had anything to do with that?"

I nodded. "I think so. I think she took one of those wire easels either from Persis' room," I glanced in the direction of the hall, wondering if Persis had crept back to listen more discreetly. "Or, maybe Ayubu's, and put it on the stairs. I think she lured Jade up there for some reason and hoped she would fall. Ayubu just happened to be there to push Jade aside." I thought for a moment. "I also know that it was Skylar who made the call of the raven that night. I found a battery operated tape player in her stuff with the tape still in it."

"Oh, my God!" Cassandra said and covered her mouth. "I can't believe we were living with her! She was...Was she crazy?"

"I don't know about crazy," I said. "That's for

psychiatrists to figure out if the authorities ever find her. And I don't think they will. If she didn't drown in Black Lake and got away somehow, she is very adept at disguising herself. She can become anyone she wants."

"But she killed people!" Carson said.

"That's what I think. The police don't feel that way," I said. "Remember, Sheriff Eckles didn't take me seriously at the hospital. And, really, the murders—the ones I'm aware of, anyway—all look like accidents. They have no reason to look for Skylar."

"She could show up at the next show we do and we might never recognize her," Cassandra mused.

We talked for a while after that, always circling around to Skylar/Lagan and the shock would be as fresh as ever. But we were all exhausted.

Ab was the first to break up the group. "I'm going up to bed. I may see you all in the morning, and I may not, depending on how early we get started. If I don't, I wish you all good luck in whatever you do next. It was a pleasure living with you."

Cassandra, Carson and I followed. I was just as tired as they but I had a report to write while it was still fresh in my mind.

It took me another hour and a half to put down all that had happened. I supposed that the case was complete, but part of me felt that it wasn't and maybe never would be. I hoped that the thefts would stop, and the murders too, though I may never know the truth of what really happened. Was it Skylar who had perpetrated the killings or was I wrong and they had been random accident and misadventure all along? For the first time in my life, I was doubting my psychic ability and that scared me more than anything that had gone before.

At last, I climbed into bed, too tired to even lie still and read.

The night passed without disturbance. No ravens, no armoire doors opening, no night light going out. Or, if anything did happen, I was, blissfully, unaware.

TWENTY-FOUR

Tuesday, July 24, 1984

T he next morning dawned as warm as the day before.

Even though I had gotten little sleep, I awoke refreshed and ready to start for home. There were some things there that needed clearing up and I wasn't sure how to go about doing them.

I found Ab and the LaChances in the kitchen. Persis was eating cereal while her parents sipped coffee. Carson was eyeing Ab's scrambled eggs.

"Hey there!" Ab said to me. "I left the last two eggs for you."

I didn't want the eggs but didn't like the idea of throwing them away. I scrambled them anyway, then offered them to Carson. He seemed delighted and scarfed them while Cassandra glowered at him.

"Before you go," I said to Persis while her parents launched into a whispered altercation. "I have something for you."

Persis seemed to have recovered from her ordeal of the day before. Either that, or she had become so adept at hiding her feelings that even I couldn't sense them. She smiled and tipped the cereal bowl to drink up the leftover milk.

I took my tea and motioned her into the living room. Our bags sat beside the front door. On top of my suitcase, I had placed a paper sack containing the glass box I had bought from our booth. I had something else, though, that I had to take care of first.

"I found this in Skylar's things, Persis," I told her and handed her the little drawing of Black Lake she had done.

She took it from me and looked at it for a long moment, then handed it back. "Will you take it? I...I don't want it. I think it will remind me."

I nodded and put my hand on her arm. The pain was still there in the form of a deep disappointment. I thought that, with time, it would fade. The trauma she had suffered had either washed away with her hysteria or was still hidden deep within her. I hoped, for her sake, that it was the former.

I bent to pick up the paper sack and handed it to Persis. She opened it, peered inside then brought out the gift.

"This is beautiful," she said, her deep voice even more hushed than usual. She turned the box over and over and ran her hands gently across the blue glass.

"It's for you to keep your Tarot cards in," I told her. "You've been keeping your cards held together with a rubber band and in your back pocket. They are too beautifully done for that kind of treatment. They deserve to live in something beautiful."

Persis' face flushed a becoming pink, but she smiled, her gaze still on the box. "It's a book made of glass," she said, looking up at me.

I nodded.

"I love it!" she said.

"When I made it, I knew that I was making it to hold something special that belonged to someone even more special. I just didn't know what or who."

She fingered the glass bevel in the center of the lid and then the blue and blue-green glass surrounding it. "You made this," she whispered. It wasn't a question. "I wish I had something to give you. Something better than that drawing."

"You already gave me something, Persis. You gave me a chance to know you. I hope you will keep in touch. I would love to know where you go with your talent."

She nodded.

"I put one of Ab's cards inside the box. If you want to get in touch with me, you can write or call Avenue Art Glass in Seattle," I told her.

She repeated the name once or twice under her breath.

Just before we left, she gave me a hug. I was surprised and grateful.

We climbed into the van and pulled out onto the street in a cloud of dust. I looked back and saw Persis watching us from the porch. I was sorry to leave. I was glad to leave.

We drove through town saying nothing and as we neared Black Lake, I asked Ab to stop. He looked at me in surprise.

"I just want to look," I told him and climbed out of the van. He followed me to the place where Persis had nearly drowned. The water was calm and inky dark. The trees shading the lake kept the air chill even though it was a warm July morning.

The sign that warned bathers was there, but as far as I was concerned, it was way too small. It should have been huge and printed with dangerous looking red letters.

As I turned to go back to the van, Ab silently followed. When we passed the Black Lake sign, he stopped me and I looked at where he was pointing. On the sign, a little higher than the final "e" in Lake, was a small red circle with a capital R in the center. It had been drawn with a felt pen and looked like the symbol for a registered trademark but I knew it wasn't. I felt the chill deepen a degree as I looked. Had it been there when I had come to save Persis? I couldn't remember even giving the sign a glance, I had been so focused on her.

Wordlessly, we got back in the van and headed on our way.

* * *

The ride home was not as harrowing as the ride down. Ab didn't have to concentrate so hard and he was in the mood to chat.

"Do you think that car that tried to run us off the road was Skylar's?" Ab asked when we began to near that same stretch of highway where the incident had happened.

"We never did get a chance to see her car, did we? I'd say, yes, it was Skylar."

"When did you first suspect that Skylar and Lagan were the same person?"

"Not as soon as I should have," I said. "I should have gotten a hint that first night that we met Skylar and she was talking about the meanings of our names. She asked me about what I did for a living when I wasn't 'helping out' at art shows."

He nodded to indicate he remembered the conversation.

"How would she know that I was just helping and

not part owner in the store or an artist in my own right unless she had been at the board meeting? She wasn't, but Lagan was. Of course, she could have spoken to any of the board members, but Dak had told me that they had been sworn to secrecy." I gave him a wry smile. "But you know how well that works."

"Don't beat yourself up," Ab said. "There are any number of ways for her to find that out. If you had asked her, she could have told you she was good friends with one of the board members and heard it from them."

"Yes," I said with a sigh. "You're right. Anyway, I was pretty sure something was up when that car tried to terrorize us on the way down. I just didn't know what." I thought for a long moment, then said, "I think it was Skylar again who hit Barbara Robertson in Seattle and killed her."

"The witness said it was a man," Ab said.

"Without her wig and with a little strategic make-up, it wouldn't be hard to make herself look like an older man." I turned to look at him. "I didn't tell you about what I saw that night that we heard the recording of the raven. After everyone had gone back to bed, I heard some footsteps or at least boards creaking in the attic. I opened my door to see if anyone was coming down from upstairs. I saw what looked like..." I stopped, realizing how insane what I was about to say would sound. "I saw what looked like a skeleton go past. It was someone who was quite small, very, very thin and completely bald. I think it was Skylar without any disguise. I went downstairs and looked around then I went up to the attic. I could tell someone had been there but that was all."

"Wow!" was all Ab had to say about that. Whether he thought it was insane or not, I didn't know.

"Skylar also left a Tarot card under Persis' door. It was the Death card, but Skylar didn't know that it isn't about death at all. She was trying to frighten Persis and she succeeded. She also left a Tarot card in Jade's armoire. It was the Devil card. She picked out the card she thought would most frighten Jade but it didn't work. Jade never saw it that I know of."

"Good thing," Ab said. "But how can you be sure it was Skylar and not Persis or Ayubu or Carson. He would have been my pick for the culprit."

"I went to the variety store in town and asked who had recently bought a pack of Tarot cards from them. They carry them, the clerk said, but they rarely sell them. She remembered who had bought those cards and described Skylar perfectly."

Ab was silent for a moment. "So, how do you think she or he..." He glanced at me.

"Let's call her 'she'," I said. I think that was the true Skylar/Lagan.

"Go over again how you think she accomplished

all these things."

"First of all, she became obsessed with someone. Women artists, it seems, were her target. I believed she watched them, perhaps for quite a long time. Then, the first step in the chain to the accomplished death was hang-up phone calls. Several of the artists reported getting them before and after shows. One even reported that the person on the other end said 'You are being watched'. That's pretty creepy on its own."

Ab nodded agreement. "How did she find out the numbers?"

"It's easy to pick up artists' business cards from their booths and save them for another time. I have at least one hundred business cards in my case right now from picking them up at the show. All four of the murdered women had received those calls. The next step was to make a mark, the circle with the R in it on a piece of their artwork. That could be accomplished by a volunteer or a patron. Attley Silverwood participated in a studio tour shortly before she was killed. Skylar could have attended it. Bliss didn't remember specifically that she was there but Skylar could have picked up a piece of barn board —Attley had lots of it lying around, and painted one."

I ruminated for a moment. "Same with Barbara Robertson. She had been part of a studio tour as well. The sign on her work was part of a complicated painting of Seattle graffiti and all Skylar would have to do is use a red pen and add the sign. Skylar could have done it when she was volunteering or at a tour."

Ab shook his head. "She had access to almost every artist's work," he said.

"Brynn Jagger had made a clay miniature of her home including the dog house," I resumed. "Skylar probably made the mark on it when she was in Brynn's booth. Maybe when she was booth-sitting. All she had to do was circle the last letter in the dog's name. Easy enough to do with a fine-tipped red felt pen."

"So, she was either a volunteer at the big shows or she was a visitor at studio tours," Ab said. "It sounds like a reason to not have tours."

I nodded. After a moment I said, "I think it was during a studio tour that Skylar tampered with the space heater that killed Ramona. Pete Rainey said that Ramona encouraged the visitors to paint small items she had made or play with the clay themselves. It's possible that Skylar saw an unfired box and picked up some red glaze and painted the sign on top of it. She hid it among some other pieces so Ramona wouldn't find it right away. When Pete found it, he didn't know that Ramona hadn't done it herself. He fired it and has kept it as a memento of Ramona." I shook my head. "I dread having to tell him."

"Don't then, babe," Ab said. "Just let it be. There's

no reason to give the guy any more grief than he already has."

"Josette Kelleher came to me at the end of the show and said she had found the sign added to one of her paintings. I think she was intended to be the next victim, but, instead, Skylar got sidetracked and tried to kill Persis."

"So, Skylar was warning these artists that she was noticing them and they were in danger," Ab said.

"Yes. They just didn't know it. If they found the circled R, they may have thought that someone had done it as a joke. A tiny act of vandalism."

"And you think the motive was simply jealousy?" Ab mused.

I nodded. "I think that, yes, it was pure, simple envy. More than that. It was deep, soul searing jealousy. I think Skylar wanted to be an artist; wanted to be famous so much that she couldn't stand to see other people living the way she wanted to live. I think the reason she singled out Persis was her winning the Emerging Artist Award. To Skylar, that was a step closer to fame and she couldn't stand it because Persis, young and just starting out, was achieving the goal that Skylar had been seeking for years."

"She could have learned, couldn't she? It seems a little extreme, killing people because you can't have what they have."

"It's extreme no matter what the motive is. When the emotion is so powerful that it's overwhelming, it can do more than ruin relationships," I said. I thought again of Easy and sighed.

We still had a way to go before reaching the cut off to I-5. I was still both eager and not eager to get home.

Ab suddenly pulled into the dirt parking lot for Ma's, the tiny diner where we had eaten the wonderful pot roast. "Ready for lunch?"

We went in and sat at the same table as before. It appeared that the same three guys were at the bar every day. Or maybe they were still there. Who knew?

We ordered the special once again, which turned out to be homemade chicken pot pie. Apparently, Ma didn't believe in serving cool food during hot weather.

"Are you ever going to tell me what's bothering you?" Ab asked after Ma had gone away with our menus.

"What on Earth do you mean?" I knew what he meant. I was simply delaying.

"You aren't you." He looked at me and I could tell that he wasn't going to let this go. "Something is wrong. I suspect it has something to do with your friend, Easy."

"We had a disagreement before I left. I don't know

if he's still mad at me, but I'm tired of being mad at him and I want our relationship to go back to the way it was." I didn't want to talk about Easy. Maybe with Molly, but not with Ab who was, after all, the subject of the 'disagreement.'

He continued to gaze at me with that "I'm waiting" look on his face.

"It was about you," I said.

"Me?"

I nodded. "He's jealous because I've been spending so much time with you and then I went on this trip to the coast with you."

"That was work. You explained that to him, I trust."

"Sure," I said. "For all the good it did."

"He loves you, babe."

"I know that. I love him too. It seems that jealousy is not the best way to show it, though."

Ab smiled and shook his head. "I have to say, I'm flattered." His smile turned to a soft laugh. "How about that? A young, good looking guy like him is jealous of me. I love it!"

"You don't have to be so happy about it," I said.

He looked at me for a moment, no longer laughing, though his smile lingered.

"If I could say that he has nothing to worry about, I would," he said. "But I'm not going to say that and that's all I'm going to say."

I regarded him for a moment too and decided it would be wise to let the subject drop.

* * *

We arrived in West Seattle in the mid-afternoon. The sun was still warm and it was a relief to get to my cool house among the trees. The argument with Easy still hung over my head and hurt my heart. I knew that in the very near future, I would have to take steps to bring it to a close one way or the other.

It was good to see my office the same, waiting for me to take up what cases came my way, some interesting, some routine. And there was always Avenue Art Glass to add the satisfaction of creativity to my life in between.

For now, I was content to stay in West Seattle with only occasional work forays away from home, but most within the city. The prospect of travel did not interest me right then. Once I had my differences with my best friend ironed out, I thought my life would once again be ideal.

On the floor, inside my front door was a blue, spiral bound notebook. I knew right away that Iola Graft had made good on her promise and had left it there. She had tucked a little note inside and pushed it through the mail slot in my door. I smiled as I picked it up and glanced through it. She thought she had a case for me, she had said. Something bad was going on in the neighborhood.

I set the notebook on the table and went to listen to my messages.

After a couple of hang-ups, which I have to say, gave me pause, there were a few messages from potential clients. I saved those for later. The next was Magda, my landlady and owner of the huge estate my house sits on. She had some bad news to tell me but didn't want to say it over the phone. Great, I thought and saved that one too. The next call was from Easy.

I was chagrined to note that my heart began a heavy pounding when I heard his voice.

"Hi, Chey," he said. "I know you're probably still mad at me since you didn't call me after we...after our discussion and I don't blame you." There was a pause and some rustling. I wondered for a second if he had written down what he wanted to say. "I've been thinking of you all week. I... I was hoping... Anyway, I'm sorry...I really am sorry. I know that I was wrong. I *do* trust you and I know I acted like—" The message cut off then. I erased it and listened to the rest of it on the next recording. This time he talked faster, maybe to get it all in before another cut off. "I have no excuse, except that I've been overwhelmed at work. I...I've been inundated with... Well, with something...Anyway I have no excuse. I know I acted like an idiot and I want very much to see you. I've cleared my schedule for Wednesday and I hope we can have dinner." Again, a delay. "Call me when you get home. Please."

Gladly, I thought and waited for the next message.

I was surprised when the last message was from Ben Graft, Iola's son.

When I hung up the phone, I could already feel the change in the air. Iola Graft was dead. Yes, she had been an old lady. Yes, she had been failing of late. Nevertheless, her death was a blow to me. I imagined that this was the sad news that Magda had wanted to tell me in person.

I made the return calls. It was a relief to talk to Easy. At first, our conversation was still a bit stiff, but almost immediately we both relaxed. The other calls, to Magda, to Ben were accomplished too. Then I phoned the clients and arranged meetings, desperate almost, for life to begin again its normal rhythm.

It wasn't until later in the day that I picked up the notebook and started reading Mrs. Graft's looping handwriting. That act was the first step in a case that I was totally unprepared for. Easy, it turned out, was already involved, though he hadn't told me. How could I know that by late summer, my own neighborhood, my own backyard would become a scene of horror?

EPILOGUE

I n 1992 the press called Aileen Wuornos the first female serial killer but, in 1984, it was widely believed that women did not serially murder. In my mind, at least, Skylar had put that theory to rest.

Of course, no one could be sure that Skylar Tarte was a woman, any more than they knew that Lagan Irshad was a man. The lines these days are more often blurred than they were in 1984. At the time, it mattered. Now it doesn't.

But was Skylar/Lagan the Raven who signed his or her work with the red circled R? I believe yes, although to this day, no one knows for sure. And was the Raven a serial killer? Again, I think yes. I think that Skylar and Lagan travelled the Northwest, volunteering at art shows, befriending artists, taking mementoes and killing when the envy was most hot and could no longer be controlled.

Did they perish in Black Lake as Persis insisted? No body was ever found. In 1995, Black Lake was dragged twice when some teenagers drowned there and the surrounding area was thoroughly searched. No trace of either Skylar/Lagan nor the young people was ever discovered. So, the question remains.

Was Lagan/Skylar telling the truth when he told Persis that he didn't know how to swim? Or was he skillful enough to swim to shore and escape into the dark forest surrounding the lake and disappear? Local legend said that Black Lake is bottomless and, looking at its murky darkness, it was easy to believe. Is Lagan's body lying in its depths? Or perhaps still drifting, drifting down and down never to find its resting place? I wonder. The question has haunted me for years.

I reconnected the stolen items I had found in Skylar's room with their owners. Of the five, only two had suspected theft, the rest had not noticed the small pieces were missing.

I called Tyler Robertson, Bliss Monahan and Rupert Jagger to tell them that their partners had most likely been murdered. Bliss was relieved. It eased her mind to know that Attley had truly been happy. Rupert seemed not to believe me. I urged him to call the Oregon State Patrol and have them begin a more thorough investigation, but he dismissed me in one or two words and was gone. Tyler took the news in stride. His wife was dead and he had chosen to believe that the Lagan part of Skylar Tarte was dead too, drowned in Black Lake. I didn't tell him of my fears that she may have gotten away. I didn't think it would change his mind at any rate and the truth would have accomplished nothing.

I debated with myself about letting Pete Rainey know and decided against it. He had been devastated enough by his wife's death which he thought of as an accident. To him, that seemed far preferable than a murder. I chose to let him heal without the truth.

I spoke to Josette Kelleher whom I believed had been Skylar's next intended victim. I told her what I knew and what I suspected and let her make her own choices. I checked in with her once a month for a little while, then, over time we lost touch. Over the years, I saw her name listed at shows on the programs Ab brought back and my mind gradually eased.

I kept in touch with Persis for many years. She grew into a poised young woman despite her rocky youth. She became an illustrator of children's books and was well known to parents and educators everywhere. She married and had two children. Does she, in the depths of her heart and in the midst of her busy life, think about those dark days when she knew Lagan and had her hopes for him? I believe she must, but, if so, she never mentioned it to me.

I always pay particular attention when I hear that an artist has died. The death of an artist in Richland, in Vancouver, in Ocean Shores may go unnoticed if there is nothing unusual about it. If the death is from illness or old age, I feel I can once again sit back and resume my own life. But if the cause is ruled an accident, misadventure or suicide, I can't help but wonder if the Raven is still out there. Still insinuating into art shows, still plotting revenge for imagined slights.

Does Skylar's jealousy grow with each passing year? Or did it die in the depths of Black Lake? Jealousy can eat into a soul and destroy it. When it becomes mixed with insecurity it can be a deadly combination. At least it was in Skylar Tarte.

In a way, Skylar had eventually gotten at least part of her wish. She didn't achieve fame, but she had wanted to be a performance artist and she succeeded. For Skylar/Lagan were artists and their shared body was the canvas.

No one saw accounts of the Raven's deeds on the news or in the newspapers. No one remembered except for the hapless men who had lost their wives. Except me. I, for one, still think, and sometimes dream about the Raven.

Cheyenne Bruce, 2020

ACKNOWLEDGEMENTS

Love and thanks to my husband, Guy, who is my editor-in -chief.

Love and thanks to my daughter, Carrie, who answers my legal questions with patience.

Love and thanks to Barb Roberts, my dear friend, for so very many things.

Line from "Stopping by the Woods on a Snowy Evening" by Robert Frost.

ABOUT THE AUTHOR

Lella Rae

Lella Rae is the pseudonym for Delores Peck.

Delores was born in Tacoma, Washington and has lived in the Pacific Northwest all of her life. She holds a Bachelor of Arts Degree in the Humanities from the Univerisity of Washington. She lives in West Seattle with her husband, Guy.

BOOKS BY THIS AUTHOR

Always A Bad Sign

In retrospect, aside from the fact that it was the last day of Jacob Levin's life, there was probably nothing unusual about that Monday in November, 1984. Until, that is, Jacob's wife, former screen star, Magda St. Martin called me for help. I was a private investigator. I was also a psychic.

Five years before, I had searched for Magda's missing teenaged daughter. I never found her and the case has haunted me for years. Now, Magda had lost two husbands and a daughter under mysterious circumstances. She wanted me to protect her from whomever was stalking her family and to independently investigate the case.

From the beginning, I knew that Magda, her secretary, Laurel and her gardener, Rolf were lying to me. As I uncovered secret after secret, I felt farther and farther from the truth until the final macabre moments.

Sign Your Life Away

I was in my car when the news came over the radio that Royal Blue was dead. Shocked, the world seemed to stop moving for a while.

Once or twice in a lifetime there arises a star the brilliance of Royal Blue. The world would eventually become used to his loss, but like the ripples on a pond, his essence would never really die. The surface of the music world would never again be still.

I drove on that day, little knowing that with the passing of years my life would become entangled with the lives of those Royal Blue had loved. Though I didn't yet know the players, they were waiting in my future to affect me to the end of my life.

And though the case was finished long ago, I dream about it still. In my sleep I'm standing on the edge of hell with a madman.

The Book Of Signs

Before the Whalesong murders, a writers' colony seemed an ideal setting; a lovely island in the Strait of Juan de Fuca, a comfortable cabin in the woods, the companionship of like-minded men and women who loved books and writing. From the moment I stepped into the case, however, and became a part of the population of its world, I felt that something was very wrong. There seemed to be darker forces afoot that were not immediately visible.

Little did I know that behind the idyll of Whalesong lurked something much more sinister than I had imagined. It was a case full of dangers, deceptions and threats that I didn't yet understand.

DISCLAIMER

The town of Oceanside does not exist. It is a distillation of many coastal towns in Washington State.

There is no Hagler County in Washington nor a Hagler County Sheriff's Office.

The Pacific Coast Arts Collective as well as the Everett Art Council do not exist and their personnel are fictitious.

Alki Spud Fish and Chips, does, however exist and has the best fish and chips in the world.

I beg the Seattle Police Department, the Everett Police Department and the Oregon Highway Patrol to forgive my liberties. I have the utmost respect for these and all law enforcement agencies.